Copyright © 2024 by C.R. Allen

All rights reserved.

No part of this publication may be reproduced, distributed, or transmitted in any form or by any means, including photocopying, recording, or other electronic or mechanical methods, without the prior written permission of the publisher, except as permitted by U.S. copyright law. For permission requests, contact crallenwrites@gmail.com.

The story, all names, characters, and incidents portrayed in this production are fictitious. No identification with actual persons (living or deceased), places, buildings, and products is intended or should be inferred.

Book Cover & Illustrations by C.R. Allen

Independently Published by Boundless Horizons LLC

1st edition 2024

ISBN: 979-8-3303-1781-3

For Grandpa Bill,

In that little barren rock cove on Lake Pleasant, you took me fishing for the first time. I think I was about six-years-old, but I remember that moment in extraordinary detail to this day.

As I got my first bite, excitement filled me. I was about to catch a fish, make you and my parents proud, but shouldn't it have been easier? The line tugged back with a force I could barely handle; it took every ounce of strength in my body not to lose my grip.

SNAP!

The fiberglass rod broke in two. I'm pretty sure I screamed as I struggled to hold on to the two pieces while whatever was hooked on the other end continued to pull me closer to the water's edge. You jumped forward, grabbing the broken end with one hand and the bare fishing line with the other, helping me haul the creature onto the boat.

It didn't look like a fish to me; it looked like a submarine with teeth. You said it was the largest catfish you had ever seen.

I watched quietly, barely able to move as you tried to get the hook out with your bare hands. The creature we had caught horrified me. The large, bulbous eyes and most unnatural whiskers were scary enough, but most of all, it was the teeth that would later give me nightmares.

Your blood mixed with the fish's blood as your hands braved the beast's razor-lined mouth. You didn't scream; you didn't even wince in pain. Your focus, your strength, and your determination narrowed onto the one harrowing task at hand, and nothing would stop you from getting the job done.

From that day onward, I knew what kind of man you were. And I also knew I would strive to be just like you.

That was one hell of a fish.

Prologue

1785

The oak leaves rustled as the light breeze made its way through the thick forest canopy, cooling Ziigwan's bronze skin and revealing the direction of the wind. She adjusted her left arm smoothly to account for it. Straight and strong, she held her bicep and forearm muscles taut, waiting for the perfect moment. They ached and fought against her will; she bided her time; they did not bend. If they slackened too early, she would miss and return a failure. Ziigwan would not allow that to happen.

When the moment arrived, two things occurred in quick succession, so quick they seemed almost simultaneous. First, the deer emerged from the safety of the tree's trunk and bent its head to the ground to nibble on a fresh blade of grass. Next, Ziigwan's arrow sprang forth, the sinew of the string unleashing a wave of energy that vibrated the surrounding air with the buzz of approaching death and pushed her black flowing hair into her face.

The deer never saw it coming. Death is like that for many of us.

Blood splattered the oak trunk as a hollow and desperate bleat scattered birds from the branches above.

She approached the carcass, her moccasin shoes silent over the dead leaves and dry twigs that littered the ground. It had taken her almost a lifetime to master walking through the forest like a jiibay, a spirit; a habit practiced in everything since she was a little. Her family had taught her that stealth was an essential skill, on the hunt and in life.

Walk softly and avoid detection.

Concealed from behind a fern, Ziigwan watched the chest of the deer, where scarlet poured like a spring from the arrow wound. The flow pulsed with each of the animal's heartbeats. As seconds passed, the pulses grew weaker and farther apart. She considered using her Kingfisher knife to slit the deer's throat, ending its suffering. However, the many-pronged antlers that it had been freshly sharpening against the tree were far too dangerous for her to consider getting any closer than she already was.

It would all be over soon. The blood loss would silently put the animal to sleep, fading away into the spirit realm, where it would rejoin the herd of its ancestors, grazing in the winter-less dream.

Its body would nourish herself and the others, an honorable ending. She would ensure its sacrifice would not go to waste.

The men hooted loudly as she entered the camp with the buck's carcass slung over her shoulders. They hadn't eaten anything other than berries and squirrels for weeks, their mouths practically dripped with saliva as the scent of fresh meat filled the clearing.

"The Indian got one!" the man named Silas yelled.

Ziigwan ignored him. He had been following her around camp for the last month, spying on her with as much stealth as a squawking wild turkey.

"Bring it over here," said the bearded man by the fire. His name was Tobias. He was the leader of these men and the only one that Ziigwan respected.

She dropped the young buck's body at his feet.

"She already cleaned it for us," Tobias said, examining it. There was a long cut along the belly of the animal, where Ziigwan had removed its digestive and waste organs carefully. They considerably lightened the carcass for transport and prevented the meat from spoiling early if burst while still inside.

"Miigwech," Tobias said to Ziigwan in her native tongue, crossing his arms across his chest with respectful gratitude. He was tall and burly. Though thick and bushy brown hair grew robustly on his jawline, none grew on his scalp. As he smiled and layered on the praise in front of his men, he reminded her of her own father. Another chief whose commitment to his people was paramount.

She had not laid eyes on her father since the previous winter and did not know whether she would ever again.

She nodded in response to the exaltations. She knew enough English to speak, but rarely chose to do so. Being amongst such strange men for so long had been lonesome, speaking a tongue other than her own only added to her longing for home, a home many days travel away.

"Is that fresh food?" said the soft voice of a woman emerging from a nearby tent. She wore an impractical dress, something Ziigwan had never seen before joining up with this band of white settlers. Clutched tight to her bosom, a baby wrapped in blankets cooed softly.

"Your ears do not deceive you, Samantha," Tobias said. "Ziigwan has brought down a deer for us."

"Thank you, my dear," Samantha said with a smile. She lowered into a slight curtsy. Ziigwan nodded in return. The thought occurred to Ziigwan that a nod was not proper etiquette in their society, but she couldn't be certain. Everything about these settlers was foreign to her. She found their customs and niceties to be foolishly eccentric.

"It's been difficult to feed the baby on biscuits and rancid berries," Samantha continued.

Ziigwan wasn't listening. Her eyes were fixed on an agate brooch on the woman's dress. It was just like the one her mother had. The smooth surface of the stone reflected the sunlight in white specks that reminded her of the sparkle of a freshly fallen snow at dawn.

Samantha noticed.

"It's quite beautiful, isn't it?" she remarked. "It was a gift from the last tribe we encountered."

The last tribe had gifted it to Tobias as part of a contract to sell their land. It had been one-sided, Tobias parting with a few modest commodities in exchange for the rights to hundreds of acres. The chief had thought it was quite a deal, since they could still live on the land as they always had. At least for the time being.

"Would you like it?" Samantha asked.

Ziigwan shook her head in the negative. She did not want the spoils of deception and the dishonor they carried.

Except a small part of her did. That sliver of shameful desire that overcomes all others in moments of weakness.

"Please, take it," Samantha said as she shifted the baby in her arms to remove the brooch and holding it out. "I insist, as thanks for keeping me and my child healthy."

Ziigwan took it immediately, knowing that if she thought about it a moment longer she would refuse it again.

"Thank you," Ziigwan said, hiding her eyes in embarrassment at anyone who would see her giving in to the darker parts of her spirit.

"Why does the savage get a bonus and we don't?" Silas whined.

"It's not a bonus," said Tobias. "It's a sign of gratitude. You should try it sometime."

Silas scoffed.

"Get this butchered and cooking," Tobias barked an order to the rest of the men, who had quickly formed a circle around the carcass. "Build a smoker so we can keep some for the next few days."

"Ain't enough meat on it for that," Silas commented. "That'll barely be enough to feed us for tonight."

"We will ration it," Tobias replied. "Won't do us any good to stuff ourselves like pigs if are stomachs empty again the next day."

Silas absconded from his protests, but only because he knew Tobias was the boss. He turned his attention back to Ziigwan.

"Looks like the native bitch is on the rag," Silas said, several men laughing with him.

Ziigwan glanced at her chest. Her leather tunic was stained red with the deer's blood, dripping onto the ground at her feet.

"Ziigwan," said Tobias. "You should get yourself cleaned up. We'll handle the rest."

She nodded at him and immediately took off for the stream she had found flowing through the forest.

"Silas, get going on felling trees for the smoker!" yelled Tobias.

As she left the clearing that served as their camp, she could hear Silas's obnoxious groans of obstinance behind her.

She stripped her clothes, and sitting on a boulder, washed them in the clear waters. The blood, still fresh, rinsed out easily, disappearing from her deer skin top with only a few rungs. Her mother had told her that the waters of this area had surprising cleansing qualities. Ziigwan was beginning to believe her.

She had told Tobias her name translated to English as 'Fresh Spring', but that was the most simplistic form that which she could communicate to them. It meant something far less literal in the native tongue of her people, the Ojibwe. To them, it signified a bringer of new ideas to the tribe. A hopeful wish of her father's that she would somehow bridge the gap with the white man.

The wish would never come to fruition. Despite learning English from the frequent missionaries, Ziigwan struggled to walk in both her tribe and the white man's worlds. Her father expected her to return to the village, to marry the strongest warrior, and assume a role of matriarchy over her people. Yet her spirit yearned for something else: to run through the forest in her own direction with no stones of home to weigh her down. So she had run away, and joined with this group of settlers as a tracker for a paltry sum, knowing they would never linger in the same place for long.

Her father had likely sent his best scouts after her, but that had been weeks ago. If they had found her, they would made their presence known. If they hadn't, they might have given up and returned home.

She hung her clothes from a branch illuminated by a break in the thick canopy. They would dry quickly thanks to the sun's warming rays, which would shine brighter today than any other day of the year. It was the summer equinox.

As she passed the time, Ziigwan examined the brooch closely in her hands, running her fingers across the smooth reddish-brown stone. Agate was the stone of change to her people, transitioning from oneself to another, a greater self. She could only hope that her path was leading her on such a journey, even as it led her far from home.

Sniffing it, she caught the distinct aroma of the woman's child lingering on it. Though not inclined to have children of her or assume that role in her tribe, she found the smell of babies attractive and enjoyable.

She put the brooch down on the rock and walked to her hanging clothes, checking their progress. She need to get back to the camp soon, before the white men wasted any of the meat.

Traveling with the settlers, she had witnessed them throwing away perfectly good organs and cuts from the animals she had caught. Their lives at home must be so different from her own, food so abundant, that such wastefulness was treated like it was nothing.

Ziigwan knew better. The brains, the tongue, the testicles; they were a rare treat in her village, usually reserved for the hunter who brought down the animal or one of the revered elders. How Tobias's men had survived in the wilderness before she joined them was curious.

With her clothes still damp, she washed her naked body in the stream.

The water was freezing cold. Summer hadn't quite warmed it enough in its long journey from high-up in the snowy mountains. The cold didn't bother her; she splashed it across her face and breasts without hesitation, taking joy in its cleansing power washing over her body.

Her mother once told her that water learns things as it travels to the great river, absorbing wisdom from the ground, the trees, the animals, and the forests. Ziigwan wasn't sure if she believed such superstitions, but she carried them with her, regardless. They were her family heirlooms, memories that reminded her of them, more precious than jewelry and more fulfilling than a warm meal.

Closing her eyes, Ziigwan focused on just listening to her surroundings. The sounds of the stream softly bubbling as it moved, the birds high above singing their songs of love and happiness, the buzzing of insects hidden amongst the branches.

This was why she loved summer. With the sun at its highest and the days at their longest, the world came alive with life eager to soak up as much of the light as it could, knowing that the darkness of winter would return.

In a few months, the weather in her Ojibwe village to the east would be miserable. In the winters, she had been stuck inside, close to the fire, listening to her mother and grandmother drone on with the same old stories about the spirits of wolves, bears, beavers, what-have-you. The world of words they weaved was wild and wondrous, but it held no stalk to the reality that she yearned for once the snows melted and the leaves returned to the trees.

A snapped twig caught her attention. Ziigwan grabbed her Kingfisher knife from her hanging shirt and held it above her head, ready to strike.

"It's just me, love," Silas said, emerging from a nearby row of bushes. He held an axe in his hands.

Ziigwan didn't lower the knife or her guard. She stood exposed in the river, attentive and weary despite being completely nude. Where she was from, the naked was not something to be shamed, and no imagined fear of embarrassment would overcome her instinct to defend herself.

"Sorry to catch you like this," Silas continued, smiling as his eyes probed her. "I was just looking for some good birch trees for the smoker."

Ziigwan knew it was a lie. There were plenty closer to camp.

"Since I am here, I wanted to thank you personally," Silas said, taking a step closer. "Just like Tobias asked me to. I realize I wasn't being friendly back there. And that would be something I would very much like us to be, friendly."

The man was only a few yards away. She tensed up, holding tighter to the knife.

"I'm not going to hurt you," he said, setting the ax head on the ground at his feet.

"Go back to camp," Ziigwan said plainly.

The sun glinted off the brooch laying on the rock next to his feet.

"What's this?" he asked, kneeling down to pick it up.

"Leave it alone," Ziigwan commanded.

He pretended not to hear her.

"Pretty thing it is," Silas said as he turned it over in his fingers. "Much like yourself."

"Give it back to me," said Ziigwan, summoning as much courage in her voice as available.

"Of course," said Silas, taking a step closer.

Each of his movements reminded Ziigwan of her own when stalking prey.

"Here, have it." He held it out at arm's length to her, beckoning her to take it from him.

She didn't want to reach; she knew it would leave her overextended. But the light glinting off the stone tugged at her thoughts. She couldn't let him pocket it. Such a beautiful, powerful object.

She was like the fox approaching the trap, aware of the looming danger, but the feeling of hunger throwing caution to the wayside.

Reaching her own hand out to his, she tried to snatch it away.

It was a stupid idea.

He had been coiled, like a viper ready to strike.

She felt him grab her wrist and pull her closer to him. Her foot slipped in the slick mud and within moments he had his arms wrapped around her, bear hugging her from behind with a vice-like grip

Ziigwan kicked and struggled, but he was bigger, stronger than her.

"Now how about you and I take a few moments to be friendly and all," he said into her ear, his breath on her cheek acrid and revolting.

Her hand holding the Kingfisher knife was free enough that she might be able to stab him in the gut with it. He'd be resigned to a slow, painful death as his insides spoiled his body from the inside-out. Except if she did, she knew the consequences. Tobias may be the leader of the white men, but he would be powerless to stop the rest if she killed or seriously injured one of their own.

Adding to her humiliation, she felt something growing in the white man's clothes, pressing against her back.

"I've got you, love," he said. "You might as well just enjoy it."

The feeling of being restricted, held in place by this most evil of men, ignited rage inside her. She couldn't risk killing him, but that didn't mean she couldn't teach him a lesson.

She swung her head back hard. Warm blood splattered on her neck and shoulders as the sound of his nose cracking erupted in the still forest air. He released her, reeling backwards in pain.

Ziigwan knew that wouldn't be enough. It would only momentarily daze him. She needed something non-lethal that would give her more time to return to the safety of the camp, and Tobias, naked or not.

The Kingfisher knife was sharp and strong, it sliced through the air with the speed of a muskellunge through the water.

Silas recoiled, clutching his face as red drops of blood splattered across his stained canvas shirt.

She had been so fast; he hadn't even seen it. Pulling his palm away and examining it, he realized from his blood drenched hand that Ziigwan's Kingfisher knife had taken a substantial chunk of flesh from his cheek.

"You bitch," he snarled. "How dare you?"

"Go back to camp," Ziigwan said defiantly. "Or I'll cut your throat."

Grabbing the axe at his feet, he swung it at her torso in a wild act of revenge. Ziigwan only barely fell backwards and into the stream in time to avoid being disemboweled.

She cursed at herself for being caught by surprise again. She hadn't expected Silas to recover so quickly.

It was a mistake she would regret.

In no time, he was on top of her. His knee slamming hard into her bare thigh and wedging it against a submerged boulder. She felt the dull end of the axe head smash her hand holding the Kingfisher knife, the cracks of bones breaking accompanied by the sharp pain filling her senses.

She yelped.

"You'll regret that," Silas grunted as drops of blood from his lacerated cheek dripped onto her face and stream.

What was the water learning from them?

Ziigwan swung her knee into his groin hard, releasing the pressure on her body momentarily. She needed to escape, but not without her weapon.

With her one remaining good hand, she grabbed the knife and jostled to her feet as Silas lay temporarily helpless, clutching his battered manhood. She considered stabbing him in the back of his neck, like she would kill a freshly caught fish as it fought to return to the water.

But she knew if she did, the others would find her and hunt her down.

So she ran.

With the wind at her back, she followed the water downstream as fast as her bare feet could take her. She hadn't gone fifteen yards before she heard Silas behind her.

"I'm going to get you," he yelled.

She didn't dare look back.

Ziigwan needed every ounce of focus on her choosing each step wisely. Traveling fast on the incline with slippery boulders and fallen tree trunks in her path, she knew her best option would be to create as much distance between Silas and herself as possible. A cut to the face, a broken nose, and a bruised ego would hardly be enough to justify a punishment from the men and Tobias.

But she couldn't return with his violent intent separating her and the camp. She needed him to cool down first.

The incline flattened as she ran until, at last, a break in the trees revealed itself.

Emerging into a sun-filled space, she greeted its warmth with thankfulness.

The stream had ended; she had followed it until it had emptied into a muddy beach that bordered a large pond. Despite her panic at being pursued, she could not help but notice how still and serene the water was. The trees swayed softly in the wind sweeping across the land, but there were virtually no waves on the pond's surface.

It almost looked like it was made of glass, with its mirror-like reflection of the sky.

"Come back here!" Silas's voice broke her train of thought.

With nothing but her knife to defend against the swings of an axe, she searched for a hiding place.

To her left, she saw a line of rocks that extended into the pond several yards. They were large enough, they might afford cover.

Swiftly, she ran over to them and dropped her body into the water until just her head was above the surface. She was amazed at how little the water rippled as she penetrated it. The surface barely registered her presence.

Just in time. From her vantage point amongst the rocks, she could see Silas appear from the tree line and come to a halt on the beach. He seemed just as stunned as she was to see such a pond in the middle of the forest.

Tightly gripped in his hand was the brooch.

"You can't hide forever," Silas yelled. She knew he hadn't spotted her yet, as his eyes darted in all directions, frantically searching.

Ziigwan slowly pulled back further behind the boulder, losing vantage of him. If she could see him, then he could see her too.

Silas continued his yelling, and Ziigwan felt a twitch of relief grow inside her as his voice grew fainter, farther away, with each bellow.

He was going the wrong way.

Something unsettling slithered around her leg. It was long and slippery. With the bright midday sun overhead, she couldn't see anything other than her own reflection in the water. It felt like an eel or snake. She considered reaching down and grabbing it but knew that if threatened; the animal was likely to strike, or at least create enough turbulence for her hiding place to be noticeable to Silas, wherever he was.

Ziigwan stayed perfectly still as the creature wrapped itself around one leg, tightened its grip, then released and did the same to the other. She held her breath at the unnerving feeling of being caressed by the unknown.

"I know you're here somewhere," Silas yelled, this time from nearby.

The slithering animal immediately retreated, whisking away towards the center of the pond, leaving the most subtle of wakes behind it.

Ziigwan closed her eyes, hoping for the best. The seconds stretched to minutes as the world seemed to slow down.

She felt like she was living in two worlds all over again, part of her submerged in the cold water of the pond while the rest warming under the sun on her face. One of quiet and death, the other of vibrant life. The spirit world and the human world.

A dark cloud must have come overhead, for the warm rays of sunshine suddenly left her face and a cold, unsettling feeling overtook her.

Ziigwan opened her eyes.

Silas stood on the rock above her, holding the axe in his hands and the brooch sticking out from his shirt pocket.

"You thought you could run, you bitch," he snarled, the wound on his face turning black.

He had the advantage. From above, he could strike without affording her the opportunity to defend herself. The Kingfisher knife in her hand would be of little use against the weight and force of Silas's cleaving axe.

She closed her eyes and prepared for the end.

It didn't come, something else did entirely.

A shower of blood rained down on Ziigwan. She screamed. Her ears rang with the sound of Silas's howls, combined with an unmistakable ripping sound, like a burlap bag being torn open.

She ducked under the water. Silas's screaming only stopped once she submerged, replaced by the strange muffled sounds of a foreign world, a spirit world.

Ziigwan heard them talking to her, songs in her native language, singing stories of her tribe from long ago. The burning in her lungs grew, her screams having emptied them of air. She thought the songs grew louder as she struggled to resist the urge to surface. As each second passed, she felt closer to death, their songs beckoning her to join the spirits.

Ziigwan flailed as something grabbed her arms and forced her to the surface. She struggled against the tight grasp. It dragged her onto the muddy beach.

With water soaking her eyes, the world above the surface was blurry and disorienting. She struggled and slashed with her knife at the shapes above her, but the grips on her arms were too tight. Her efforts were in vain. She could barely move.

"Ziigwan!" a voice yelled. "Ziigwan!"

She knew that voice; it was Tobias.

As the shape above her grew more defined, she saw his face take form.

"What happened?" Tobias asked her. He looked frightened.

"Silas, he attacked me," Ziigwan panted before spewing forth a deluge of water from her lungs onto the muddy ground.

"He attacked you? Why?" Tobias questioned again, the creases in his forehead betraying more than just concern.

"He followed me, he tried to..." the words got lost as she looked around.

The entire camp of men stood in a large circle on the beach. Their faces betraying nothing other than varying degrees of shock.

"I ran," Ziigwan continued. "Then..."

"Then what?" Tobias asked, his voice on the verge of desperation.

"I don't know," Ziigwan said.

Tobias's face didn't change. He looked shocked, scared, and concerned all at once.

Then she saw why. Strewn along the beach every few yards, were bits and pieces of flesh. An arm, then a leg, a loose eyeball in between them. Streaks of red blood soaked into the brown mud, glistening in the light. Everywhere she looked, she saw parts of what used to be a human body, parts of Silas.

Dead in the center, the agate brooch lay crushed into the clay underneath an enormous paw print.

1

2023

Asher should be asleep. It was early in the morning, too early, in fact. The summer sun in Wisconsin typically was peeking its head out from the horizon by five, yet no hints of light had penetrated the crack in his curtains yet. The sounds of crickets and owls that dominated the hours of twilights were slowly ceding ground to the welcome creatures of the day. A bluejay in the distance sang a forlorn song to a lost loved one, probably lost to the neighbor's ever patient cat. A chattering squirrel celebrated a freshly harvested acorn that it would bury in the ground in preparation for the brutal winter it knew would come.

Sleepily, the world outside was waking up, but not Asher. It felt like he had been awake for hours.

He was too excited. He had been looking forward to this day all week, a welcome break from the monotony of the typically boring small town summer he had thus far, been forced to endure.

Asher sat up in bed. He thought he heard something, something very unnatural from outside his window. Completely still, he sharpened his senses as he listened. It took only a few seconds to recognize it. The rattling of cans and clinking of bottles as the recycle bin his father had put out the night before was lifted high into the sky and deposited into the back of the garbage truck. The engine whirled to life as it strained to accelerate the colossal vehicle forward just another thirty feet to the next bin, then the next one, and the next one. Asher could relate to the repletively mundane life of the poor hauler. It could have been on Ice Road Truckers or the center star of a stadium of cheering fans at one of the countless monster truck rallies that travelled the country. Except it was stuck here, in boring old Tranquility Pond, fated to a life of prosaic routine, just like Asher.

He couldn't help but feel disappointed.

Unable to sit still a moment longer, he checked his phone. The screen informed him it was a little after four in the morning. Not his usual wake up time while on summer break from school. Laying down, he considered closing his eyes again, letting sleep retake him until it was a more reasonable hour.

His excitement temporarily abated, he let himself quietly drift into a state of drowsiness. Much like the world outside his window, he was halfway between two worlds, one of the waking and one of dreams. The sounds of the birds and squirrels became muffled. The garbage truck finished its route on his street and took its clinking and clanking to another neighborhood. A stillness took over his senses.

Waking up with a jolt, he wondered if the sound like a gunshot he had heard was just a dream or if he really heard it. He pulled open the curtains slightly, still too dark to see more than his own reflection in the glass. The sky was devoid of stars, a dull matte black that somehow glowed with the approaching sun.

A light blinked to life at the base of Asher's bedroom door, the narrow slit casting an eerie ray of yellow into his room. He thought about getting out of bed to investigate, but the quickly growing congregation of shadows in the hallway dissuaded him.

He could hear their faint whispers.

"It's so early," he heard his mother say. "Can't we let him sleep in? What would a few more hours matter?"

"We can't miss our chance," the voice of Asher's grandfather replied. "We need to be out on the water before the sun is in the sky."

"I'm so worried and nervous," his mother added.

"You know how old he is. It's time."

"But shouldn't he—"

"We're going," his Grandpa Joe cut her off. "Now, how about something to eat? Something quick."

The door suddenly opened, the hinges creaking loud, and Asher shut his eyes tight, pretending to still be asleep, not wanting to betray his deception.

"Asher," his mother's soft, sweet voice said. "It's time to wake up."

Asher groaned.

"Honey," she said again. "Grandpa Joe is here to take you fishing."

With feigned exhaustion, Asher sat up and dragged himself out of bed. At nine years old, he dare not betray to his parents just how excited he truly was.

The sound of a fiddle accompanied by a deep melodic voice played on the radio in his grandfather's old blue truck as they drove down the highway. Grandpa Joe hummed along happily to the tune as Asher watched the countryside pass-by. Movement from the driver's seat caught his eye.

It was Grandpa Joe, rubbing at his chest uncomfortably.

"Are you alright?" Asher asked.

"Just a little indigestion," Grandpa said. "Your mother makes one hell of a breakfast."

"I liked the bacon," Asher said with a smile.

"Nothing in life quite like bacon and a fresh cup of coffee," his grandfather said, unable to hide the visible discomfort in his face as the rubbing seemed to have no effect on the pain.

"Coffee is gross."

"I said the same thing when I was your age. I eventually learned to love it."

"When will I like coffee?"

"When you're ready."

Asher noticed a fresh grease stain on his own overalls, a consequence of his rush to chow down breakfast like a soldier at mess. His mother had insisted they devour a small feast before departing. An enormous platter of scrambled eggs, a plate stacked with bacon, bowls of hash browns, and more dishes magically appearing on the table, as they had sat mostly in silence. Asher's chewing the loudest noise apart from Grandpa's protestations that they were going to miss first light.

It reminded Asher of the big dinner his mother had made for his older brothers before they left for college, each course arriving just as you thought you couldn't swallow another bite, as if she hoped the extended meal would delay their inevitable departure or dissuade them at the last moment.

The truck passed a boarded up convenience store. Faded banner advertisements for cold beer and discount cigarettes still hung from the walls. When Asher was younger, he remembered frequenting it with his grandmother. She would often steal him away in the summers for their own little adventures. Trips to the library, to the old movie theater, even to the Ladies Auxiliary were welcome departures from sitting at home, and always accompanied by whatever sweets he wanted. His own parents' obsession with eating a healthy diet gave each trip down the candy aisle an aura of daring excitement at breaking the rules. It had been a rare treat. He wondered if a horde of candy remained inside, hidden behind the graffitied plywood covered windows, just waiting to be discovered and feasted upon.

"Do you miss grandma?" Asher asked, echoing his own painful emotion aloud.

"Every day, my boy," his grandfather replied. "I still talk to her, pretend she's here with us."

"I know, I hear you sometimes," said Asher. "I think about her a lot too."

Even as a frail old woman, she had been incredibly beautiful. Kind and sweet, their trips to the convenience store for confectionery treats had always been a little secret, and he had never tattled. But now that she was gone, candy just didn't have the same allure it once had. It was like her energy had been what made the flavor so enjoyable and fulfilling.

"Have you seen any of your friends from school since summer started?" Grandfather asked, trying to change the subject.

"Just Stu," replied Asher. "And only once. He's been following this girl everywhere around town. She's a junior and talks non-stop. I think she's annoying, but he won't listen."

"Well, I guess he's about that age," grandfather commented with a grin. "I was thirteen too when I started paying attention to girls in earnest."

Stu and Asher were only friends because their dads were on the same bowling team. It was a friendship of convenience. Forced into play dates with one another as their mothers gossiped in the kitchen. They had very little natural chemistry. Just about the only interest they shared was playing video games, which they did together begrudgingly in silence. At least they used to.

In a small town like Tranquility Pond, with no other kids his own age, Grandpa Joe was just about the closest thing Asher had to a best friend.

"Girls are gross," Asher replied. "I've just been playing Nightstalker 4 most of the summer."

"That's that video game that Mary's dad got you?"

"Yes, Grandpa Craig sent it as an early birthday present. It's pretty fun."

Grandpa Craig always got Asher the cool presents for birthdays and holidays. But since he lived in Florida, it was almost like the expensive video games and toys were his way of making up for the fact that he barely knew his grandson. Meanwhile, his Grandpa Joe never got him video games but would take him on adventures all the time; camping, hiking, star-gazing. They practically lived in the forest during the summer months. But what Asher loved the most about hanging out with his Grandpa Joe was the stories. Staying up late to listen to tales of ghosts, wendigos, and werewolves; it was about the coolest thing he could think of. It beat hanging out with Stu any day.

Asher put his hand over his face to block the first ray of light to appear on the horizon. It had somehow found him through the branches and leaves of the forest.

"Why haven't you taken me fishing before grandpa?" Asher asked.

"You weren't old enough yet," Grandpa Joe replied.

"But Stu's dad takes him fishing every weekend."

"Stu's four years older than you. And his dad takes him two hours south to go fishing in one of those stocked lakes. Hardly much sport in dropping a line into the water and pulling a fish out immediately."

"The school told us the pond is dangerous. That runoff from the old plant made the water toxic."

"They told me something similar when I was a kid. Never stopped me, though. Ain't nothing toxic in that water, probably cleaner than what you get out of the tap on account of how untouched it is."

"Then how come more people don't fish there?"

"The town likes to keep it a secret. Don't want the whole place swarming with folks from Chicago or Milwaukee, turning it into some tourist trap."

"But wouldn't that be a good thing? You know, all that money from the cities."

"Not everything in life is about the money. Don't you worry about it."

But Asher did worry about it. More than a nine-year-old probably should.

He liked to listen in on adult conversations. They spoke in riddles and used words he didn't understand, like 'tariffs' and 'outsourcing'. Asher loved trying to figure out what they were really talking about, decipher the code. He would often sneak out of his room at night and from the top step of the stairwell, listen to his parents gossip and argue.

Just last night, Asher had overheard them talking about how there weren't many jobs left since the plant shut down. That the town's population had been cut in half as young families moved to the city, just like Asher's older brothers, who had gone to work in Atlanta and New York after college and didn't even visit at Christmas.

People in Tranquility Pond were like the hair on Grandpa Joe's head, falling out follicle by follicle until only a few sparse gray ones remained.

"I heard mom and dad talking about Cathy Stevens," said Asher. "They said she's pregnant."

Grandpa Joe just nodded.

"They also said she's moving to Green Bay to have the baby," Asher continued.

"I heard the same."

"Why doesn't she stay?"

"They have better health care in the city."

"So why not go there and have the baby and then come back?"

Grandpa Joe thought hard on how to answer.

"Well, I guess Tranquility Pond reminds her a bit too much of her older sister. Sometimes old wounds like that are best left out of sight to avoid re-opening them."

"What happened to her sister?"

"She went missing seventeen years ago."

"Where'd she go?"

Grandpa flinched. He was having a hard time figuring out how to explain it to a nine-year-old.

"Probably ran away. Sometimes kids do that."

"But why wouldn't she—"

"I love this song," Grandpa Joe said, interrupted him, turning the volume knob up.

Asher wanted to turn the radio back down. He wanted to learn more about what happened to the girl that went missing, but he could tell Grandpa Joe wasn't going to tell him. At least not yet, but maybe he would out on the water. His grandfather exercised fantastic tact and reserve most of the time, but after a few beers he knew the words would start flowing and be difficult to stop.

His grandfather nodded his head to the music. His blue hat that said 'I'm not old, I'm a classic' embroidered on it, bobbed with the beat.

Asher resigned himself to staring back out the window of the truck at the emerging world passing him by. Colorful wildflowers grew unchecked on the side of the road, a cornucopia of reds, blues, pinks and yellows that extended into long, narrow meadows eventually swallowed up by the dense temperate forest.

"We're here," Grandpa Joe said as they pulled off onto a dirt side road.

Asher was relieved. He really had to pee.

The water of Tranquility Pond was still and quiet as the truck came to a stop in the parking area just outside the river bank. It wasn't a developed parking lot, but just a clearing with grass that had been flattened by the crosswind blowing in from the body of water and allowed vehicle access without having to brave the treacherous silty mud that encapsulated the pond's banks.

To Asher's surprise, two trucks were parked and waiting for them.

Grandfather didn't look pleased as he turned off the engine and got out. Asher followed suit.

Two men stood outside the vehicles, apparently waiting for them. One was a familiar old man who wore a cowboy hat, jeans, and smoked a cigarette. The other was younger, probably early thirties, with dark skin and long hair that hung down to his chest in braids.

"Rufus," Grandpa Joe said as he walked up with an outstretched hand to the older gentlemen. "Got to say I'm a bit surprised to see you here today. Didn't think you came out to the pond anymore."

"That's Mayor Hatchwell to you, Jonah," the man in the cowboy hat replied in a standoffish tone, taking grandpa's hand aggressively. Despite the beer belly and hunched posture, Asher could tell the old man used to be very strong and athletic. Wide shoulders, a thick neck, even his hands dwarfed grandpa's.

The old men stared at one another, not speaking. Both had stern expressions and Asher could clearly see Grandpa Joe's knuckles turning white as he tried to match the strength of his adversary.

Without warning, both of them laughed and wrapped their arms around the other in a friendly embrace.

"Good to see you, old friend," Rufus said with a smile.

"You too Rufus," Grandpa Joe replied. "You remember my grandson, Asher?"

"How could I not?" The old man in the cowboy hat leaned down onto one knee so he was eye-level with Asher. "You look just like your grandfather did when he was your age."

"Why did you call him Jonah?" Asher remarked. "His name is Grandpa Joe."

The old men chuckled loudly as the mayor snuffed out his cigarette in the dirt.

"Clever as a whip," the mayor said with a pleasing smile. "I heard you have a birthday coming up. How old will you be?"

"Ten," Asher answered.

"Ten," the mayor repeated. "That's a big step in a young man's life."

Asher caught the mayor shoot a strange glance at Grandpa Joe as he said it.

"Here, I got something for you," said the mayor, fishing in his shirt pocket and pulling out a lollipop still in its wrapper. "Never too old for one of these."

He handed it to Asher, who took it and thanked him. He didn't really want it; it felt so juvenile, but his mother had taught him to be gracious when accepting gifts.

The younger, dark-skinned man, who had been quiet thus far, stepped forward.

"Ian Nibiikwe," he introduced himself, offering his hand to Grandpa Joe. "I'm here on behalf of the tribe."

"Nibiikwe," Grandpa Joe repeated out loud. "I heard what happened. I'm sorry for your loss."

The dark-skinned man didn't reply, he just nodded silently.

"I'm afraid I can't let you go out there today," he said, nervously glancing at Asher as he spoke, as if afraid to say the wrong thing in front of the boy. "These waters and the animals that live in them are sacred to my people. It would be disrespectful."

Grandpa Joe narrowed his eyes.

"I remember your uncle," Grandpa Joe said, his eyes sharp and narrow as he eyed the other man. "He was a good man, a good officer."

"Thank you," Ian said. "I still can't allow you to proceed."

"How old are you?"

"Thirty-two."

"Gosh," Grandpa Joe remarked. "What I wouldn't give to be thirty-two again. I've lived here my entire life, swam in that pond more times than I can count. I've fished there, I've hunted in these woods, lived amongst the trees since the day I was born. It's sacred to me, too."

"We were here first," Ian retorted.

"Not you though," Grandpa Joe said quickly. "I don't think there's anyone left in your tribe as old as me, is there?"

Ian shook his head, his eyes fixed on grandpa's.

"And isn't your land miles from here? I can't remember the last time your people even stepped foot in town."

There was no reply.

"Then as far I'm concerned, I have as much right to be here as you or anyone else," Grandpa Joe said with determination. "Maybe even more, based on what I've had to go through."

Both men stared at each other. Asher could feel the heat from the tension that radiated between them.

"Jonah, maybe we could go for a quick walk," Mayor Hatchwell said, stepping between them and blocking their staring contest with his bulky frame. "A private talk. Ian, you wouldn't mind watching over the boy for a few minutes while we do that, would you?"

"Not a problem," the dark-skinned man said, his face turned into a scowl.

Mayor Rufus Hatchwell led Grandpa Joe away and out of earshot. Ian and Asher stood quietly as they watched the two men walk along the muddy bank in intense conversation. They appeared to be arguing.

"How come I've never seen you before?" Asher asked, curious about the man he had just met.

"I live on the reservation," Ian replied, turning his gaze to the young boy.

"My grandpa says people on the reservation like to keep to themselves."

"We do."

"But don't you like coming to town? There's a movie theater, an arcade, and—"

"We aren't always welcome."

Asher couldn't see why they wouldn't be, but adults sometimes made up funny excuses to not do stuff.

"Do you have any kids?" He asked.

Ian looked at him for a long moment.

"A son," Ian said at last. "He would be ten years old next month."

"Where is he? I'd certainly like to meet him. There aren't any other kids my age in town, and the older kids think I'm annoying."

Ian's eyes suddenly grew glassy, even as the rest of his face betrayed no signs of emotion.

"He died," Ian said flatly. "Last month. A drunk driver from out of town."

Each word sounded more painful than the previous as he spoke.

Asher's heart sunk in his chest. He hadn't intended to bring such a painful memory to the forefront like he had. He had just gotten so excited to hear that there was another kid around that was closer in age to him than Stu. Genuine remorse overtook him.

"I'm sorry," Asher said, resting his hand on Ian's arm. He didn't know why he did it, it just felt like the right thing to do.

Ian looked down at him with those wet eyes, simultaneously unwilling to cry and unable to hold back the desire to. Asher couldn't help but relate to the feeling. He felt the same way when the older kids told him he was too young to hang out with them.

He tried to remember what had made him feel better after his dog had died after a Timber Rattler bite.

"Grandpa Joe always tells me that those who die still hang around us in spirit," said Asher. "Your son is probably listening to us right now, probably going to go fishing with Grandpa and I. I bet your son loved stories, and Grandpa Joe tells the best ones. My favorite one is about a goblin that lives under a bridge that…"

"Is everything alright?" the mayor asked as he returned, a fresh cigarette in his mouth.

Ian gave the boy one last look before sniffing and addressing the mayor.

"Everything is just fine," Ian said.

Grandpa Joe slowly strolled up to join them.

"Listen Ian," the mayor began. "I'm afraid Jonah here is a stubborn old bastard. He says there ain't nothing to change his mind about going out there today with his grandson. Now I feel for your people's concerns and all, but this is public land. He has every right to be here as you do. My hands are tied."

Ian looked at both the older men one more time.

"Alright," Ian said. "But be warned that the spirits of the water and the land that live here are powerful. They should not be underestimated."

"What kind of spirits?" Asher asked excitedly.

"I don't believe in spirits," Grandpa Joe replied, ignoring his grandson. "Only in flesh and blood. I came prepared."

He tilted his head slightly to the truck bed where all their fishing gear was. The man from the tribe walked over and peered inside before returning.

Asher noticed a slight flicker to the dark-skinned man's eyes as he nodded to grandpa. They must have come to some unspoken agreement or understanding, though Asher was clueless to what it was. Another one of those ways grown-ups communicate in code so that kids won't understand what they are talking about.

"If I can not stop you," said Ian before making his way to the back of his own truck. "At least allow me to provide a gift."

He rummaged around in a pack before turning around and getting down to one knee so he could be eye level with Asher.

Ian held out an open hand. In it sat a small knife, unlike anything Asher had ever seen before.

"I wanted to give this to my boy when he was old enough," Ian said. "But he is gone, and my wife can no longer bear children. You remind me of him. I would like you to have it."

"I don't think giving the boy a knife is a good—" Mayor Hatchwell began, but stopped when Grandpa Joe held up his hand.

"I appreciate your honorable gift," Grandpa Joe said to Ian. "And I'm certain Asher shares in my gratitude."

"You mean I can have it?!" Asher asked ecstatically.

Asher reached out and lifted the knife by the hilt.

"It is known as a Kingfisher blade," Ian said. "How it is made, or from what exactly has been lost to my people. All I know is that our tribe's greatest warriors have wielded it going back hundreds of years. They say it is so deadly that it can even pierce shadow."

"Thank you," Asher said. He was doing his best to not yelp in excitement.

"Good luck," Ian said, standing back to his full height. "I hope to hear of your success tomorrow."

He nodded at Grandpa Joe, who nodded back respectfully.

"And Asher," the dark-skinned man added. "Keep it close. You never know when it might come in handy."

Asher was too enthralled with his new knife to listen.

"Be careful with that thing," Grandpa Joe warned as Asher fiddled with the blade. "It's very old. You don't want to break it."

The boat they sat in barely bobbed on the stillness of Tranquility Pond. Grandpa busied himself setting up the fishing poles, bait, and other tools they would need, a half empty beer wedged between his legs. The dew from which beading on the aluminum and staining his pants dark.

The Kingfisher knife felt light in Asher's hands, lighter than the buck knife he got for Christmas. Yet somehow it was sturdier, stronger. The blade did not bend, no matter how much pressure he placed on it. It was also completely black, but not like it was anodized. A few uses and anodized coatings scraped away. If this blade was indeed as old as Ian said it was, then it would have been worn down to bare metal by now. Instead, it looked almost brand new, the deep black so reflective that it caught and shot back glints of the sun from the few rays that penetrated the cloud cover.

Running his fingers along the wooden handle, he expected it to be rough or splintered from its age, but it was a smooth to the touch. The wood was of a grain and color that Asher did not recognize, not ash or hickory like he had seen before, something he could not recognize.

"What's it made from grandpa?" Asher asked.

Grandpa Joe took it and examined the knife up close.

"Looks like stone," he said. "Obsidian or slate, maybe. I've heard of those used as blades for primitive weapons."

"It doesn't feel primitive. How'd they get it to be so shiny?."

"Enough polishing will do that."

"Feels really light to be made of rock."

"What do you think it is?"

"Bone. It reminds me of that eagle talon we found last summer."

"Doesn't look like any bone I've ever seen before."

He handed the knife back to Asher and returned to threading the fishing line into the hooks. His hands trembled as he worked the intricate loops. Every time he missed the loop or fumbled with a piece, he would swear under his breath, then take a long swig of his beer. Asher wondered if the alcohol helped him with the arthritis.

Not wanting anything to happen to his new treasure, Asher searched for something to wrap it in until he could find a proper sheath for it back home. He rummaged in the long leather pack that Grandpa had unloaded from the truck that contained the fishing poles. His hand felt something long, round, and heavy inside. Pulling away the leather flap, he saw the barrel of the largest gun he had ever seen.

It wasn't his first time seeing a gun; they went shooting together often, but typically with a small .22 rifle, light enough for Asher to handle. The guns Grandpa had packed for their fishing trip were easily double the size of the .22. It looked like something straight out of Call of Duty. The bullets sat loose next to it, bigger than Asher's thumb. He reached for the barrel; he felt a strange fascination with touching it.

His Grandfather's hand grabbed his wrist, startling him. Despite his age, the old man still had his lightning quick reflexes.

"You know better than to play with guns," Grandpa Joe said, a stern look on his face.

"I didn't know we were going shooting today," Asher replied.

"We're not."

"Then why did you bring them?"

"In case of bears."

"There are bears in the woods?!"

Asher grew excited at the thought of not only seeing one, but getting to take a shot.

"Better safe than sorry."

Grandpa Joe released Asher's wrist, then returned to his hooks. Asher checked the tackle box next.

"What's this?" Asher asked, pulling a triangular shaped item wrapped in an old rag.

His grandfather peered at him without responding, eyes narrow and cautious.

Asher unwrapped it from the dirty, fish-gut stained cloth.

The item inside was metal, about the size of his palm. From the yellowish tint, Asher guessed gold or copper. It was flat and triangular, with a slight curvature to it. One side had very subtle, minuscule depressions in it, like little craters that created a slightly bumpy surface. But turned over, the other side was flawless and smooth.

"Is this a fish lure?" Asher asked.

He peered at his grandfather, who had taken the opportunity to finish his beer in one long drink. He crushed the cans between his hands and dropped it to the floor of the boat.

"I found it a long time ago," Grandpa Joe spoke. "I keep it as a reminder."

"A reminder of what?" Asher asked.

Grandpa Joe didn't respond, instead he stared out over the pond. His hands trembled between his knees. His arthritis must really be acting up.

"Are you ok grandpa?"

Suddenly turning, Grandpa Joe noticed Asher staring at him with concern.

"I'm fine, just getting old," he said with a smile before pulling a fresh beer from the cooler and popping it open.

Asher shrugged. Finding another old rag in the depths of the tackle box, he pulled it out and wrapped the blade in it for safekeeping; dropping the bundle into the chest pocket of his overalls.

With no waves and the dawn's light still shy as it hid behind the thick cloud cover, Asher could see deep into the water below. As he peered over the side of the boat, he imagined finding pirate treasure chests overflowing with gold, or maybe a shiny white skeleton of someone drowned long ago for crimes most nefarious. But there were no skeletons or treasure chests. However, he could see vast schools of fish darting back and forth in the faint light. Mostly minnows, but every few seconds a long slender muskellunge would swim past, forcing the orderly schools to scatter and descend into chaos.

Before too long, they both had their lines in the water and Asher sat silently watching the bobber float on the surface, still and lifeless.

Time passed slow. Asher was getting antsy. Going to one of those stocked lakes like Stu's dad did to fish sounded a whole lot more fun than this.

"I'm getting bored, Grandpa," Asher said with a groan.

"But it's so beautiful out here," he replied. "Don't you enjoy it?"

"I do, but I'm bored."

"That's part of the joy of fishing. Lots of time waiting patiently, time to settle your mind and reflect. I know it's not as fast-paced and exciting as Nightwalker 7..."

"Nightstalker 4."

Grandpa Joe laughed and Asher realized he had said the name of Asher's favorite video game wrong on purpose.

"Being out here, I like to look back at my life and remember moments that were most important to me."

Asher noticed his eyes cast down as he spoke. It was the face Grandpa Joe made when he thought about Grandma. He didn't like it when Grandpa was sad.

"Can you tell me a story?" Asher asked, hoping to change the subject and get improve his grandfather's spirits.

"That's a grand idea," replied Grandpa Joe. "I have one about—"

"Tell me the one about the convict, the guy who escaped prison with the hook for a hand."

"Maybe another time, I was thinking—"

"Ooh, I know. Tell me the one about the Wendigo again. The one that eats orphaned boys."

"Actually, I want to tell you about—"

"No, wait, tell me the one—"

"Asher!"

His grandfather's stern voice interrupted his racing mind.

"Sorry grandpa," Asher said, turning red.

"It's alright," said Grandpa Joe, patting the boy's shoulder affectionately. "Today, I want to tell you a story that I've never told you before. This one is a true story."

"Sure," Asher replied sarcastically. He knew none of Grandpa's stories were real.

"I swear. This one really happened."

"What's it about?"

"It's about family, it's about love," Grandpa Joe began, but paused when he noticed Asher's eyes roll. "And it's about the creature that lives in this pond."

"What creature?" Asher said, as his eyes got wide.

"The story begins when I was a teenager, back in 1972..."

Even the buzzing of insects and chirping of birds grew quiet as Grandpa Joe spoke, like they were just as eager to listen to the fantastic tale as the young boy was.

2

1972

"Have you heard Bowie's new album?" Diane asked the other girls as she adjusted her swimsuit straps. It was a red polka dot one-piece, almost the same shade of red as her hair. Red was her color. Everything from her lipstick, nail polish, and even her beach towel all matched. Diane was the type of girl who was always over-dressed for the occasion. Sitting on the dock made of rotten planks that hung out over the muddy waters of Tranquility Pond, she looked out of place, better suited to a Hollywood pool party at a ritzy hotel.

"Not yet," replied Olivia from the shore. Laying on her towel, she was trying desperately to get a tan without turning the shade of a lobster. Her long blonde hair tied up into a neat bun on her head, exposed her shoulders to the sun's rays. "My mom won't let me. She thinks his voice is going to lure me away to some concert in Chicago and she'll never see me again. Like he's some demon or devil from hell sent to Earth to corrupt young girls."

"Devil or not," added the third girl of the group, Stephanie. "I'd like to see what he's hiding in those tight pants."

The rest of the girls giggled.

Stephanie wore square, white-framed sunglasses that contrasted nicely against her jet black hair. Sitting next to Olivia, she was having a far more successful time absorbing the sunlight, her skin turning a pleasing golden hue already.

"I like how he doesn't fit the gender norms," said the brunette and last member of the circle of friends. This was Darci and she sat in the grass under a tree, reading a book. She wore bellbottom jeans and a conservative blouse. With her frizzy hair and thick reading glasses, she looked very out of place compared to the others.

"What are you reading?" asked Olivia.

"War and Peace," Darci replied, holding up the thick volume. "Mrs. Applebee recommended it as light summer reading. She said it will give me a leg up on English and History classes in the fall."

"Light reading, right..." said Olivia with a smile.

The girls continued chatting and laughing. After a frigid Wisconsin winter spent mostly indoors, they were all just happy to be outside, enjoying nature.

At school, they were considered the popular girls, commanding reverence from their classmates and transcending the common social archetypes of the time. Their undisputed leader was Stephanie. She was tall, athletic, and attractive; but those traits paled in comparison to how smart she was. Quick, witty, and blessed with an innate ability to always know exactly what to say; her personality had a gravity to if that naturally drew others into her orbit.

Diane was the model and movie star in training, more obsessed with her appearance and social standing than her studies. She obsessed over movies like Breakfast at Tiffany's, dreaming of being discovered in their small town and being whisked away to New York or Los Angeles by some wealthy businessman or talent scout. Not that she needed it. Her family was wealthy by comparison to the rest of the town; evidenced by the pink convertible Ford Mustang her father gifted her when she had turned sixteen.

Outsiders saw Olivia as the quietest and most timid of the group, the quintessential girl next door type. However, once in the confidence of the others, she was as chatty as any of them. Her dreams and aspirations were less lofty than her friends. She had considered leaving town for college but decided against it, unwilling to generate too much distance between herself and her mother. Starting a family and living a quiet life was all she had ever wanted.

Darci had been introduced to the girls after agreeing to tutor Diane and afterwards just kind of stuck around. Though not sharing many interests with the rest, she had proven a loyal friend to each of them; cementing her status amongst them. Her bookish nature proving exceptionally helpful if any of them needed help with studying or homework assignments.

As the sun continued its sleepy summer rise above the horizon, the chirps of the doves, finches, and robins filled the air with joyful song. Freshly returned from their seasonal trips to the south, the birds busied themselves making merriment and swapping stories of potential partners, much like the girls on the bank. It was pleasant background music as the slow march of summer break carried on. It could have been a Monday or a Thursday or maybe even Saturday; in the stressless bliss of these untroubled months, they did not know or care.

The forest that watched over the small pond was old. Its oak trees, nourished by the nutrient-rich waters, grew thick canopies that blocked almost all light to the forest floor. Their thick trunks providing ample hiding places for shadows. None of the young female quartet heard the sound of a twig snapping coming from its depths. Carefree laughter, the hallmark of uncorrupted youth, deafened their ears from the approaching intruder. Silently from the bushes, eyes watched them, patiently waiting for a chance to strike.

"Pass me that copy of Seventeen," Olivia asked.

"I'm not done with it yet," remarked Stephanie.

"I can't believe you want to read that thing," added Darci. "It's hyper sexualizing women!"

"We wouldn't want that now," laughed Stephanie as she adjusted her top to better support her ample breasts.

"I like the articles," Olivia commented innocently.

"It's just makeup and gossip and..." Darci began, but she paused. "Did you hear that?"

"Hear what?" said Diane.

"I thought I heard something," Darci added.

"There's nothing out here except us," remarked Stephanie. "The mayor has everyone on high alert about an algae bloom or something."

"I suppose so," Darci said, but her voice reflected little comfort.

They returned to their discussions of boys and celebrities.

"Do you want to go see the new Robert Redford movie this weekend?" asked Olivia.

"Oh, would I!" remarked Diane, her head popping up at the mere mention of the heart throb's name.

"He's so dreamy," began Stephanie. "I would love—"

She never finished her statement.

Without warning, a figure emerged from the bushes and charged the girls.

Stephanie screamed and tried to jump to her feet, slipping in the mud and landing hard on her shoulder. Darci held up her open book as a shield, as if the thick volume could somehow protect her. Olivia grabbed Stephanie, trying to help her friend.

Poor Dianne was left exposed on the rickety dock that stretched out over the water.

She hit the water with a scream and a loud splash; the ambusher tackling her head on and knocking her in.

The serene waters of the pond became frothy and violent from the panicked flailing of arms and splashing of water. Diane's red head barely staying above the surface as she struggled to free herself from the assailant.

Another figure emerged from the forest and chased after them, stopping at the edge of the dock. It was a teenage boy with auburn hair. In the bright mid-morning light, the girls could recognize him immediately. It was Steve, the quarterback of their school football team, the Tranquility Pond Pioneers.

"Craig!" Steve yelled at the boy in the water, still wrestling with Diane. "Stop being a creep."

"I'm just having a little fun," said the square face of a muscular, blonde teenage boy that bobbed on the surface. Diane emerged shortly after him, her red hair clumped into strands around her shoulders like a crimson octopus wig. Craig chortled at her as she slapped at his shoulders weakly.

"You asshole!" Diane yelled at him.

"Come on," Craig remarked. "You looked hot. I didn't want you to burn."

"There's an algae bloom!" Diane said angrily back at him as she frantically swam for the ladder attached to the dock.

"Bullshit," said Craig as he helped hoist her out of the water, then himself. "The water looks the same as last summer. They just wanted us to stay inside and read for school or something."

Diane ran to her towel and quickly wrapped her hair.

Standing next to one another, it was clear Steve was slightly taller. With a lean, toned chest and well-defined arms forged from years of varsity sports, he was handsome and charming. Almost every girl in school had a crush on him. Craig was stockier. He played fullback, which warranted bulky pectorals, thick biceps, and thighs as thick as Diane's waist. Even wet, his blond hair maintained its form. Cut in a flat top style, he looked like the human equivalent of the eraser on a no. 2 pencil.

"Oh my god," Diane suddenly burst out. "My eyes, I can't see! My skin, it feels like it's on fire!"

Her hands trembled in front of her face.

Craig's playful expression suddenly changed to one of panic.

"I don't feel anything," said Craig, his voice betraying a growing nervousness. "Are you sure—"

She keeled over, clutching her stomach, a gurgling sound emanating from her throat.

Craig's face turned white as he knelt next to her, looking terrified and lost.

"What can I... But it can't be... It's just algae, it can't hurt—"

His stuttering stopped as he realized the gurgling sound had been replaced by that of Diane's laughter. Standing up straight again, she cackled at Craig, who looked clueless to what was going on.

"Not cool," Craig said, the blood returning to his face and turning it red in embarrassment.

"Turn about is fair play," Diane remarked.

"I told you, the algae can't hurt you," he replied defiantly.

"What are you, a biologist?" Darci said, walking up to join them. She had a smirk on her face. "I seem to remember you getting a D in Mr. West's class."

"D+," Craig corrected her. "I did an extra credit paper."

"On what?" Darci whipped back.

"Sexual reproduction," he replied in a playful tone. "Interested in learning more?"

He flexed his muscles and posed as he said it. Darci wrinkled her nose in disgust at the comment.

"We're really sorry about him," Steve said, stepping between the two. "He's just having a little fun."

"What were you guys doing hiding in the bushes?" Diane asked in an annoyed voice. "Peeping?"

"No, no no," Steve replied. "Well, Craig was. I was trying to stop him."

"Sure," remarked Stephanie in a sarcastic tone. She looked annoyed as she tried to wipe the mud from her arm and shoulder with the muddy towel, only succeeding in smearing it further.

"Let me help you with that," Steve said, practically bounding to help her.

"You said 'we're really sorry about him'," Darci said with a curious expression. "Who's we?"

As if on cue, two more teenage boys emerged from the forest.

"What did Craig do now?" said the skinny one of the pair.

"Made an ass of himself," answered Steve. "Hey Jonah, would you mind lending Stephanie your towel?"

Jonah stepped forward with his backpack in hand and fished inside. It was a tracker's pack that had belonged to his father. With ample space and plenty of pockets, he had taken it camping countless times. Within, he had packed two towels, a change of clothes, his pocketknife, a bag of Bugles, some Twinkies, and a couple of lukewarm Cokes. A little overkill for a couple of hours out on the pond, but his dad had taught him to always come prepared.

Finding the towels, he considered giving Steve the one with a brightly colored Donald Duck embroidered on it that belonged to his younger brother, Levi. Not wanting to show that one off in front of the girls, he handed over the plain blue one instead.

"Thanks Jonah," Steve replied.

Jonah wished Steve would call him Joe like he wanted, but it never stuck. Steve had told him he didn't look like a Joe, so he called him Jonah. Which meant everyone else also called him Jonah.

They had grown up together, living across from each other on their quiet neighborhood street as long as they could both remember. Steve was two-years older, about to become a senior, but that didn't seem to matter to him. They were best friends, practically brothers. Steve looked out for him and he looked out for Steve where he could. Their relationship only became stressed over the last year, when their interest diverged. Steve played football, Jonah didn't play any sports. Steve wanted to chase girls by the diner. Jonah wanted to go hiking or camping. Filling those gaps, Craig had appeared more and more often, his interests more aligned with Steve's.

"That was nice of you," said a soft voice that swam in Jonah's ears.

It was Olivia's.

She had recovered from her initial shock at Craig's surprise attack and had wrapped herself in her towel, betraying her hallmark modesty.

Olivia was the youngest of the girls in the group, the same age as Jonah. They shared many classes together. Jonah had taken home economics for the chance that they would be assigned as partners taking care of a flour sack baby. They hadn't been assigned as partners. Of course, she had aced that easily, her flour sack child being returned in perfect condition. Jonah's unfortunately hadn't survived Levi's impromptu play sessions, a majority of the flour finding its way onto the living room carpet. His mother hadn't been able to decide what she was more angry with him about, the colossal mess or his failing grade.

Jonah struggled to think of something clever to say. Should he tell her how beautiful her hair looked? It was tied back in a ponytail. Should he ask if she's enjoying the weather? Of course she was. Why else would she be out here? Every idea that passed through his mind sounded stupid, bordering on moronic. Meanwhile, she just stared back at him, smiling, waiting for his reply.

He was about to say something, anything, to break the silence when Milton beat him to it.

"You should really put more sunscreen on," Milton said. "You're starting to burn."

"Thank you Milton," Olivia replied, diverting her attention and smile to the other boy Jonah had arrived with.

Jonah felt relief that the spotlight had been taken off him, but also regret that he hadn't capitalized on his moment to chat with her.

Milton was short, with black hair styled into a comb-over and held firmly in place with thick hair gel. Even less attuned to sports than Jonah, he wasn't attuned to the outdoors either. With his round shape, stocky legs, and strange waddle to his steps, he was almost comical in any physical activity. He complained constantly about bugs and allergies. Jonah felt it strange he had even agreed to join them. However, for the last few years, Milton had been the complimentary third wheel to Jonah's and Steve's activities. Often staying up late to watch horror movie marathons, quick to provide insights and hilarious commentary on the ridiculousness of slasher and monster films.

"We could get really sick from the algae," Milton said, walking carefully to the edge of the water. "It can cause skin irritation, respiratory problems, and even liver damage."

"I told you," said Craig. "It's just a load of bull. The mayor just doesn't want anyone to have any fun."

"Is this what you call fun?" Darci remarked. "Jumping out of the woods and scaring the bejesus out of us."

"We were just going for a nature hike," Steve said, not wanting the contention between Darci and Craig to escalate further. "Sorry to bother you."

"You aren't really a bother," added Stephanie, batting her eyelashes at him. It was apparent she was enjoying the attention he was giving her as he helped clean off the mud from her skin.

"Mind if we stick around then?" asked Steve. "We promise we won't be a problem."

Stephanie seemed to think for a moment.

"Fine, but no more throwing us into the water," she said.

"Scout's honor," Steve said with a wink.

The sun traversed the sky, and soon it was afternoon. The teenage boys passed the time rough housing in the pond with the girls faking cries of protest when caught in the splash zone. Though not trying to get wet, they didn't retreat further inland with each 'unintended' misting or spray.

Jonah was starting to agree with Craig. There was no algae bloom. The water, though muddy, was not bright green. The rocks and pebbles under his feet were barren and jagged, not smooth as one would expect.

He went to go grab a Twinkie from his pack and took a seat on a boulder to eat it. From there, he could see the group of teenagers slowly fragment as individuals broke off and paired up with one another.

Craig treaded water as he suspended himself just off the edge of the dock with his chin resting on the wood. A couple feet away, Diane lay on her towel, her hair slow to dry. Surprisingly, she was smiling and laughing heartily at his jokes, her anger with him a distant memory already. Jonah couldn't help but think that her feigned disgust and anger towards him earlier had been just attempts to conceal her attraction to him. She always did like being the center of attention.

Farther along the beach, Darci and Milton sat under the shade of an enormous birch tree, engaging in a fierce debate over the Vietnam War. Nothing about the way they talked or their body language indicated anything going on between them other than a mutual interest in intellectual conversation. Steve, only a year away from eligibility for the draft, and Jonah, with his own personal tragedy tied to the conflict, refused to discuss the war with their friend; so Milton had resorted to the always feisty Darci to share his opinion with. She was not the type to listen without sharing her own in kind.

"It's necessary that we undertake such measures to stem the tide of communism in Asia," Jonah over heard Milton say.

"At the expense of America's youth?" Darci replied with exacerbation. "You know many of your friends, maybe even you, will be drafted next year and sent overseas to fight a war they know little about."

"But it's always been like that. Why should this be any different?"

"Shouldn't we have evolved past that primitive concept by now? Plus, what's so wrong with communism? It's a viable alternative to…"

Jonah zoned out as their topic meandered to economic policy, something he was even more out of touch with.

His own views on the war were convoluted and tainted by painful memories. Hadn't it already taken enough from this town?

"So who's watching your brother?" Olivia asked. Jonah was so startled he nearly slipped from the boulder.

Recovering quickly, he tried to pretend his heart hadn't just skipped a beat.

"I convinced my neighbor that I wasn't feeling great and needed to rest," Jonah answered quickly, not wanting to waste another opportunity. "So she's watching him."

She stood there smiling at him, then Jonah realized she was waiting for him to scoot over so she could sit next to him.

"Sorry," he said as he slid sideways.

"It's okay," she answered as she sat. "Do you have any more Twinkies? My mother says sweets are bad for my figure. I haven't had one in ages."

"Of course," Jonah said, pulling a fresh package from his pack and handing it to her.

"Thank you," she said, tearing it open. "You know you really shouldn't lie to Mrs. O'Leary."

"Just a little white lie," Jonah replied nervously.

"My mother always told me it was the little lies that always get you. They grow so big that they swallow you whole."

She had a point.

"I know. I just haven't been able to spend much time with Steve this summer. He's at the gym, training with Craig and the football team every morning. Then they go to Appleton for camp in a few weeks. I just couldn't spend another day couped up inside that house watching some four-year-old play with blocks."

"I'd watch him. I love kids."

"Of course, me too..."

Jonah lied. He didn't want to admit that he found his 4-year-old little brother Levi to be the most annoying human being on the entire planet. He only hoped she wouldn't see right through him.

Jonah loved being this close to her, close enough to see the little details that he hadn't noticed before, like the dimples in her cheeks or the hint of brown that flecked her otherwise green eyes. There were freckles on her shoulders that she tried to cover with her towel, but it kept falling down and forcing her to pull it back up. Even as she noisily chewed on the yellow cream-filled pastry, she seemed more perfect than ever.

"Your brother is only a few years old, right?" She said in between bites. "I still feel like I never saw you around in the summers before that even."

"I would usually go camping with my dead," Jonah replied.

"Aren't you worried about bears?"

"Not really. As long as you are careful, they'll leave you alone."

"I love the outdoors. I saw a herd of deer drinking from the lake when we got here."

"I saw them too!" Jonah exclaimed. "They just walked on by like we were nothing to be afraid of. People must not hunt in this area too often."

"I went hunting with my dad once while my mom was visiting her sisters," Olivia began. "We didn't get anything, but it was just nice being out there with him."

Jonah noticed the sadness growing in the girl's eyes as she mentioned her father. He felt it too. It was a feeling he was all too familiar with.

"My dad used to say, the real trophy is not the deer, but the experience."

"Mine too."

They both descended into silence, staring at the ground in mimicked moments of reflection and memory.

"How's your mom holding up?" Jonah asked, breaking the silence.

"She's doing alright," Olivia replied. "I've been staying home a lot to spend time with her. She doesn't like to go out, afraid something will happen to her."

"That's silly. This is the safest town in the entire country. Have you seen Sheriff Holmes? Spends more time at his desk napping than chasing criminals."

"I know, but I just can't convince her everything will be fine. She won't let me out of her sight unless Darci comes. I'm all she has left."

Jonah knew what she was talking about. If it wasn't for Levi, he would be the only family his mother had left too. Guilt at leaving Levi behind tugged at him.

"Oh my god, are you seeing this?" Olivia suddenly exclaimed, breaking his chain of thought.

Jonah followed her eyes to the water, where two heads bobbed on the surface about ten feet out from the shore. It was Steve and Stephanie, their lips locked as they kissed.

"Free show" yelled Craig.

The two broke off their kissing to stare back at their audience with blushed cheeks.

"He started it," Stephanie said as she swam back to shore.

"That's my boy," egged on Craig, smiling from ear to ear.

Everyone's attention diverted to Milton, who suddenly let out a loud yelp.

"Fudge!" he exclaimed.

Attempting to stand up, he clumsily batted at the layers of mud clinging to his shorts.

"It's just mud," said Craig.

"It's not just mud, you neanderthal," Milton replied. "These are my favorite shorts. My mom is going to kill me."

"Just wash them off in the lake and hang them to dry."

"And run around in my underwear? I don't think so."

Milton was one of those kids that hated gym class, at least in part because of the requirements of changing in a public locker room. He complained to the nurses about imagined maladies so often that they got tired of it and just gave him a note whenever he asked, excusing him from exercise.

"I got an extra towel you can borrow," Jonah said. "It's Levi's, but I brought it just in case."

Milton seemed to mull it over for a moment before agreeing.

"It's in here," said Jonah, handing over the backpack.

Milton wandered away from the group, following the shoreline. He would search for a secluded spot to change. Somewhere so far that there was almost no chance that anyone or anything could see him. Jonah just hoped that he wouldn't get lost.

"That was nice of you," Olivia said.

The compliment made Jonah feel like a superhero even if just for a moment.

Something over Olivia's shoulder caught his eye.

"Shhh," he hushed to her. "Check it out."

Nodding to behind her, Olivia turned her head and covered her mouth with her hands to keep from squealing.

Stephanie and Steve had used Milton's commotion as the opportunity to emerge from the water and sneak away into the forest for privacy, hand in hand.

"I can't believe her," Olivia whispered. "She's always talking about how much of a jerk he can be."

"Well, she obviously see's something in him," replied Jonah.

"Did you know that she told me I'd be her maid of honor one day?"

"Quite the honor. Steve said the same thing, I'd be his best man when he got married."

Olivia laughed.

"Could you imagine those two at the altar and us next to them? I bet she'd want a super traditional wedding. All the bells and whistles."

"Steve wouldn't mind. He'd be too busy counting down the seconds until he could get her back to their room alone."

"I was reading this interesting article in Seventeen today."

"What's that?"

"They were saying that it's tradition for the best man and the maid of honor, to, you know..."

Jonah's eyes few wide and his jaw dropped. His brain raced as he tried to think of something to say.

Play it cool, you've got to play it cool. He thought to himself.

He never got the opportunity to reply.

Steve and Stephanie emerged from the seclusion of the forest prematurely, both looking much less joyous than they had been upon entering it.

Jonah could see why.

Three large teenage boys walked shoulder to shoulder towards them as they retreated.

Jonah knew them well already.

The two boys on each side were Neil and Nathan, thick-skulled members of the wrestling team. Both had shaved their heads and their scalps looked like one of Levi's connect the dots activity books as the hair stubbornly grew back.

In the between them was Rufus Hatchwell. He stood almost a head taller than Jonah, with broad shoulders and thick arms. He was the captain of the wrestling team and two-time state champion. His hair was the same jet-black color as Stephanie's, the likeness would have been remarkable if one didn't know that they were twins.

"What are you doing with him?" Rufus snarled.

Steve took a step forward towards the boy, but Stephanie found a way to wedge herself between them.

"We were just talking, Rufus," Stephanie pleaded.

"I got this," Steve said. "I'm not afraid of him.'

Maybe he should be. Steve was tall and strong, but next to Rufus, he looked any old kid in school.

Regardless, Steve was not deterred. He tensed his face and neck in defiance with an unflinching gaze that could stare down a charging lion.

"Why don't you mind your own business?" Steve said.

"My sister is my business," replied Rufus, his fists clenched at his sides.

Jonah knew this could only end one way.

Abandoning concern for his own well-being, Jonah burst into a run towards the boys. He arrived at Steve's side, ready to help, but noticed Craig had beaten him there despite doing the same only after Jonah had taken off. It was like Craig had waited to see what Jonah would do before he decided to rush forward himself.

In terms of numbers, the boys were even. But in terms of weight class, they were over-matched. Craig was about the same size as Neil or Nathan, but Jonah was thirty or forty pounds lighter than either. He wouldn't be too useful in a fight, either. He had done alright when play fighting with Steve as kids, though he was pretty sure Steve had let him win a few times.

He wished Milton would be back soon. They were going to need him if they hoped to survive this.

Rufus struck first, pushing his sister out of the way before tackling Steve around the waist with his state championship caliber take-down. Jonah dove at them but found himself unable to move as one of Rufus's lackeys, either Nathan or Neil, grabbed him by the back of the neck and put him into a headlock.

Jonah turned purple as he struggled to breathe. Thankfully, Craig landed a punch to his assailant's face that freed Jonah, at least temporarily.

The six teenagers continued their scuffle on the shoreline while the girls screamed for them to stop. Violent waves rippled across the pond's surface as bodies and limbs flung and flailed with one another. Red streaks of blood found their way into the pond, suspended in the water like oil, until a mysterious current swept them into the depths.

3

1972

Jonah winced as the isopropyl alcohol stung at the skin of his face, dabbed against a small gash that sat between his temple and ear.
"That hurts," he hissed.

"Stop being a baby," his mother replied as she dipped fresh gauze into the bowl to soak up the disinfectant. "You deserve it."

The pain returned as he clutched tight to the seat of the dining chair in the kitchen, the waning light of the afternoon shining through the window above the sink.

"Please be gentle," he asked. "That really hurts."

As if his request was somehow offensive, his mother dragged the wound maliciously with the gauze. She had the bedside demeanor of Nurse Ratched.

He jumped from the chair and cursed, pacing the kitchen with heavy breaths.

"Quiet, Levi is in the next room," she scolded him. "Sit back down and let me finish cleaning the wound."

"You're being rough on purpose!"

"I'm trying to get the dirt and sand out before it gets infected. You're the one who decided to use his face as a plow."

"I didn't—" he tried to reply, but she had already approached him with a freshly soaked ball of gauze, ready to attack his injury with renewed fervor. He let out a deep sigh and gave up, holding still to let her work.

"You'll be lucky if this doesn't leave a scar," she said. "We have no money to even think about going to the hospital in Madison for stitches."

She hadn't always been this way. Growing up, he remembered her as a sweet and loving woman who always babied him when he got hurt. She was colder than he remembered, short on patience and quick to anger. They didn't talk about it much, but the last four years had been really hard on them both.

"I had to give up my shift at the diner tonight," his mother told him as she tossed a stained red ball of gauze into the open trash. "The dinner rush Jonah, the dinner rush. Do you know how much that will cost me in tips?"

With her arms crossed in front of her and her neck tensed, her anger was palpable.

"I already said I'm sorry," said Jonah. "I don't know what else you want from me. I didn't start the fight, it was all—"

"You're just like your father. Running head first into everything. Look where that got him! Look where that got us!"

"You didn't have to come home. I could have taken care of myself."

"Oh really? When I got here, you had already made a bloody mess of the kitchen. What were you doing at the pond, anyway? The mayor told everyone to stay away cause of the algae build up. Lord knows whatever else the plant has been dumping in there. What were you thinking?"

Jonah opened his mouth to refute the mayor's claim of algae, but decided against it. It wouldn't have mattered.

"And leaving Levi with a neighbor when it was your responsibility to watch him? Lying to Mrs. O'Leary? Did you know she runs my bible study group? Every week I sit with her and a dozen other moms to talk about sin and now she knows you were straight up lying. I'm never going to hear the end of it. This is why I won't let you get your license yet. I can't trust you not to—"

She droned on, scolding him for being reckless and irresponsible. It wasn't the first time he had heard her tirade like this, and he knew it wouldn't be the last.

Jonah wasn't really listening. He tried to contain his own anger, his anger at being forced to give up his summer, possibly his last summer with his best friend, to play babysitter. He tried to think of something else, something adequate enough to cool the heat growing in his chest before he exploded. One thought immediately came to mind.

It's tradition for the best man and the maid of honor, to, you know...

"Earth to Jonah," his mother said, knocking him in the back of the head. "Are you listening to me?"

"What?"

"I asked you a question. Where's Dad's watch? I'm heading to the repair shop in Madison tomorrow and I'll drop it off."

"Oh, it's..."

Jonah's mind raced, trying to think of where he had left it.

It was the only intact remnant of his father they had found after the landmine had gone off. The only physical part of the man to make it back from Southeast Asia. Despite being broken and having a cracked face, Jonah insisted on wearing it practically everywhere. He had put it on after waking up that morning, that he remembered clearly. He continued to sift through thoughts, pulling details as best he could from the fog. Still on his wrist at breakfast, still on his wrist when Steve picked him up, still on his wrist in the forest.

Then he remembered.

He had taken it off and put it in his backpack when they got to the pond. Knowing his friends, he didn't want to risk losing amongst the endless attempts to throw each other off the dock or dunk heads under the water. The same backpack Milton had taken with him when he went off into the forest to change.

"It's in my backpack," Jonah told her. "I left it in Steve's truck."

He lied.

"Well, you better go get it," his mother said, putting away the first aid kit. "I've got to get dinner started."

She walked to the sink and started filling a pot with water. "Dinner's at six. Be home by then."

"Yes, mom," Jonah said, heading towards the hallway as fast as he could. Milton lived on the opposite end of town. If he hurried and left on his bike now, he could make it back just in time.

With one hand on the front doorknob, something caught his eye. He stopped.

With the light shining through the living room window, the glass of the picture frames containing family photos that lined the hallway cast crystal-clear reflections almost as good as a mirror. Jonah saw his. His hair was dirty and unkept, the gash on his face oozed drips of blood, a flush of purple grew around his cheeks and under his left eye, the precursor to the inevitable bruising to come. He looked like a boxer in between rounds of a heavyweight fight. He only hoped that Rufus and his numb-skull cronies had got it worse.

A cloud passed in front of the sun, dimming the light, and revealing the picture in the frame that he had been using as his makeshift looking glass. His father's smiling face stared back at him. The man's hair was short, kept in the military style. His uniform, recently pressed with perfect folds, proudly showed off his array of military honors. Unit citations, service ribbons, medals; it was a cornucopia of honor. They hardly seemed like worthwhile recompense to his family, who needed him, not useless decorations, to continue the life they had started together.

The photo was taken right after volunteering to go to Vietnam. Volunteered, that's right. Jonah's father had survived the Korean War and fifteen years later didn't even hesitate to go back into the fray. Would he have been smiling if he had known that it would be the last photo he would ever take?

Jonah's family wasn't the only one.

The town had organized a huge block party the day before the men shipped out. Some of the others were drafted, but most had chosen to enlist. They were all full of excitement, everyone in town showing up to pat them on the back, cheers with them, put them on a pedestal as American heroes. Olivia's father had been one of them. They were about to go off and fight the Viet Cong, to fight the Reds, to fight for America. The death totals hadn't accumulated yet, the public hadn't soured on a war fought in a country most couldn't find on a map. The protest and anti-war movement were still only whispers behind closed doors, not gaining steam into the grand marches that now popped up all over the country.

Jonah remembered his mother smiling from ear to ear, laughing and joking with the other wives of the soldiers, her belly sticking out proudly under her shirt, Levi nestled safely inside.

The men about to go off to war held cold cans of cold beer, smoked cigars, and told lewd jokes from boot camp.

None of them were quite ready to replace the beer with grenades, the cigars with dope, and the jokes with hushed worries of where Charlie would be hiding next.

It was the last time Jonah had seen his dad, the body the military had sent back was too eviscerated by a grenade for an open casket.

He wondered how different it could have been if he hadn't volunteered. How much happier his mom would still be. If the war hadn't taken the man in the picture with the friendly smile and in the aftermath left nothing but a vast canyon of nothingness, impossible to fill.

Even the ones who returned came back missing something; physical or mental, never to be whole again.

A war thousands of miles away, across continents and oceans, had torn the tiny town of Tranquility Pond apart just the same as if it was being fought on main street. Levi was the youngest child left, with most of the young men overseas, dead, or recovering from devastating injuries; no one had been spared to start the next generation. The elementary school grounds were sparse and quiet while diapers collected dust on shelves. It would be years before a baby's cry would be heard again.

"Jonah have a boo-boo?" a small voice asked behind him, breaking his train of thought.

Jonah turned to face the four-year-old Levi. The boy had bright green eyes and short hair the same color as Jonah's. He refused to wear shorts or pants when hanging around the house, so he stood in his underwear bought at the Sears in Madison and a plain red t-shirt. In his arms were his blanket and a teddy bear; both looked like they had seen better days.

"I'll be ok," Jonah reassured him, but the boy wasn't convinced.

"Go to doctor?" Levi asked.

"Not this time."

"I fix."

Levi offered up his blanket to Jonah. It was almost brown with dirt from being dragged around the yard all morning, twigs and grass clung to it. Levi carried it and the stuffed animal with him everywhere, refusing to part with them under almost any circumstance. Neither Jonah nor his mother risked the screaming tantrum that would ensue if they tried.

"No, thank you. I've got to go."

"No go, stay. Play blocks with me."

"I can't play blocks right now."

"Then play war with Levi."

Whomever had taught Levi that game had unwittingly unleashed a cruel joke upon their home.

"I'll play with you after dinner. I promise. Be good for mom while I'm gone."

Jonah passed the boy a reassuring smile, but it didn't ease the child's discomforting gaze.

Turning, he reached for the doorknob and stopped again, feeling a tug on the back of his t-shirt.

Levi wasn't the kind of child to take no for an answer.

"I really have to…" Jonah began, but couldn't finish his words. Levi was holding up his blanket, his most prized possession.

"Thank you, but I don't need a blanket right now," Jonah said, not trying to upset his brother.

"Protect Jonah," said Levi plainly.

"You really don't have to."

"Blankie protect Jonah."

Jonah thought about just ignoring him and leaving, but the conviction in the four-year-olds voice was absolute. If he didn't accept it, he knew Levi would be devastated.

Jonah took it from him.

"Thank you," he said, forcing a smile.

"Blankie protect Jonah," Levi repeated, smiling back.

Jonah threw the blanket into the cab of Steve's truck as he jumped inside. After the delay at the house, there was no way he would make it to Milton's and back in time before dinner. Lucky for him, Steve was home and was looking for any excuse to get away from the angry eyes of his mother.

She apparently was just as unhappy for her son to come home bloodied and bruised as Jonah's was.

Steve drove them to Milton's house. It took about fifteen minutes. Despite both sporting some serious bandages and open wounds, they laughed and joked on the trip like nothing had happened. The stinging pain a long forgotten memory already.

Milton's mother answered the door when Jonah knocked. He turned his head to the side, hoping to block the big cut Rufus had given him from her view.

"Evening Jonah," Milton's mother said with a smile. She was a short, round woman, with her dark hair done up into a beehive on her head.

She looked so much like her son that they would be almost impossible to differentiate if not for the different hair and clothes.

"Hello Mrs. Sandberg, is Milton around?" Jonah asked, eager to get the backpack and return home before he angered his mother any further.

"I thought he was still out with you and your friends."

Jonah cocked his head to the side.

"He was, earlier," Jonah said quickly, not wanting to get Milton in trouble. "He probably just got sidetracked on his way home."

"How long ago was that?" she asked, the concern in her voice growing.

"Just a little while ago. Nothing to worry about. I'll just see him tomorrow."

He turned to head back to the truck.

"Oh my god, you're bleeding," she exclaimed.

"Oh this," Jonah said, touching his cut. "I fell, that's all."

He felt a hand on his shoulder.

"Is Milton ok?"

The woman's voice suddenly turning frail.

"Of course he is. Why wouldn't he be?"

She didn't respond. He thought he could hear a slight sniffle behind him.

"I'll tell him to come home right away if I see him," he said, hoping to not get her worried.

Slowly, she released his shoulder.

Almost running back to the truck, he jumped into the passenger side of the idling vehicle.

"What is it?" asked Steve.

"Just go," Jonah answered.

Steve put the truck into gear and pulled away, the loud exhaust backfiring.

Jonah looked back at Milton's mother, still standing in the doorway, watching with her face contorted into an uneasy feeling of helplessness until she was nothing but a speck in the distance.

"What happened?" Steve asked.

"He's not home," replied Jonah.

"I figured that. Where is he?"

"She thought he was with us."

"Where is he then?"

"I don't know."

They drove to Darci's house. She lived a few blocks away. Maybe the two were continuing their debate from earlier and lost track of time.

Except he wasn't there. Darci called around to the other girls. None of them had seen him. They left Darci's with concern only growing and time running out before Jonah had to be home for dinner.

"Where do you think he is?" Steve asked first.

"Well, I don't really remember much from after the fight," stated Jonah.

"When Rufus pulled that knife, everyone kind of scattered."

"I've never seen the girls run so fast."

"Me neither."

He laughed, but it was short and unsure.

"He was changing or something, right?"

"With my backpack."

"So maybe he came back and everyone was already gone."

"Not everyone."

Jonah's eyes narrowed.

"Rufus and his meatheads were still there when we left, weren't they?"

"Yep," answered Steve. "They were pissed off that we had run. Rufus most of all."

"So Milton comes back, finds us gone and..." Jonah's voice trailed off.

"Rufus waiting for him with a knife."

They both looked at each other for a long moment.

"You think they hurt him?" asked Steve.

"I mean," Jonah contemplated it. "It's a possibility. Should we call the police?"

"You kidding?" said Steve. "And get us all into even more trouble? Rufus is a bastard, but he's just trying to protect his sister. He wouldn't really hurt anyone, least of all Milton. At least I don't think he would."

Jonah traced the cut on his face. He begged to differ.

"What if Milton slipped and hurt himself?" Proposed Jonah. "It's not like he's the most rugged outdoorsmen."

"Like twisted an ankle?"

"My best guess."

"So where is he, then?"

Both looked at each other, then straight ahead, where the narrow highway disappeared into the forest.

A sign stood at the corner.
Tranquility Pond Access Road, 3 Miles.

Earlier that day, the measly dock where they had spent the afternoon with the girls was bright and vibrant, filled with playfulness and laughter. But at dusk, with the sun hiding just behind the trees and the full moon growing brighter by the second, it was still and eerie. The muddy beach was so devoid of any signs of life that they could hear each other's heavy breathing as they traversed the tall grass and reeds.

Thankfully, Steve had two flashlights in his glove box, or else they would have been reliant on the moonlight alone to light their way.

"This must have been where Rufus tackled me," Steve said, pointing the beam of his light onto several wide depressions in the mud mixed with footprints.

"I think so," added Jonah. "Look at the prints. You can almost see what happened."

It was true. You didn't need to be Tonto to track the steps that led from the treeline where Steve and Stephanie had tried to slip off to, back to this spot on the shore, Jonah and Craig's own quickly joining the fray. Darci, Olivia, and Diane's dainty impressions followed before whisking Stephanie away from the melee.

"These are ours," Steve said, referring to the prints leading back towards where Steve had parked his truck earlier. Craig's expensive Adidas shoe print was undeniable (he had the only pair in town).

"These must be Rufus and his goons then," Jonah said, pointing to three more generic shoe prints that disappeared in the short grass.

"It can't tell where they went after this."

"They could have circled around to come looking for us again, to get the drop on us."

"But we were gone."

"Not all of us."

Jonah paused to process the thought.

"Milton!" both of them began yelling at the top of their lungs, hoping, praying for an answer.

After five minutes, their voices were growing hoarse.

"He could be unconscious," Jonah remarked.

"Or worse," Steve said, letting his words kind of trail off. "Even if they just cut him a little, you know him. He passes out at the sight of blood."

"I'll head this direction," Jonah said, referring to the shoreline they had last seen Milton walk away on.

"I'll go the opposite," replied Steve. "Call out if you find him, otherwise we'll meet on the other side."

Jonah didn't want to admit to Steve he felt nervous about splitting up. He took a deep breath and tried to muster his courage. He thought of his dad, who had never been afraid of anything or anyone in his entire life.

Meanwhile, Steve didn't want to admit to Jonah that he was terrified of being out there alone, that despite being almost eighteen years old, despite being quarterback of the football team, he was still scared of the dark.

"Great idea," Jonah said.

"See you in a few," replied Steve.

Both friends split up and began walking in opposite directions.

The full moon in the sky cast an endless army of shadows across the shoreline as Jonah walked carefully. Knowing how slick the grass and mud was, he wanted to avoid slipping and falling into the cold water. With no wind, the surface of Tranquility Pond was as still as he had ever seen it before. A perfect mirrored surface that reflected the reverse world of his own, one where tall grass and trees grew upside down in the sky and the stars shined from the ground.

He wondered how far Milton would have traveled carrying Jonah's backpack in order to feel he had enough privacy to change. Ten yards? Twenty? A half-mile? In gym class, Milton refused to shower with the rest of them and would only change after the locker rooms were empty.

He may have gone quite far.

A hooting owl startled Jonah. Stumbling, his toes felt instant cold as the pond's water filled the gaps between them.

"Damnit," Jonah cursed, pulling his foot out.

The ripples of his intrusion traveled from the shore in steady waves. With no competition to stop them, they would travel all the way until they were absorbed into the shoreline on the other side.

Whether it was the sudden cold or something else entirely, Jonah couldn't help but feel like he had disturbed something.

Too many late nights watching horror movie marathons. He thought to himself, shaking off the images of The Creature from the Black Lagoon, Loch Ness, and Bigfoot that lurked in his imagination.

Milton would have been looking for a more secluded spot anyway, not wide open on the beach like this.

Up ahead, about twenty yards, there it was.

Three large boulders extended from the tree line into the water, each one about shoulder height. It would be the perfect place for someone who was overly modest but also very paranoid to change while also keeping a close eye out for any possible intruders. The exact place Milton would pick.

He approached slowly. That illogical terror of the unknown that grips children staring into dark closets creeped at his resolve.

"Milton!" he yelled, hoping that magically his friend would jump out from behind the three gray stones like a magician's assistant reappearing after the magic trick.

No movement nor sound greeted him. Tranquility Pond well-earning its namesake.

The moment had come. Jonah stood in front of the row of boulders. If he just leaned over one, he could see whatever might be hiding from him on the other side. Would it be the boogeyman or his friend's body, hopefully still breathing?

He swallowed his own hesitation and peered over.

There was nothing there, no monster, no body, no anything. Just the same muddy shore with the waves of the pond softly crashing against it.

Wait, the waves?

While his footstep had created a small ripple that carried to the far shore, something far larger had caused this disturbance.

And for a second, Jonah thought he heard something. It was faint, but distinct in the eerie silence.

It sounded like someone swimming.

He shined his flashlight into the pond, hoping to illuminate the cause of the noise, but with the suddenly violent waves now emanating across it, all he saw was the rhythmic rising and falling of the water.

"Steve!" he yelled. "Is that you?!"

It wouldn't be the first time Steve had pulled an inappropriate prank.

"Cut it out," Jonah yelled again.

No response.

His eye caught something floating on the surface.

Jonah's guts turned over inside of him, the first thought in his head being that it was Milton's lifeless body. But as he stood and examined it under his flashlight's beam, he began to realize that it couldn't be a body.

Milton had been wearing a white shirt. He would stick out on the dark water like a sore thumb. Whatever was floating about ten yards out from the shore was dark as night and unreflective of both his flashlight and the moon's glow.

It looked like a log, a rotted old log, bobbing on the surface.

He let out a loud sigh and shook his head at himself. He had gotten himself all worked up over nothing. Milton wasn't here, just him and Steve acting like idiots, per usual.

Not thinking, letting the moment of silliness overtake him, Jonah picked up a flat rock from the shore and skipped it towards the log, as if hitting it would somehow recover some of his dignity for being so unabashedly afraid of nothing.

His aim was true. After several skips, it bounced off the log with a strange, metallic, dinging sound.

Jonah flinched as two orange eyes appeared, bright jewels floating in the darkness of what he now knew was no log at all. They watched him silently, and with each passing second chilly tendrils stabbed at his chest, seizing his muscles as the fear he was so quick to write off returned with a vengeance.

He stumbled backwards, simultaneously unable to run or stay put in the same spot. Unable to watch his step, his eyes refusing to break with the orange ones that watched him, he tripped on a rock and fell to the muddy shore.

Dazed from the fall, his senses swirled with sensations. He thought he heard loud splashing, splashing that grew in volume and intensity with each passing moment. Whatever he had seen out on the pond, it was coming.

The waves were too violent for him to see it, but the white frothing splashes of water rising into the air told him all he needed to know. He pushed himself backwards, hoping to put as much distance between himself and the pond as he could.

It moved fast, faster than he could hope to escape from.

The mist got into his eyes and blurred his vision. Whatever it was, it was close now. The violent splashing like gongs in his ears.

He closed his eyes.

It gripped his shoulders first, lifting him from the ground before shaking him back and forth violently.

"Jonah, Jonah!" Steve's voice yelled from directly in front of him.

Jonah opened his eyes to find Steve's distinct auburn hair right in front of him.

"Oh Steve," Jonah exclaimed, letting out a long held breath. "Thank god it's you. There's something—"

"Stop messing around," Steve scolded him.

His vision improved enough that he could see more details of Steve's face. His eyes had materialized, and they stared back at him, wet and glassy. Tears glistened his cheeks, he looked most un-Steve-like.

"What is it?" Jonah asked.

"I found him," Steve said, with a voice that broke like it had when Steve had first hit puberty. "I found Milton. He's dead."

4

2023

"Woah!" Asher exclaimed. "You found a dead body? That's so cool."

"I didn't find it, Steve did," Grandpa Joe replied.

The boat floated sleepily on Tranquility Pond, not quite awake yet with the sun tucked discreetly behind thick cloud cover.

"Did you get to see it? Was it purple and bloated like on the TV shows?"

"There wasn't much left to see."

"Was it bloody and gross?"

"Stop, relax."

Grandpa Joe reached into the small cooler between them and pulled out a soft drink, tossing it to the boy, who caught it excitedly, then pulled out a beer for himself.

"What I'm trying to explain," Grandpa began, the can's top hissing as it popped open. "Is that there wasn't really a body to find, only pieces."

The comment made Asher gasp. Soda gushed from his nose. He leaned over the side of the boat, trying to get it all out. Tears in his eyes, his grandfather comforted him with soft pats on the back.

"How many pieces?" Asher asked he regained the ability to speak.

"Over a dozen," Grandpa Joe replied. "Of course, that wasn't all of him. Just all they could find. We think some animals got to some of him before we got there. It was right over there, actually."

He pointed to a stretch of bare, nondescript shore where a black willow tree overhanging the water was the only distinguishable feature.

"Do you think we could go look?" Asher asked, way too excited about being in the same place as a dead body as a nine-year-old should be.

"Do your parents let you watch those murder TV shows?" Grandpa Joe asked.

"Not really. I usually watch them when—"

Without warning, the water next to them erupted. Asher let out a short shrill shriek as he jumped backwards, landing on the floorboard of the boat.

Grandpa Joe was ready, already expecting it, and his hands moved instantly to unfurl the bag of rifles and shotguns he had packed. Pulling one up to his sights, he pointed it at the disturbance in the water. His thumb released the safety. He had pre-loaded them; he was ready to fire.

Asher watched from the floor of the boat, watched his grandpa act with so much calm and determination under even the most nerve-wracking of conditions. Despite his age, despite his sciatica, despite his arthritis, despite his heart condition; Grandpa Joe seemed just as young in that moment as he would have been as a teenager.

Asher covered his ears, bracing for the loud gunshots.

Except they never came. The only muffled sound he could hear through his palms clasped tight over his ears was his grandfather's signature belly laughter.

With trepidation, Asher slowly rolled to his knees and peeked over the side of the boat and into the water.

The surface frothed white as the fish attached to Asher's line struggled against the hook stuck deep in its mouth, jumping from the water in a fruitless attempt to escape its inevitable demise.

"You want to reel that in?" Grandpa Joe asked between laughs.

Asher grabbed the rod mounted to the side of the boat and turned the reel just like he had seen in the movies, his grandfather moving beside him to guide him. Together, they pulled the fish out of the water and into the waiting net.

"Looks like a fine first catch to me," Grandpa Joe said, holding the fish up for Asher to examine.

The boy leaned in close, eager to learn more about the strange creature that a few moments ago was staring back at him from under the surface. A sudden jerk of the fish's tail sent Asher reeling back again into his seat.

"It's just a fish," Grandpa Joe remarked with a smile before holding the fish tight to the side of the boat and rummaging around in his overall pocket for his knife. Asher couldn't help but notice the fish's mouth gulping for air as it stared at him, its eyes calm and unfeeling, even as its death approached. With one quick stab of Grandpa's knife, it was over. The fish was sent to the big lake in the sky.

"Want a picture with it?" Grandpa asked.

"I don't think so," Asher replied, diverting his eyes away from the now dead animal.

"You sure? You can post it to TikTrack or Faceboot."

Asher wanted to laugh at his grandfather but couldn't muster it. He felt sad about the fish.

Opening another cooler, this one filled with nothing but crushed ice, Grandpa Joe threw the body inside before closing it tight.

"That'll make a fine fish fry tonight," he said, casting a reassuring smile to the still panting Asher.

"Grandpa," Asher said tentatively, his voice scared and small.

"What is it?"

"Why didn't it fight back when you held it?"

"Well, I suppose it couldn't. I have a firm grip."

"I don't think so. I looked into its eyes. It looked like it had given up, like it knew it was time for it to go."

Grandpa Joe gave the boy a peculiar look as he mulled the boy's words in his head.

"I suppose that's probably the case," he said at last. "Acceptance. Sometimes you just have to know when you're beat, know when there ain't nothing that can keep you from your fate. When that happens, that makes it time to just play nice, not make it too messy for everyone involved."

Asher nodded in agreement. He supposed that made sense.

Grandpa Joe examined Asher's face. He sensed that there was something else troubling the boy.

"Come on Asher," he began with a friendly voice. "I know when something's bothering you. Why don't you just come out and say it? Get it out in the open."

Asher considered it for a moment before speaking.

"How come I never heard about your brother Levi before?"

Grandpa Joe took a big swig from his beer can, almost downing it in one gulp.

"I guess I'll need to continue the story to explain."

As the commotion of the caught fish subsided, and the pond returned to its natural state of stillness, Asher listened intently as his grandfather picked up where he had left off.

5

1972

It was after midnight. Despite the heavy fatigue Jonah felt in just about every muscle of his body, the bright florescent lights of the police station made it almost impossible for him to do anything other than sit uncomfortably. It didn't seem to be a problem for Steve; he snored loudly, his head tilted back, almost falling out of the chair in front of Sheriff Holmes's desk.

Jonah considered getting up, walking around the station, just to pass the time. They had already been there hours, told to wait patiently until the Sheriff got back from the crime scene. It was so quiet inside, the half a dozen desks for clerks and deputies behind them empty since four o'clock the previous afternoon. Right around the time he was being patched up by his mother.

He was startled and the peacefulness abruptly interrupted when the doors of the station swung open and almost a dozen men swarmed inside. None of them seemed to notice the bewildered Jonah or the still sleeping Steve, their focus intently on the big-bellied, handle-bar mustache clad officer at the lead. Jonah noticed the sheriff's scowl betraying no attempt to hide his displeasure at being chased into his own henhouse. Of course, Sheriff Holmes was always scowling, so that might have just been how he looked.

"I told you all," Sheriff Holmes said, suddenly turning to the group. "Go home. I'll be making a statement in the morning."

"Can you tell us anything about the boy who was killed?" asked an overly eager man that had elbowed his way in front of the rest of the swarming crowd. He was the only one that Jonah didn't recognize in the slightest.

"Who are you?" the sheriff asked.

"Bill Bradley, The Capital Times," the man replied. He didn't look like any reporter that Jonah had ever seen before. He always imagined newspapermen wore brown, over-sized suits and Trilby hats with pencils stuffed behind their ears. This one wore a Hawaiian shirt, jeans, and his graying hair was visible behind a receding hairline.

"How'd you get here so fast?" The Sheriff asked him. "Madison is almost an hour away."

"I was heading to the Dells to visit family," the reporter replied. "I stopped at the diner for dinner and, well, word travels fast around here."

The sheriff gave a loud grunt.

"We'll have a statement prepared for the morning," he said, sounding annoyed. "Until then, no comment."

"Can you at least recommend a good motel in town?" Bill asked.

"No," Sheriff Holmes said abruptly. "Now clear out."

The reporter smiled. He obviously wasn't fazed by the sheriff's rudeness, he looked like he was used to it. He separated from the crowd and disappeared through the front doors.

Jonah recognized several of the men who remained. One was the sheriff's deputy, his skin a greenish-tint, dabbing a white handkerchief to his mouth.

"Go to the bathroom and get yourself cleaned up, will you?" the sheriff told him.

Jonah noticed several dark stains on the deputy's shirt as he practically sprinted to the restroom.

"Now that the reporter is gone, what can you tell us?" said an old man, still in his pajamas.

"Not much," the sheriff told him. "We identified the victim as Milton Sandberg. That's the extent of it."

"Are you absolutely sure it's him? Couldn't it be a someone else from out of town?" another old man asked.

"His parents are on their way now to confirm his identity, but trust me, it's him. There's not much left, but enough. I have the rest of my deputies out there searching for the rest of him as we speak."

The group of old, white-haired men who had shown up erupted into murmurs and whispers with one another.

"Gentlemen, please calm down," Sheriff Holmes said, raising his arms and using his authoritative voice. "We've just started the investigation. You'll know once I know more. Now, if you'll please excuse me, I need to call Madison and ask them to send a forensics team as soon as possible."

"Sheriff," said a calm, frail voice.

Like Moses parting the Red Sea, the group of old men split apart and a well-dressed man wearing a suit and derby hat hobbled forward unsteadily on a cane. It was the mayor.

He usually held court at the Elk's Lodge, where everyone from the head of the school board to the man who owned the plant would visit to consult with him. Jonah had only seen him a handful of times, the last time being his father's funeral when the mayor had given him a reassuring pat on the shoulder and thanked him for his family's sacrifice.

Sacrifice, Jonah was beginning to hate the word.

"If we could speak in private for a moment," the mayor said. "Perhaps I can offer my insights on how to handle the situation."

"Of course sir," said Sheriff Holmes.

The mayor and the sheriff disappeared into the quiet of the interrogation room, while the crowd of old men filed through the front door and out of the station.

The station returned to silence except for the faint sounds of the deputy's retching from the bathroom and Steve's snores. Jonah's friend could sleep through a gunfight.

Jonah felt bad for the officer in the bathroom. Whatever was happening to him sounded just awful. He knew the feeling, too. When Steve had showed him the scene under the black willow tree where Milton's limbs and organs were arranged like a macabre Easter egg hunt, he too had felt like expelling the contents of his stomach. If he had stuck around to have dinner with his mother, he might have done just that.

It wasn't long before the mayor and the sheriff re-emerged from the interrogation room.

"We can discuss further tomorrow," the mayor said as he hobbled towards the front door. Passing Jonah and Steve, the old man paused a moment.

Jonah felt the man's hand on his shoulder, strong even in its frailty.

"I'm sorry about your friend," the mayor said. "Please stay away from the pond for the rest of the summer, for your own good."

"Yes, sir," Jonah replied, almost instinctively.

The old man slowly hobbled out the door, the station returning to a quiet state where only Steve's snoring and the sheriff's heavy breaths broke the silence of the night air.

The sheriff sat down at his desk in front of them. He looked annoyed, to say the least, as if Milton's death was an annoying change of pace from his usual routine.

He cleared his throat before lifting a torn backpack from under the desk.

"Is this his?" The sheriff asked.

"It's mine actually," Jonah replied.

Steve kept on snoring.

Jonah jabbed him in the ribs, but Steve only brushed him off, mumbling something under his breath before going back to sleep.

Sheriff Holmes gave Jonah a look before slamming the pack down back onto the desk. The noise sounded as loud as if the sheriff had fired his revolver into the air.

Steve nearly fell out of his chair as he woke up with a start.

"Glad you could get your beauty rest," the sheriff said with a faked smile.

"Now, I'd like to hear your story one more time. Starting from the beginning this time."

For the next hour, Steve and Jonah recounted the events of the previous day in extraordinary detail. From the style of eggs his mother had made for him that morning to the color of the girl's swimsuits. Jonah left out only one detail, one he hadn't even told Steve about yet, the thing he thought he had seen in the pond: the two glowing orange eyes.

After all, he probably just imagined them. The light plays tricks on you at night when it reflects off the water.

"So, your theory is that Rufus Hatchwell and his buddies killed Milton?" The sheriff said back to them, his eyes stony and unrevealing.

"Yes," Steve and Jonah said, almost in unison.

"Because you guys got into a fight earlier," the sheriff said, his monotone voice hard to decipher.

They both nodded.

The sheriff leaned back in his chair, his enormous belly jiggling slightly as it fell from the desktop to his lap.

"Do you have anyone who can corroborate your story?" he asked.

"Ask any of the girls or Craig," Steve replied. "They'll tell you the same thing."

"Anyone who's not one of your friends?"

Steve and Jonah looked at each other, trying to think.

"The Sandbergs can tell you they saw us, when we came looking for Milton," Jonah said as soon as it crossed his mind.

"Good," said the sheriff. "I'll ask them right now."

Panic struck Jonah as he heard the front door of the station open.

"Brian," the sheriff said, standing up. "Please take these boys home."

The deputy who had spent the better part of half an hour in the bathroom appeared immediately.

"Come on, kids," the deputy said. "Follow me."

Steve stood, excited to leave the station, but Jonah remained seated.

"Sheriff," he said, his voice tentative.

"Hmmm?" the sheriff grunted in response.

"Do you think I could have my backpack back? My father's watch is—"

"I'm afraid not. The backpack and all its contents are evidence. You'll get personal effects back after we close the investigation. Now it's best you two get going unless you want to sleep in a cell tonight."

Jonah wanted to argue, but perhaps it was the exhaustion that had overtaken him that took all the will to fight out of him. He quickly joined Steve beside the deputy as they walked towards the front doors.

"Oh, and Brian," the sheriff yelled from behind them. "You left the evidence locker open again, anybody could have waltzed right in and taken something. Please be more careful next time."

"Yes sir," the deputy stammered out.

Jonah saw the room in question as they walked, the large sign above it identifying it as the Evidence Locker. Through the glass window, he dared a peek inside. It was absolutely stuffed to the gills with guns of all shapes and size: handguns with extended mag clips, rifles for large game, and even a few cans with pins attached to their tops that looked suspiciously like grenades.

The deputy must have noticed his curiosity.

"We confiscate a lot of illegal weapons around here," he said. "Wannabe big game hunters from the city come up here and like to pretend they Hemingway or something."

Jonah nodded.

He would have asked another question about such an interesting arsenal of firearms if he hadn't been shocked by the item laying on a table in the center of the room: the bloody and ripped to shred remains of his brother Levi's towel.

Jonah felt a pit form in his stomach and he hurried after the deputy and Steve as they made their way to the lobby, eager to escape the grisly sight.

Only waiting in the lobby, he found something worse.

Mr. Sandberg sat in a thin plastic chair with his hands on his lap, staring straight forward, his face emotionless and drained of all color. He was so still, not even acknowledging them as they passed. He could have been mistaken for a wax sculpture.

Next to him, Mrs. Sandberg sat with her head buried in a handkerchief soaked with tears. She looked up at him. Her red eyes with deep bags under them pierced him more than he ever thought they would.

"Is Milton ok?"

"Of course he is. Why wouldn't he be?"

Jonah's own words of encouragement echoed back to him, hitting him with a tidal wave of guilt.

Steve and Jonah had left Milton behind after all, too concerned with saving their own skin to be concerned for their friend.

Some friends we are.

Steve fell asleep in the back of the police car almost as soon as the door was closed, leaving Jonah and the deputy sitting silently as the officer drove slowly on the deserted night roads.

The deputy held the wheel firmly with both hands, as if afraid if at any moment that it might slip from his grasp and send them into a streetlight or into a neighbor's yard.

Peering into the rear-view mirror, he strained to read the deputy's name tag.

"Deputy Brian Nibiikwe," Jonah said aloud. From the man's dark complexion and last name, it appeared he had come from one of the nearby tribes.

The deputy only nodded in response. His eyes were bloodshot, clearly strained from his exertions in the restroom.

"Which tribe are you from?" Jonah asked, trying to make conversation to mask Steve's snores.

The deputy peered at him before speaking.

"Ojibwe," he said.

Jonah understood why he had spoken little until now. The moment the deputy opened his mouth, the car immediately stank of alcohol. It reminded him of how Steve's dad smelled coming home after a late night at the bar. Combined with the thick layer of sweat on the man's forehead, the slow and methodical focus on driving, it suddenly made sense. The deputy hadn't been sick from the crime scene. He had been drinking all night.

The deputy suddenly looked very self conscious, aware that his appearance was telling.

"What will happen now?" Jonah asked, hoping to draw attention away from the deputy.

"There will be an investigation," the deputy said. They sat at a red light, no other traffic at this time of day passing by. Most cops or residents would have just driven through it.

"Probably bring you in a few more times for additional questioning."

"Will you bring in Rufus?"

"He's already been picked up, just heard it on the radio. He and his friends are on their way in."

"Are you arresting him?"

The deputy peered at him in the rear-view mirror with a curious look.

"Why would we? There's no evidence it was him."

"There's what we told you."

"I'm sorry, kid, but just because you got into a fight earlier today doesn't mean he killed your friend."

Jonah sighed. He knew the deputy was right. Milton's severed head hung in the back of his mind. He needed to keep talking, get his mind to move on to something, anything.

"Why aren't you working at the station on the reservation?" Jonah asked. Few Ojibwe hung out in town, much less worked there.

"I'm no longer part of the tribe," the deputy replied.

"I'm sorry to hear that."

"It is what it is."

"What happened?"

Maybe if Jonah wasn't so tired, wasn't so desperate for anything to get his mind off of Milton, he would have known how incredibly rude his question was.

The deputy looked taken aback for a moment, but then answered

"It's a long story."

Jonah peered up at the light, still red.

"Looks like we have time."

"The Ogimaa, the chief, made it clear I was no longer welcome."

"What about your family? Didn't they stand up for you?"

"My brother is the Ogimaa."

"Oh."

The police car descended back into the uncomfortable silence as the light turned green and the cruiser slowly pulled forward at a snail's pace.

Deputy Nibiikwe was sweating profusely, wiping at his brow with his sleeve. Jonah wondered if it was just the alcohol or if he was nervous about something else. Had he been kicked out of the tribe because of the drinking?

"I'm sorry about your brother," said Jonah, trying to comfort the deputy. "I have a little brother myself. My mother hates it when we fight."

"All mothers do," the deputy replied. "How old is your brother?"

"Four, almost five. He's the youngest kid in town, which means not a lot of others his age to play with. I get stuck with him all the time. My mom works at the diner so I—"

"We're here," the deputy said, interrupting him.

Pulling up to Steve's house, Jonah pulled on the door handle but soon discovered that obviously the backdoors of police cars only opened from the outside.

"Well, thanks for the ride," Jonah said awkwardly, waiting for the deputy to let them out.

Except the deputy didn't move.

"You really need to stay away from the pond this summer," the Deputy said. There was a coldness to his voice.

"I know, I know. The algae bloom. The mayor told us."

"Especially your brother."

Jonah thought the comment peculiar. What did his brother had to do with this?

"I don't understand."

Suddenly, the deputy turned around and faced Jonah, his bloodshot eyes betraying no emotion.

"My people have many legends about that water," he began. "Going back farther than our tribe has existed. The water is dangerous."

The orange eyes in the water hung in Jonah's mind. He tried to push them out of his thoughts. It was nothing; it had been nothing, right?

"It didn't seem that dangerous," Jonah replied.

"How old are you?"

"Fifteen. I turn sixteen in September."

The Deputy seemed to nod at his response.

"Then you weren't here seventeen years ago. I was. I was just a boy, but I heard about the family that died out there. I heard about what happened."

"What happened?"

The Deputy began to speak again but stopped himself, almost like he was remembering something mid thought.

"Forget I said anything," he said, getting out of the car.

"But wait," Jonah said, but it was too late. The deputy couldn't hear him.

The back door opened and the sleeping Steve nearly hit his head on the curb as he fell out of the car. Immediately lights on in Steve's house turned on downstairs and the shadows of his parents materialized in the open doorway.

Jonah tried not to look at them. He didn't want to carry their expressions of disappointment and anger with him. He knew he would get his fair share as soon as he got home.

Jonah didn't emerge from the police car until Steve was inside his house, the door slamming shut behind him.

When he did, he stopped to look at Deputy Nibiikwe, hoping for one more chance to learn more about the family that had died on the pond.

The deputy looked tired. The long night of drinking and then going to work had worn him down. Maybe that was why he had slipped up.

"Thanks for the ride," Jonah said, using his waning energy to force a smile. "But can you tell me more about—"

"I can tell you no more," the deputy said.

"What about—"

"I can tell you no more."

Jonah nodded and turned to walk towards his house next door.

"Jonah," the deputy called for him after he was a few yards down the sidewalk.

Jonah turned his head, his eyebrows raised.

"Stay away from Tranquility Pond. For your own good and your brother's."

"Do you know how long I've been waiting up for you?!" His mother exclaimed as he walked through the door. "When Sheriff Holmes called and said he was taking you in, he wouldn't tell me anything other than you'd be back in a few hours. I didn't know he meant you'd be walking in the door at three in the morning!"

"I'm sorry, mom," Jonah managed to say. He felt so tired.

"You're sorry?! Where were you? What happened?"

Jonah considered sitting down to tell her everything, tell her about Milton and the pond and what he thought he saw in it. He knew it wouldn't matter. She was angry. No explanation in the world would calm her down. He just wanted to sleep.

"Can we talk in the morning?" he asked.

"No, we can not," she replied.

She was turning beet red, preparing to explode in anger. He didn't care. All he wanted was to feel the softness of his pillow under his face and the sweet embrace of his mattress.

"Don't you walk away from me…"

But he did, right up the stairs and into the hallway that led to his bedroom.

To his surprise, a pair of eyes stared at him from a crack in the door across the hall.

It was Levi.

"Mom's going to kill you if she finds out you are still awake," Jonah said with half-open eyes.

"I can't sleep," Levi stated, his head emerging from the darkness.

"We've been over this. There aren't any monsters in your closet or under your bed. Monsters aren't real."

"Yes, they are."

"No, they're not."

"I'm scared. Can I sleep with you?"

Jonah didn't care how scared Levi was. He didn't care if the kid didn't sleep all night. He just wanted to fall into his bed and close his eyes, alone.

"No."

"Where's blankie?"

"What?"

"Blankie, where's blankie?!"

Levi was growing more agitated, so was Jonah.

"I don't know where your stupid blanket is!"

He didn't mean to yell, but being this tired had dulled his ability to hold back his temper.

Levi recoiled into the darkness of his room and slammed the door shut.

Jonah immediately felt bad.

He paused with his hand on the doorknob as he mulled over entering. Putting his ear up to the thin wood panel, he listened. He could hear whimpers emanating from the other side. Levi was crying. He considered apologizing, telling Levi he was sorry. But his own bedroom was just a few yards away, his bed clearly visible, calling to him, beckoning him to its comforting embrace.

Jonah hit the pillow and was asleep within moments. That dreamless sleep that only exhaustion can bring on, and it was a good thing too. If he had any dreams, they would most certainly have been about those glowing orange eyes.

6

1972

"Jonah, you have a friend here to see you!" his mother yelled from the other side of his bedroom door, banging on it harshly and startling him from his dreamy haze. It had been several days since coming home from the police station, and his mother's furious anger with him had only partially subsided.

Jonah glanced at the clock by his bed. It was seven in the morning; he had only been asleep a few hours. Since he was grounded, he had nothing better to do the night before except stay up late watching the horror movie marathon playing on television.

It had been a pleasant break from the stress of the previous few days and his own private tribute to Milton, who loved trashy horror movies. "Dr. Terror's House of Horrors", "The Haunting", and "The Man with the X-Ray Eyes" were the appetizers, all building up to main course, Milton's all-time favorite movie, "Night of the Living Dead".

Jonah pulled a dirty shirt over his head as he got up and headed towards the door.

Unlocking it, he wasn't surprised to find his mother waiting for him in the upstairs hallway.

"You are still grounded," she said, her eyes stern.

"I know," Jonah said through a yawn.

"I wouldn't have let them in if they didn't tell me it was for school."

Jonah's eyebrow perked up. That was interesting.

"Who is it?"

She ignored his question.

"I'm going to give you five minutes, that's it. Then their gone. Do you hear me?"

"Yes, yes, I hear you."

"And don't forget, you're watching your brother tonight."

Jonah groaned from the top of the stairs.

"I don't want to hear it, young man. You have no idea how hard I work to put food on the table, take care of you, take care of your..."

Her voice faded as he descended the stairs sleepily.

Jonah wondered who would be visiting him this early. Maybe it was Steve, or one of the girls: Darci or Stephanie; maybe even Olivia.

The thought of his crush dropping in suddenly made him very aware of his own appearance. With his messy hair cow-licked straight up like Alfalfa and his filthy clothes stained from raiding the kitchen at midnight; he must look like a complete slob.

But it was too late. He was already at the base of the stairs. Instinctively, he slid his hands through his hair, hoping it would do something, anything, to improve his appearance, before turning to face this unexpected caller.

It wasn't Olivia. It wasn't Diane. It wasn't Darci or Stephanie either.

Staring back at him was Rufus Hatchwell, and by his expression, he was not too happy.

"What are you doing here?" Jonah asked, his mind not quite registering reality yet.

"You've got some nerve," Rufus replied. His fists clenched tight at his sides. His black eyebrows prominently angled into a grimace sat stark against his rapidly reddening forehead.

"What are you talking about?"

"Telling the sheriff you think I killed your friend."

Jonah stared back at him, not wanting to betray any of the fear and anxiety growing inside of him. The almost healed wound on the side of his face pulsated with each heartbeat. It was its first time facing its maker since its creation.

"Well, did you?" Jonah asked.

"Are you kidding?" Rufus scoffed. "I had nothing against that nerd other than he liked to hang out with a couple of losers."

"Say that to my face."

Jonah took a step closer, trying to match the toughness projected in his voice with his body language.

Rufus took another step forward as well.

"I just did," Rufus replied. There was not even a hint of fear in the older boy's voice.

"So what do you want, then?"

"They called me into the police station, had to sit there and answer questions all day. They filed a report based on what you and that panty-stain Steve told them about the fight. Apparently word has already got to Madison. Some reporter in town called it in and my name was in the newspaper this morning. The university is reconsidering the scholarship."

His voice hung there for a moment. Jonah could sense the bubbling anger inside Rufus, the human equivalent of a volcano building up to eruption.

"Well, you shouldn't be starting fights then," Jonah said. Whether he was still groggy from the early wake-up or just that stupid; he was dangerously close to pushing Rufus over the edge.

"My sister is out of your friend's league. He has no business hanging around her."

"She's her own person. She can hang out with who she wants to and so can Steve. What are you doing here anyway? Too afraid to tell this to Steve's face?"

Rufus grunted like a bull holding back the urge to charge.

"His mother wouldn't let me talk to him. Since you're his little lackey, I figured you could relay the message."

"And what message is that?" Jonah asked, ignoring the comment.

"If I lose my scholarship or I find out he's hanging around Stephanie again, I'm going to kill you both."

Jonah considered the threat. If Rufus was innocent, then it was empty. But if Rufus was guilty...

How would his father had responded? His dad would have cracked a joke in the face of anything, even the most dire of danger.

"You better calm down there," Jonah said with a smile. "Wouldn't want Sheriff Holmes to hear about you talking like that."

Rufus looked ready to lunge for him.

The ringing of the telephone filled the house with noise, but Jonah barely registered it. He was too busy staring down the larger, older boy.

"This is your last warning, both of you," Rufus snarled.

"You can take that warning and shove it up your—"

"Jonah!" his mother exclaimed from the top of the stairs. "What is going on here?"

"Mom, um," Jonah struggled to find the words.

"Nothing's wrong, mam," Rufus said, the anger in his eyes suddenly gone and a smile on his face. "Jonah and I were just chatting about next year's classes."

Rufus went from Attila the Hun to Beaver Cleaver in no time flat. It was a rare trait in boys their age who, like Jonah, tended to wear emotions on their sleeves. He would make a great politician one day with skills like that.

"That's good," Jonah's mother said with a smile as she stood behind Jonah. "Unfortunately, I need to cut this short. Jonah has to run out for a bit."

Jonah looked at her with a confused expression.

She escorted Rufus out the front door. Only when she wasn't looking, did Rufus look back at Jonah with a flash of those rage-filled eyes and mouth two words that Jonah was certain he meant with every ounce of his being.

"You're dead."

With the door safely closed, Jonah relaxed his shoulders. He considered hugging his mother, who unwittingly may have saved her son's life, but she was too busy looking at him with concern.

"I just spoke to the mayor," she said. "He would like a word with you."

"The mayor?" Jonah asked.

"He's waiting for you at the Elk's Lodge. I told him you'll be down shortly."

"What does he want to talk to me about?"

"I don't know," his mother replied, putting her hand to her brow and closing her eyes. She was holding back the urge to cry, Jonah could tell. She always did after bouts of being stern or yelling at Jonah, like the whole exercise of simultaneously playing the role of good guy and bad guy exhausted her.

"Just don't make this any worse, please," she added.

He considered giving her that hug after all, wrapping her arms around her and letting her cry on his shoulder, just like dad had done before getting blown up in Vietnam. Jonah was tall enough now, as tall as his father had been and the same lean build. Maybe he could recreate his dad in himself like he just been trying to do in front of Rufus.

Something held him back, as if there was some invisible barrier between them that repelled every thought of moving closer to her. He quickly gave up on trying.

Jonah ascended the stairs towards his room.

"Change before you go," his mother yelled after him. "You smell like you slept in a pile of garbage last night."

Jonah instinctively sniffed at his armpit after she said it. She wasn't wrong.

7

1972

The Elk's Lodge bustled with activity as Jonah walked inside. Filled with tables and chairs, almost no seat was vacant as veterans and old-timers played cards and discussed the good old-days with one another. Everywhere, loud hoarse voices competed with the shuffling of decks and clattering of glassware for space in the domed hall that echoed the noise surprisingly well. The walls were lined with photos and portraits of previous members and annual gatherings. Little American flags stuck from flowerpots in the center of the tables. Almost everyone wore a hat, whether to identify their affiliations or to hide gray and balding scalps.

When Jonah first came into view, a strange quiet overcame the room. Only a few hushed conversations lingered, of which he distinctly heard his father's name mentioned.

"Jonah," said an old voice that felt like it reverberated against every surface in the establishment. "Please join us."

"Yes, sir," Jonah replied, seeing the mayor standing up and beckoning him over to a long table at the far end of the hall.

He hadn't known what to expect at the Elk's Lodge. Though everyone knew about it, none of his friends ever talked about what happened inside. They all assumed it was just a place for old men to hang out, but in that moment, it felt like so much more.

Jonah walked down a center aisle, the only path to the long table at the end. Every single person at the table sat quietly and stared at him with intrigue as he walked, like he had stood up to protest a wedding when the officiant asked for anyone to speak now or forever hold their peace.

He took notice of the various groups that made up the Elk's Lodge members. The World War II veterans clumped together in several tables weren't wearing their uniforms but were easily identifiable from their caps, some with pins or patches that indicated their rank, unit, or branch. A smaller group behind them, tucked almost into a corner, were the ones who made it out of World War I. They looked almost half-way to the grave already, their skin wrinkled and sunken. Most sat in wheelchairs with a few nurses watching dutifully nearby. The little old men from the Shriners club watched him with beady eyes from under their funny little hats.

Two men in particular peered at him with stares that made his stomach flip over. Jonah recognized them. It was the school principal and head football coach. The short walk was beginning to feel like a mile.

Arriving at the long table with the mayor, he noticed it sat slightly higher than the others throughout the hall, giving it an aura of importance. Stacks of folders filled with papers were arranged across it, some bearing the stamps and seals of official documents.

"Please take a seat, Jonah," the mayor said, his body tremoring slightly as he sat back down. Jonah imagined with that wiry, old frame that the mayor must have incredible difficulty moving around.

Jonah sat in the chair opposite. It was an ordinary chair, with a back that stopped right below his shoulders and no armrests. By comparison, the mayor's chair was more comparable to a throne, with a wood back that extended above his head and wide, cushioned armrests of rich violet velvet.

He didn't recognize the others at the table, but it wouldn't take Sherlock Holmes to figure out who they were. Fur caps, orange vests with N.R.A. patches on them, and the long rifles held at their sides gave way to the impression they were a hunting party of some sort. None of them spoke. Electing to watch him with keen, calculating eyes, like a deer in their sights.

The hall sat quietly behind him, but Jonah could still feel their gaze intently on him, bearing down with an imagined heat like fire. They might as well had shown a spotlight on him as soon as he had walked through the door. He would have felt less conspicuous.

The mayor's gaze felt less intense by comparison. Of everyone in the room, he looked the least intimidating. His thin neck, barely able to hold up his round head, was neatly crowned by a silly derby. His hands rested on a cane that was nestled between his legs to steady him as he leaned forward, without which he might topple over.

For the first time, Jonah got to see the mayor in such close proximity and under circumstances that afforded him the ability to examine the old man. A scar under the man's left cheekbone ran down his neck and disappeared below his collar. His hands bore more scars, more than Jonah could count.

They slashed back and forth across his skin in long, smooth streaks; only interrupted by oil spots and deep wrinkles that betrayed just how close to death's embrace the man probably was. Jonah tried to guess which war the mayor had fought in, by how old the man looked, it could have been the civil war for all Jonah knew.

But it was the man's cane that caught Jonah's eye almost immediately. The mahogany stalk connected to a copper metal head that was shaped into the head of a panther. Inlaid into that were a pair of emerald eyes that shined brilliantly. It must have cost a fortune.

Jonah sat, waiting for the mayor to say something, and not sure what to say himself. What could he say, for that matter? The mayor had summoned him.

The mayor's eyes narrowed, studying him. Jonah couldn't help but feel like the emerald eyes on the cane watched him too.

"I'm sorry about your friend," the mayor said. As if everyone in the room had been collectively holding their breath, the regular bustle that Jonah had perceived prior to him being noticed returned and the room erupted into talk and laughter once again.

"Thank you sir," Jonah replied.

"I spoke with the sheriff. He tells me you think it was one of the other boys from school."

"I just told him what I thought," said Jonah, feeling defensive. He still thought Rufus was capable of it, even if he had no proof, but the more the rest of the town questioned it, the more improbably it sounded.

"Well, I've known the Hatchwells for a long time. I've known Rufus since he and his sister were born. I can assure you that they are incapable of such an evil act."

"You should have seen him at the pond—"

"At the pond that I strictly forbid anyone from visiting."

Jonah gulped.

"But he pulled a knife on us. He was furious, he was angry, he was—"

The mayor held up his hand, and Jonah cut himself off immediately.

"Holding a knife and using a knife are two very different things. Believe me, on that."

Jonah's eyes moved to the scars on the mayor's hands and face. The man must have even more than he shows. Why else would he wear a full suit on a hot summer day?

"What happened to poor Mr. Sandberg is a travesty," the mayor continued. "Members of the lodge have already started the wheels in motion for the funeral arrangements and other preparations to assist the family through this difficult time."

Jonah nodded, he was happy to hear that Milton's mother and father were getting help. He would never forget their devastated faces as he was marched out of the station.

"Meanwhile, young Rufus has a bright future ahead of him. A full ride to college is a special opportunity for a young man like himself. It would be awful if rumor and speculation undid such a thing."

Jonah tried to think about what his father would do if he was sitting there in his stead.

"If it wasn't Rufus, then who was it?" Jonah asked.

The mayor's expression was ironclad, except for one slight movement. It was a flinch, suppressed well, but Jonah still noticed it in the man's left ear, which had twitched slightly.

"It's not a matter of who," the mayor replied, his voice remaining calm and steadfast. "It is known that Grizzly Bears from Canada travel farther south every year in search of new foodsources. After consultation with the sheriff, we have decided that is the most logical solution."

He waved at the assortment of hunters that sat at the table with him.

"Shouldn't you wait until you hear from the forensics team from Madison? They might have a different explanation."

"Unnecessary. They have already been told that the case is closed."

"What about the autopsy? I'm sure that—"

"There won't be an autopsy," the mayor interrupted him again. "His body will be cremated in accordance with his family's wishes later this week."

Jonah opened his mouth to protest, but the mayor's face let him know it would be futile to argue. He knew adults were exceptionally good at ignoring others, especially teenagers.

"I've been mayor for almost forty years now. I've seen a lot of things happen to this town in my time. We've sent many men overseas, like your father. Too many never came home, too many to count. We survived the depression. We've survived harsh winters, droughts, and floods. But if there's one thing I've learned more than anything else in my time, is that we can only survive through sacrifice."

Jonah's eyebrows jerked up in confusion immediately. What did he mean by that?

"Sacrifice requires a great many things; compromise, struggle, and, most importantly, unwavering commitment to the greater good. Believe it or not, I was once a young man like yourself. Those words meant little to me at the time, just like they mean little to you now. But one day you'll understand. It might be when you're old like me or much sooner, but we all learn, eventually."

Jonah couldn't hold his words back any longer.

"So, what are you trying to tell me? To just shut up about Milton?"

The mayor's eyes narrowed.

"I'm asking you to not ruin another boy's future with wild accusations. I'm asking you not to search for answers that need not be found. Searching for meaning in death is in itself meaningless."

"So why all this talk of sacrifice? You're talking in riddles. Why did you really call me here today?"

The mayor cleared his throat and took a deep breath.

"I am old. One day I won't be able to guide this town anymore. There are other men, much younger than myself, who must pick up the torch and lead us into the future. It is part of my job to shape such men. And there are precious few left to do so. I believe you might be one of them, one day at least. I called you here to see for myself."

Jonah was taken aback. He wasn't a leader.

It's all misdirection, he thought to himself. For whatever reason, the mayor just wanted him to shut up about Rufus so that the brute could go off to some school out of town. Promises and flattery were just part of his repertoire. It didn't matter if Rufus killed Milton or not. The mayor had no intention of discovering the truth.

"So is the truth meaningless, then?" Jonah asked.

The mayor audibly sighed.

"The truth is a fickle friend. As much likely to bite the wielder as it would a foe."

Another riddle. Somehow, the comment only infuriated Jonah more. If he were a kettle on the stove, he would be whistling loud enough to wake the dead.

What would his father do?

"Is that what you did with that family's death seventeen years ago? Hide the truth?"

The mayor's ear twitched again. The hall grew silent immediately. One of the World War I veterans suddenly burst into a uncontrollable hacking cough.

"Who told you about that?" The mayor asked with authority in his voice, more an order than a question.

"I've heard it around town," Jonah lied. He didn't want to get the deputy in trouble.

"It was another Grizzly Bear attack, nothing more."

"Everyone in school knows there aren't any Grizzly Bear around here. It's a bunch of malarkey you made up, just like the algae bloom."

He hoped he had mustered enough confidence for the mayor to believe his lie. The fact was, no one in school talked about any of it; their interests focused more on dating and movies.

"Jonah," the mayor said, his voice suddenly soft and measured. "Are you sure you want to know the truth?"

"Yes," Jonah replied without hesitation.

The mayor took another deep breath.

"The truth is that the man took his family into those woods. The truth is that he was deeply disturbed. The truth is that he hacked up his wife and his kids with a hatchet. The truth is that there was almost nothing left of their six-month-old baby for us to find. The truth is that his widowed sister from Buffalo, who had six children of her own, was his sole remaining beneficiary for his life insurance. The truth is that if it had been discovered he had killed his family and then himself, the policy would have nullified and she would have gotten nothing."

The mayor's breaths hastened, as if saying it out loud somehow exhausted him beyond his breaking point. Though already sitting, he collapsed backwards into his chair and put his hand to his face, covering it from Jonah's eyes.

Jonah didn't know what to say. He sat there unsure of what to do next, stunned into inaction by the revelation.

It was the mayor, who was the first to break the silence that had descended on them.

"Your father had been so quick to run into danger, to test the unknown, I had hoped that his son would have learned his lesson. I may have misjudged your character. Time will tell. You may leave."

The words of this man who Jonah barely knew, who he had met only a few times in his life, somehow stung him deeper than he could possibly have imagined. Holding back the urge to flee from the room in tears, he stood up slowly. He could feel the muscles in his arms and legs trembling, making it hard to walk as he slowly staggered down the aisle towards the door.

If the eyes of the men of the Elk's Lodge had been oppressive on his arrival, they were near piercing on his departure.

He was almost to the door when he heard the mayor speak up one more time.

"Jonah," the man beckoned.

Jonah forced himself to turn and face the old man from across the room.

Loud enough for all to hear, the mayor spoke.

"Never forget what I told you of sacrifice. You may think you've seen the worst of it already. But if life has taught me anything, the older you get, the more it will take from you. The person inside you who decides whether to flee from it or embrace it will be the man you become."

8

1972

Jonah dropped his bike haphazardly on the front porch and walked inside. The entire ride home from the Elk's Lodge, his emotions had swirled with anger, grief, and disappointment. Anger at the mayor for being so quick to move on from Milton's death; passing it off as just some accident. Grief that Milton, the most genuinely nice guy he had ever met, was gone. And disappointment, not at the mayor or the sheriff's department, but in himself and how poorly he seemed to be living up to his father's legacy.

Levi was on sitting in the living room building towers from colored wooden blocks engraved with animals, shapes, and letters.

"Hi Jonah," Levi said excitedly. Though Jonah hadn't apologized for being rude, his young boy had seemingly forgiven him.

"Oh, hi," Jonah replied, his voice absent of Levi's youthful warmth. After everything that happened today, he just wanted to get out of the house with Steve and his friends. The last thing he wanted to do was sit absentmindedly with Levi and let his mind wander.

"Good, you're home," Jonah's mother said from behind him.

He turned to find her on the stairwell, fastening on a set of earrings. Her hair was done up and held in place by a braided headband, a sensible style she had adopted after getting the job at the diner.

Jonah noticed the wrinkles forming around her eyes, visible signs of stress that were absent just half a decade prior. Apparently, working late nights while trying to raise a teenager and a toddler was taking its toll. Jonah felt a twinge of guilt for how difficult he made it for her sometimes. The fight with Rufus, leaving Levi with the neighbor; neither was intended to add to her strain, but it did regardless.

"What did the mayor want?" She asked, checking her reflection in the glass of his father's picture frame, just like Jonah had.

"Nothing," Jonah replied, not wanting to discuss the details with her.

"Come on, Jonah," she said, adjusting her hair and rubbing the outline of her lips. "The mayor doesn't call out of nowhere to just have a chat."

Jonah tried to think of a worthy lie.

"He just wanted to talk about Dad."

His mother immediately stopped fussing with her hair and makeup and peered back at him through the reflection. He saw the smallest hint of a tear form in one of her eyes, a droplet of moisture that threatened to undo all her work to get ready. In a flash, the tear was gone, his mother's expression of sadness replaced by with one of the stern, tough mother figure.

"Just tell me later," she said before kissing two of her fingers and tapping them on the glass, right onto Dad's forehead in the picture.

"When will you be back?" Jonah asked her as she hopped on one foot, trying to slip on a shoe.

"Late. There's some new illusionist having a show tonight at the movie theater. I expect a late rush after that gets out. Don't wait up."

"I won't."

Fully shoed and content with her hair and makeup, she crossed the room and kneeled on the carpet next to Levi, who was counting the blocks as he stacked them.

"You be so good for your brother, little one," she said, wrapping her arms around him and pulling him in tight for a hug. "Jonah is going to keep you safe all night long until I get back."

Levi squealed with glee. Jonah didn't understand why the little boy got so excited to spend time with him. They had nothing in common and Jonah barely paid him any mind.

She stood up and turned to him.

"There's macaroni on the counter," she said. "Just follow the instructions and don't burn the house down."

"Alright mom," Jonah practically groaned back at her.

"And no horror movies. Last time he walked in on you and Steve watching television, it took a week to convince him to sleep in his own bed again."

"Alright mom."

"And no friends over. You're still grounded."

"Alright mom."

She must have gotten the hint as she opened the front door to leave. At the last second, she paused and looked back at him.

"Just know that I appreciate this," she said. "I know it's been hard, but every day I look at you, I just can't help but think about how much you've transformed into the spitting image of your father."

Jonah didn't want to think about it, nor talk about it. The conversation with the mayor had been more than enough for him. So he stood there silently, staring at the ground.

His mother made a noise like she was going to say something else, but decided against it. The front door shut and the sound of the car backfiring soon followed.

The rest of the evening with Levi flew by uneventfully. Jonah cooked up the macaroni and they ate it on the couch in front of the television. It was a little overcooked, Jonah had left it on too long after walking away to read a comic book in his room and forgotten all about it. It wasn't until Levi had come looking for him to ask if it was ready yet did he remember and by then the noodles were throughly soggy.

The transgression against pasta was soon forgotten.

As shows like The Flintstones and Scooby-Doo played, Levi watched with unflinching enjoyment.

"Ruh-roh," Levi said in his best impression of Scooby-Doo. A silly attempt to make Jonah laugh, but Jonah didn't even notice. Levi eventually gave up and returned his stare to the screen.

Jonah was too busy thinking about Olivia. As an only child, she certainly didn't have to worry about watching a little sister or brother. He imagined what she would be doing at that very moment. Would she be getting ready to go out with Diane, Darci, and Stephanie? Perhaps they would just drive around in Diane's convertible with the top down. He pictured her in his mind, her hair flowing elegantly behind her as the world flew by. The soft skin of her shoulders visible in a sleeveless tank top, the only way to stay cool on a warm summer evening. The smile on her face charming anyone and everyone that passed by.

He grinned as his mind wandered, until he became aware of a faint hissing sound coming from the stairwell. Levi didn't notice it, he was hypnotized by the bright colors dancing on the screen. Looking up, a face stared at Jonah from the top of the stairwell.

It was Steve.

With a hand gesture, he beckoned him upstairs.

Jonah looked at Levi nervously.

"I'll be right back," Jonah said, standing up. "I need to use the bathroom."

Levi grunted in response, never taking his eyes off the screen.

Carefully, Jonah crept up the stairs, trying to be as quiet as possible until he was safely in his room, where Steve spun around in his chair, making swishing noises with his mouth. Jonah shut the door behind him.

"What are you doing here?" Jonah asked. "Aren't you grounded?"

"Oh ya, totally," Steve replied. "Except my parents went to see that illusionist at the theater and left me alone."

Steve's parents did this a lot, announce a grand punishment for misbehavior, but after a couple days they'd forget about it and let him do whatever he wanted again. Jonah's mother was not as lackadaisical.

"Well, I'm still grounded and watching Levi tonight," Jonah replied. "If you want to come over and watch movies after he goes to bed, that would be fine."

"I don't want to watch movies," said Steve.

"Then what are you going to do?"

Steve stopped spinning in the chair and faced Jonah.

"What if I told you that there's going to be a party tonight?"

"Town is practically on lock down by the sheriff and the mayor, who's stupid enough to throw a party at their house?"

"Not at a house, at the old well."

Jonah knew of where he spoke of well. It was 15 minutes walk from Jonah's house, straight into the woods behind it. The clearing where the old well had been built years ago was easy to find if you knew where you were going, but near impossible if you didn't. It would be well insulated from the attentive eyes and ears of anyone in town. Even if someone did tip them off, the sheriff would be hard pressed to find it without a guide.

As kids, it had been their own secret hideout. A hidden place where they had pretended they were pirates, staging kidnappings of action figures and threatening them with walking the plank if they didn't reveal where the buried treasure was. The plank being an old board they positioned over the well's entrance. It was at least a thirty-foot drop into the cold, dark water at the bottom. After one G.I. Joe in particular had refused to divulge the location, he had fallen to his watery grave only to curiously be found in a nearby streamed the next day. Jonah's dad had told him the entire area was snaked with subterranean tunnels and waterways that fed Tranquility Pond. The revelation only added to the intrigue at what other secrets may be hiding down there.

"Craig was able to nick a keg from the grocery without anyone noticing," Steve continued. "Word has already gotten around town."

"You really think that's a good idea?" asked Jonah, he remember his conversation with the mayor. "With Grizzlies or whatever else is out in the forest, should we really be out there too?"

"Oh, come on. No one's seen a bear that close to town in decades. Stop being a pansy. It'll be fun."

"I can't go, I'm watching Levi."

"Levi is going to bed soon, and you were just telling me the other day how great it is he sleeps through the night on his own now. Leave him here and be back before your mother gets home. No one will know the better."

"I don't know."

"What if we make it about Milton, a big kegger to celebrate his life?"

"Milton didn't drink."

"Fine, but I already talked to the girls. They told me they'll be there. Olivia too."

Just the mention of Olivia's name gave Jonah's heart a flutter. He had thought that nothing could get him to risk betraying his mother's trust again, not after what he had just put her through. But Levi did sleep like a rock these days, even falling asleep on a blanket in the town square as fireworks went off on July 4th. After bedtime Jonah would just be in his room watching horror movie marathons again, alone. It wouldn't hurt to go out for a few hours.

"Alright, fine, I'll go as soon as Levi falls asleep."

"Excellent, bring a flashlight."

Both boys looked up suddenly at the sound of footsteps approaching on the stairs. Steve bolted to the window like an action movie star ready to dive through it.

"Jonah?" said the small voice of Levi from the other side of his bedroom door.

Both boys took a breath of relief.

"Be right there," Jonah yelled back.

Steve muffled his laughter.

"See you later?" He asked in a whisper.

Jonah nodded.

In a flash, Steve disappeared out the window.

Jonah walked to the door and opened it to find Levi standing with teary eyes on the other side.

"I was scared," Levi said.

"I was just getting something from my room," Jonah answered.

"Who were you talking to?"

"No one."

"I thought I heard someone."

"Nope, just me. You're just tired. Let's get you to bed."

"Where's blankie?"

Still in Steve's truck, on its way to the party in the woods.

"I'll get it for you tomorrow."

"I want it now!"

"I can't get it right now. You'll have to wait."

"I want it now!"

Jonah was growing impatient. The thoughts of Olivia drinking a beer under the moonlight were swirling in his mind. He needed to go before someone else charmed her away into a rendezvous in the woods.

Lifting Levi up, he carried him forcibly to the boy's room across the hall and practically threw him onto the bed.

"Ow," Levi yelped as he landed awkwardly.

"You'll live," replied Jonah, rushing to pull the blankets over the boy. "There, I'll see you in the morning."

"Bedtime story!" Levi demanded.

Jonah groaned.

"Ugh, not tonight Levi."

"Milk!"

Jonah practically sprinted down the stairs to fill up a sippy cup with milk from the fridge before returning at an equally expedited pace.

"There you go, milk. Now go to bed," Jonah commanded, hurrying to the door frame and switching off the light.

The door was almost closed before he heard a voice squeak from inside that caused him to pause.

"Jonah," Levi said.

"What is it?" Jonah sighed.

"I'm scared."

"Of what? There's nothing to be scared of."

"I don't want to be alone. Can I sleep with you?"

"No, you can not."

"I miss momma."

"She'll be back by the time you wake up."

"I miss dadda."

A lump formed in Jonah's throat. He did not have any retort for that. He tried to think of something to say, something comforting that a four-year-old boy would understand, but nothing seemed right.

He couldn't exactly explain that a bunch of old men in a room at the Pentagon decided one day to send a bunch of younger men off to fight a war in a country 10,000 miles away.. That their dad, who had barely survived Korea, had volunteered to go back to the front lines. That once there, the South Vietnamese liaison assigned to their platoon, who was secretly a spy for the north, sent them on patrol into an area he had known was littered with landmines and enemy ambushes. That their dad had insisted he lead the patrol, insisted he be at the forefront of the danger despite having a son at home and another on the way. That the landmine that had ended their father's life was actually manufactured by French colonialists.

It barely made sense to Jonah, how would it make sense to a four-year-old kid?

"Just go to bed," said Jonah before shutting the door.

Waiting several minutes, he made sure that Levi didn't get out of bed to ask him more questions. Content that the boy had gone to sleep, he hustled to his room and changed into his Led Zepplin t-shirt, the cleanest one he had, and pulled on a pair of jeans.

In no time flat, he was out the window and taking off into the woods in the direction of the old well where he hoped the beautiful Olivia would be waiting for him.

From Levi's bedroom window behind him, the young boy watched his older brother disappear into the forest.

9

1972

Jonah arrived at the old well, surprised to see almost a dozen vehicles already parked and a radio blasting "Schools Out" by Alice Cooper at full volume. Circles of teenage girls stood gossiping and chatting with one another while groups of drunk teenage boys watched them from the backs of truck beds with lustful eyes. The scent of alcohol hung heavy in the air already. A freshman was puking behind a tree. Members of the football team in their varsity jackets hooted and hollered as they passed a football back and forth, cheering one another on as they attempted to catch it one handed without spilling their beer. Someone had started a bonfire that illuminated the forest clearing with a warm, inviting light silhouetted by dancing shadows.

The scene was as far from what Milton would have enjoyed as it could be.

Jonah scanned the crowd of teenagers talking excitedly amongst themselves. He was searching for Steve.

"Jonah!" Craig bellowed, catching his attention. Craig was standing next to the keg, distributing beer into cups, and talking merrily amongst a group of recently graduated seniors. Despite the sultry summer air and the close proximity to the roaring bonfire, Craig wore his varsity letterman jacket covered in various patches and proudly displaying his captain designation for the football team.

Jonah approached, and Craig handed him a full plastic cup of beer.

"Isn't this place great?" Craig asked, his words slurring slightly as he talked.

"Totally," Jonah replied half-heartedly. It had been great, better even when it was just Jonah and Steve who knew about it.

"So groovy that Steve found it," Craig commented.

"Steve and I both found it."

"What was that?"

Craig's attention had already been diverted to a couple of pretty juniors who had approached looking for a refill.

Jonah tried to ignore the comment. He didn't quite understand what Steve saw in the obnoxious jock.

With Craig no longer acknowledging his existence, Jonah snuck away to look at the old well.

He had no idea when it was originally constructed. The round barrier stood about four feet tall and was made from a mix of stones and mud. His best guess was that it was originally built by the settlers who had founded the town. A chain and bucket were attached via an old rusted metal bracket embedded in the stone wall.

As children, their parents had forbid them from playing near it. Jonah's mother had even gone as far as to instruct his father to board it up for their own safety.

"If there isn't a little danger in life, they'll never learn anything," his dad had said, never getting around to actually doing anything about it.

It felt silly then and silly now that his mother had been so deathly afraid of one of them falling inside. It was just a relic, an old hole in the ground, probably didn't even have any water anymore.

Pulling a penny from his pocket, Jonah wrapped it tightly in his fist and held it over the dark opening.

I wish that I will kiss Olivia tonight.

He repeated the words in his head over and over again with his eyes shut tight, then opened his palm and let the coin fall.

The penny fell straight down and disappeared into the veil of darkness.

Listening close, he waited for the sound of the penny hitting the water or clanging against the old stone.

Ding, ding.

It didn't sound like water at all, or stone, for that matter. It sounded metallic, the sound of metal hitting metal.

Intrigued, Jonah leaned his head over the opening and peered down.

Too dark to see anything.

Pulling his flashlight from his pocket, he shined it down the well, trying to see what the penny could have deflected off of. It was no use. His flashlight was not nearly powerful enough to penetrate that deep to see the bottom.

He flicked it off, expecting the bottom to return to just a formless mass of black.

Except staring back at him were those orange eyes he remembered from the pond.

Jonah froze, afraid to move and lose sight of what he had tried so hard to convince himself the last few days was just his imagination.

Locked in each other's gaze, neither of them blinked nor moved. Moments passed, an impromptu staring contest.

Jonah jumped when he felt hands on his shoulders.

"What are you doing?" Steve said, laughing.

Jonah breathed heavily as he tried to think of words to describe what he had seen down in the depths.

"Are you ok?" Steve asked.

Jonah looked around and realized he was dripping with sweat. Several of the partygoers were looking at him strangely, Craig amongst them.

"I thought I saw something down in the well," Jonah managed to sputter out.

To his great alarm, Steve leaned over and peered inside the opening. His head disappearing into the darkness at the neck.

Jonah wanted to reach out and pull him away from the danger, but before he could move Steve let out a loud yell.

"Yodel-Lay-Hee-Hoo!" he screamed, it echoed throughout the darkness.

Relief fell over Jonah as Steve's head emerged intact from the hole.

"I don't see anything," he said, with only a slight slur to his speech.

"You guys having fun over here?" Craig said as he approached, a dark stain from a freshly spilled beer on his shirt.

"Jonah and I used to have a blast playing out here," Steve said with a smile, patting Jonah on the shoulder.

"Dude I'm serious," Jonah replied. "I saw something down there."

"Well, I didn't see anything," said Steve with a shrug.

"What are you trying to tell me, Lassie?" Craig said mockingly to Jonah. "Did little Timmy fall down the well?"

Craig proceeded to prance around the two, imitating a dog and egged on by the chorus of laughter from the rapidly growing group of teenage onlookers.

Jonah was most unhappy to see Steve laughing along with them.

"Come on dude," Jonah said quietly to Steve, feeling embarrassed.

"What? It's funny!" his friend replied. "Ah, don't be a stick in the mud. Besides, I have someone I'm sure you want to come see."

Jonah's heart skipped a beat in his chest as Steve led him, thankfully out of earshot of Craig's howling, to find Stephanie, Diane, and Olivia sitting on the hood of his truck. They all wore bell bottoms and low-cut tops. Olivia's was a brilliant forest green and her hair was partially braided, hanging at the side of her face, giving him a full view of her brilliantly bright eyes. The worry over what he saw in the well somehow evaporated instantly.

"What's that all about?" Diane asked, peering over their shoulders at Craig in the distance.

"Oh, just your boyfriend making a fool of himself," Steve replied.

"He's not my boyfriend," Diane said quickly. "He's just nice to look at."

The girls all giggled and Jonah suddenly felt self conscious about whether he had sweated through his shirt already in the humid summer night air.

"Where's Darcy?" Jonah asked, curious where their usual fourth member of the quartet was.

"She didn't think it was appropriate to be out celebrating so soon after Milton, you know," Stephanie replied.

The girl's giggles subsided as quiet overtook the group.

Jonah shared their melancholy.

"Well, I for one think," Steve began, raising his half-drank cup of beer. "That he would want us to be out, having a good time in his name. To Milton."

"To Milton," the rest of them repeated in unison, with their cups raised. Beer splashed and spilled as the plastic containers clinked together.

As he cautiously sipped at his beer, a thought suddenly occurred to him that caused him to look around the clearing nervously. *Where was Rufus?*

Stephanie noticed his concern.

"Don't worry," Stephanie said with a smile at Steve and Jonah both. "Rufus went to bed early. He's got to be in Madison to meet with the wrestling coaches first thing in the morning. We are all in the clear."

Jonah let out a breath of relief.

"It's got to be tough having an overbearing older brother like that," commented Jonah as he rubbed the cut on the side of his head. Though it was healing, he could still feel the raised scab.

"Rufus isn't all that bad," Stephanie replied. "He's just feeling protective and a nervous about college next year. You'd be surprised how much pressure everyone in town is putting on him. Even the mayor came to visit the other day to talk to him about staying out of trouble."

"That's no reason to start a fight and pull a knife," said Jonah.

"Hey guys," Craig's voice appeared. "Have I got a treat for all of you."

Jonah could smell it without even turning around. The joint Craig held between his fingertips was already lit and filled the space with its signature skunky smell.

"Finally," Diane said, hopping off the hood of the car. "I've been jonesing for a hit all night."

Craig handed her the spliff and, without hesitation, she took a big hit. Smoke billowed from her mouth as she hacked and coughed.

"That's it baby," Craig said, putting his arm around her waist. She didn't seem to mind.

Diane passed it to Stephanie next, then Steve.

Steve held the joint out in the air, offering it to Jonah.

"What about you Jonah?" Craig said with devious looking eyes. "You want to smoke the grass like the rest of us?"

Jonah had never smoked before, not even cigarettes. He didn't really want to start now, but with the eyes of the rest of the group staring at him, he felt the sudden need to at least try it.

"I'll try it," Olivia said unexpectedly, and she plucked the blunt from Craig's hand and put it to her mouth, inhaling gingerly.

Jonah's jaw just about dropped as he watched her suppress a cute, quaint little cough before handing it to Craig.

"Jonah's turn," Craig said, his grin widening.

"Come on Jonah," said Steve. "It's only a little pot. Not going to hurt you or anything."

Jonah picked the joint from Craig's hand and held it several inches from his mouth as he tried to muster enough courage to try it.

The chanting began with Craig, of course, but it quickly spread to the rest of the girls.

"Jonah, Jonah, Jonah…"

It wasn't until Olivia joined in that he felt no choice but to place it to his lips and inhale.

"Jonah?" said a small, frail voice behind him.

Jonah turned around abruptly and coughed up an enormous cloud of smoke as he looked at Levi, holding a teddy bear, staring up at him. The young boy must have followed him into the woods and, judging by the mud smears on his socks, he hadn't bothered to put on his shoes.

"What the hell are you doing here?" Jonah exclaimed before coughing.

The harsh tone scared Levi as the little boy recoiled.

"I was scared in my room," Levi said. "So I went looking for you and you weren't there. So I followed you."

"Goddamnit, Levi," Jonah said, as he tried to take deep breaths to calm his anger. "Why couldn't you just stay home?"

"I'm sorry. I was scared."

"You're always scared, ever since Dad died."

Levi started to sob quietly into his teddy bear.

Jonah immediately felt bad. He was the one in the wrong, smoking pot and drinking in the forest when he should have been home.

"I got to get you home before mom does," Jonah said.

Though his hit was brief, he was already starting to feel a slight, disorientating effect. He turned around several times, trying to discern in the darkness which trail led back to his house.

"It's this way," Olivia said, jumping off the hood of Steve's truck and grabbing Levi by the hand. "I'll walk you guys back."

Levi immediately stopped crying at her touch.

Jonah would have felt embarrassed, except a big part of him was far too excited at the prospect of being alone with Olivia, well almost alone.

He took off after Olivia and Levi, ignoring the snickering of Steve and Craig behind him.

Jonah tried to keep his cool as the three of them walked the faint trail back to his house by the light of his cheap K-Mart flashlight. Whatever effects he thought marijuana would have on him were nothing compared to the actual.

While Olivia asked Levi sweet questions about his favorite shows like Scooby-Doo and The Brady Brunch, Jonah couldn't help but grow paranoid that he would return home too late and find his mother waiting for him. A situation only worsened by the presence of a girl accompanying him, Levi's clearly dirty state, and her son high as a kite.

Despite his growing anxiety, his mind still found the capacity to appreciate how sweet Olivia was with Levi. Though she had no brothers or sisters, she looked like a complete natural with kids. Levi was loving it too, he was smiling from ear to ear as he talked and talked and talked at length about everything that mattered in his little world.

And everything about how she was with him, from her voice to her laugh, every ounce of it, felt authentic; a stark contrast to Jonah's own regular feigned interest in his little brother's life.

He was so enamored by the two that he didn't see a gnarled root sticking out of the ground and proceeded to trip over it, falling flat onto his face.

Momentarily dazed, and partially incapacitated by his high, he laid there on the ground motionless until he felt the warm touch of Olivia on the skin of his arm. That touch, that feeling, felt better than anything else he had yet experienced in his life.

Jumping to his feet, he tried to regain his composure, brushing the leaves and dirt from his Led Zeppelin shirt. Thinking he had done a good job, he put on a face of dignity that quickly melted when he realized that both Levi and Olivia were laughing at him hysterically.

"What is it?" he said, not sure what they found so humorous.

"One second," replied Olivia, as she approached close. He could smell her perfume and see the faint moonlight reflecting on her golden blonde hair as she reached a hand forward, brushing up against his cheek, and pulling from above his earlobe a rather large twig with leaves still attached to it.

If it hadn't been so dark out, she would have seen Jonah turning bright red.

The rest of the walk didn't take long, and they soon found themselves at Jonah's back porch. A moment Jonah had both expected and dreaded the entire hike, the moment he knew she would say goodbye and return to the party without him.

"Well, aren't you just filthy," Olivia said, kneeling next to Levi before looking up at Jonah.

"You want help giving him a bath?" she asked, her face a glow in the porch light.

He had never responded in the affirmative so quickly before in his entire life.

"Lead the way, Levi!" Olivia said excitedly as the little boy joyfully bounded into the house ahead of them.

It took almost every speck of willpower Jonah had, not to jump for joy himself.

The arrival of Levi had led to an unfortunate departure of his friend Jonah from the party, but it turned out to be a blessing in disguise for Steve. It reduced the number of watchful eyes by two and, thanks to Diane and Craig now getting stoned by the fire, his arm over her shoulder, Steve and Stephanie were at last left alone.

They didn't need to talk about it, there was no discussion necessary. By the look in each other's eyes, they both knew what the other wanted.

Steve double and triple-checked that no one was watching, and only when he was absolutely certain, did he lead Stephanie by the hand around to the back of his truck and onto the truck bed. He had squeezed his truck between two thick tree trunks just in case this scenario presented itself. Thanks to the branches and darkness of the night, they found themselves secluded from the rest of the teenagers, with only the faint sound of drunken laughter behind them.

It wasn't long before their lips had found each others and their tongues began a delicate dance that both had been painfully anticipating with the other for several days now.

As Steve's hands roamed, pushing the boundaries of unexplored territories on Stephanie's body, he worried he had gone too far when she sat up suddenly.

"What's wrong?" he asked.

"Nothing," Stephanie replied. "I'm just cold."

Shit, the one thing he had forgotten to bring was a blanket.

He could kick himself for being that stupid. If he wanted one now, he'd have to go back to the party and ask around. The moment would be completely ruined.

Wait, there was something.

Reaching through the sliding back window, he rummaged on the seat until his hands grasped something soft and fluffy. Pulling it out, he lofted it into the air until it spread out and fluttered silently onto Stephanie's body. She immediately curled it around her, embracing it.

"A little small," Stephanie said with a smirk. Indeed, it only covered her from her knees to her shoulders.

"It's all I got, baby," Steve said, returning her smirk with a wide, charming grin. "I bet I can help keep the rest of you warm."

Stephanie giggled in agreement as their kissing continued and their thoughts intertwined, soon to be followed by their bodies, Levi's precious blankie draped over them.

"Vroooooom!" Levi yelled as he swung the wooden airplane through the air in the bathtub. Olivia giggled in response as she splashed at the toy and making a whistling sound imitating the harsh winds of a storm.

Jonah watched from the doorway, leaning against the frame, his hands folded in front of his chest.

He had liked Olivia since the moment he met her, he had dared to use the words 'Love at first sight' only in the seclusion of his own thoughts, and from that moment on, he had never thought there could be anything she could ever do to endear herself more to him.

He had been wrong.

Watching her play with Levi, smile with him, laugh with him; new feelings grew inside him he didn't know existed. They weren't sexual feelings, the often mis-categorized explorative lustfulness of youth, they felt like so much more.

"Time to get out Levi," she said playfully.

"Not yet!" Levi shouted back, continuing his plane's daring maneuvers up, down, and into the waves of the bathtub.

"It's really late," she said, in the same distinctive motherly tone that Jonah remembered his own mother having when he was a kid. It was a tone that was sweet, passive, but also almost impossible to say no to.

"Ok," Levi said, giving in to her request and standing up.

A few minutes later, dried and wearing fresh pajamas, Levi lay in his bed clutching his teddy bear.

"Blankie?" he muttered, his eyes half closed.

Olivia looked back at Jonah, hoping for help.

"Sorry buddy," Jonah replied. "It's still in Steve's truck. I promise I'll get it for you tomorrow."

Expecting another tirade of outrage at being denied his prized possession, Jonah was surprised when Levi replied softly and sweetly.

"That's alright."

Olivia giggled.

"Olivia?" Levi asked, his consciousness somewhere halfway between waking and the dreamworld.

"Yes, Levi?" Olivia answered.

"Can you come back and play with me?"

"Only if it's ok with your brother."

"I'm sure he will say yes."

Levi's voice extended out as he yawned. His eyes were closed.

"Why is that?" Olivia asked, stroking the boy's hair softly.

"Cause he likes you," Levi said.

Jonah's jaw dropped as he immediately went into panic mode, expecting Olivia to run from the house, fleeing his affection in terror.

Olivia didn't even flinch. She remained on her knees, softly stroking Levi's hair as she hummed a soft lullaby.

It took only seconds for the room to be filled with the sound of Levi's snoring. Jonah and Olivia silently closed the door behind them and tiptoed downstairs.

"I'm really sorry about that," Jonah said, rubbing the back of his hair nervously.

"It's alright," Olivia replied.

"So you're going back to the party?"

"No."

"Why not?"

"I don't know. I guess I'm not really in the mood. I think I'll just go home."

"I can walk you home," Jonah said excitedly.

Olivia laughed.

"You, sir, are on babysitting duty," she said, smiling and tapping his chest with her forefinger.

Jonah laughed with her.

"I guess you're right," he said before adding. "Can I see you tomorrow?"

"Probably," she said sheepishly as he opened the front door for her.

He expected her to walk out and into the night, but she didn't. Instead, she stood there in front of the open door, only a few feet from him, hesitating.

"You should know," she said quietly, a decibel above a whisper. "That I like you too."

Jonah felt like cold water had been splashed on his face. His eyes were wide and his muscles tensed in complete and utter shock.

After all of his numb-skull, amateur pot-smoking, and overall awkwardness that night and before; she still liked him back?!

He didn't have time to dwell on it.

"Well, good night!" Olivia said, before leaning close and giving him a short but sweet kiss on the lips. An instant later, she was out the door and walking down the sidewalk, heading home.

Jonah must have let in a thousand insects, as he stood with the door wide open, his mind completely frozen, unable to comprehend his first kiss with the girl of his dreams. When the gears in his head finally began working again, they were gunked up with all sorts of thoughts of Olivia, reliving that moment over and over. It was only from sheer exhaustion that he managed to drag his lovesick body up the stairs and crawl into bed.

There was only one thing on his mind that night as he closed his eyes and drifted off to sleep. The beautiful, fair, blonde Olivia, the sole star and one-woman-show of the theater that was his dreams.

Rufus rolled up his sleeves as he approached the bonfire burning in the forest. An even hotter flame burned in his chest as he went on the hunt for the one person he knew needed an ass-beating.

The crowd of sophomores and juniors parted their ranks as he walked through the center of the clearing, the look on his face the only warning sign any of them needed to know that danger was approaching. One of the more inebriated ones was too slow, and Rufus knocked him over with barely a nudge from his shoulder, sending the underclassman sprawling to the ground, wondering how he had been hit by a freight train in the middle of the forest.

Next to the keg, Steve's football buddy, Craig stood drunkenly joking and putting on a show for the others as he chugged beer after beer. That little wannabe socialite Diane was next to him, cheering him on.

Craig caught sight of Rufus, spitting out his last gulp of beer in a spray over the onlookers as he tried to retreat backwards. Fortunately, he was cornered by the fire and there was nowhere for him to run.

Rufus rushed forward, tackling Craig and pinning to the ground with his knee on the football player's neck. Though equally matched in size, Rufus wasn't the state champion without reason, and Craig's attempts to dislodge him were futile.

"Where's my sister?!" Rufus yelled, his saliva frothy and spraying with each word.

It was an anger he had been building up since waking to find his sister's room empty. It had taken several phone calls to find out where she had gone. But once he knew she was with Steve, he had no choice but to go out and find her, and find him. The mayor's warnings be damned.

"I don't know, man," Craig said, his usually confident voice suddenly timid and scared.

Just as Rufus thought, the jock was nothing without a helmet and pads to protect him.

"You're always following him around," Rufus snarled. "You know where he is. Tell me now and I won't break your neck."

Diane was screaming, but none of the other onlookers dared to jump into the fray and risk being the next target of Rufus's wrath. The crowd slowly inched backwards, simultaneously enthralled by the altercation but also fearful it would erupt into their own ranks.

Rufus exerted more pressure on the teenage boy's neck. The boy's cheeks were turning purple.

"They were by his truck, by his truck," Craig squealed as the popping sound of bones intermingled with the popping sounds of the fire.

Rufus stood up, freeing Craig, who coughed and choked as he tried to catch his breath. He would deal with him later, first he needed to find his sister.

Locating Steve's truck, he grabbed a nearby rock and threw it at the windshield of the Chevrolet. It crashed hard against the glass, creating a dense spiderweb of cracks from the center of impact.

"Get out of there now," Rufus commanded as he waited by the driver's side door, ready to grab the fleeing Steve by the neck the moment he showed his face.

The crowd of teenagers had gone silent, watching the ordeal unfold with astonished reverence.

"You've got five seconds before I break down the windshield and drag you out by your dick," Rufus threatened again. "Five."

No movement whatsoever from inside the truck.

"Four."

Still nothing.

"Three."

He could hear Diane crying as she attended to the hacking and coughing Craig.

"Two."

Rufus couldn't wait to show Stephanie what a pitiful choice of a human she had gotten herself involved with.

"One."

Giving them ample time to give themselves up, he put a hand on the driver's side door handle and pulled.

To his surprise, the door was unlocked. Swinging open with ease, it revealed nothing more than stacks of fast food wrappers and empty bottles of Gatorade. Leaning his head inside to investigate further, he noticed the sliding window behind the seat pulled wide open.

Grunting angrily, he slammed the door shut before walking around the tree and to the rear. Perhaps they were still in the truckbed.

If he found Steve back there, he would drag the boy out to the middle forest, far from the eyes of the party witnesses. Once they were alone, he would make sure the overconfident jock became very well acquainted with Rufus' trusty switchblade. He wouldn't kill him, wouldn't cut him either, but he would scare him. Scare him good enough that Steve wouldn't dare even look at his sister the wrong way ever again.

Bingo.

Steve was there, hiding under some child's blanket.

What an idiot. Did he really think that the small fabric could hide him? His feet stuck out from the bottom as the coward covered his head with the colorful fabric.

"Got you," Rufus said, cruel satisfaction in his voice.

Pulling the corner of the blanket away, he prepared to slam his fist into Steve's chest.

Instead, he froze in place.

Steve had been under the blanket alright, at least what was left of him. His head looked like it had been removed and then put back on crooked and sideways. Flaps of bloody skin hung loosely from gashes in the boy's forehead and cheeks. His jaw was gone, a gaping hole remained where his pearly white teeth had once been. A pool of blood several inches deep had formed underneath the body.

Rufus stumbled backwards. He opened his mouth to scream, but nothing came out. Each breath he took felt more labored, like some invisible anaconda had wrapped itself around his chest and was slowly squeezing the air from his body.

He tried to regain his senses. Whatever had done this to Steve was still out there. There was no sign of Stephanie. He still needed to find his sister.

Rufus pulled his switchblade from his pocket and held it out in front of him defensively, not sure it would be effective against whatever had attacked Steve.

Every sound in the surrounding forest was amplified tenfold in his ears. The gentle rustle of branches as they swayed in the breeze, the snap of a small twig; every noise filled his imagination with visions of what monster lurked in the darkness, stalking him.

Rufus spun in circles, not wanting to be caught off guard.

His foot inadvertently kicked something round, possibly a soccer ball, that rolled several feet until it came to a rest under the darkness of a thick bush.

Surprised and bewildered, he leaned down and reached for the unknown object.

Wet and slippery, he struggled to get a good grip. Finding one at last, he lifted it into the pale moonlight that broke through the canopy.

It was like looking into a mirror. The eyes, the ears, the nose, the mouth, the dark black hair; they were more than familiar. He had looked at those exact features every day since he was born.

A moment passed as he struggled to understand what was happening, but when it did finally hit him; he was ill-prepared to cope.

Falling to his knees, he wished this was all just a bad dream. That he was still in bed, resting before his big trip to the college the next morning. But most of all, he wished he wasn't holding in his hands the head of his twin sister Stephanie.

His tears fell from his cheeks and onto his dear sister's dark, lush hair.

Rufus was too overcome with sorrow and shock to hear the eruption of screams from the clearing behind him, as the throng of teenagers frantically ran in every direction, fleeing for their lives. He didn't register the dark silhouette of a creature, that was most certainly not a grizzly bear, standing in front of the fire; its slender shape and long tail, equally mesmerizing and terrifying. Most of all, he didn't notice the orange glowing eyes that hovered in the darkness of the creature's face, right above where its teeth dripped with the blood of a fresh kill.

10

2023

"I don't know if I liked that part, Grandpa," Asher said, with a confused look on his face. "I mean, the blood and guts were cool, but there was an awful lot of kissing going on. And what is marijuana?"

Grandpa Joe was barely able to stop himself from spitting out his beer.

"Something I'm sure you'll learn more about when you're older," he reassured his grandson.

"The marijuana or the kissing?"

"I expect both. Plus, I warned you, this story was really about love."

Asher purposely contorted his face until he looked like he had just smelled a skunk walking past.

For a moment, Grandpa Joe had forgotten why they were there. He had let himself get caught up in the story and in doing so, one of the bobber floats on the water had begun jerking violently. Who knows for how long.

"My arthritis is acting up," Grandpa Joe said, his serious expression returning at once. "Would you mind pulling this one in?"

"Would I?!" Asher replied enthusiastically, tipping the boat slightly as he jumped forward to grasp the pole and pulling it. The boy was a natural for fishing, just like his grandpa.

Grandpa Joe watched the water carefully, with one hand gripping the rifle tightly at his side. He felt a trickle of sweat drip down his neck. He hadn't realized how nervous he was.

It had been seventeen years since he last fished on Tranquility Pond, and there had been another seventeen years prior to that since his previous visit. The pond never changed. It looked the exact same as it had when he was a teenager.

His fear of what lurked hadn't changed either.

"Darn, it got away," Asher remarked as the splashing stopped.

"Put some new bait on the hook and try again," Grandpa Joe said.

"But I wanted that one, and it got away!"

"Sometimes that's just the way things go."

"What do you mean?"

Grandpa Joe tried to think of a way to explain failure to a video game addicted nine-year-old used to every challenge being offset by an infinite count of lives.

"I mean, sometimes you just get one shot to win," he said. "And if you miss it, well, you might not get another one for a very long time, maybe never."

"Well, that's stupid," Asher said as he fiddled with the worm wiggling in his fingers as he tried to impale it with the hook.

Grandpa Joe shook his head, but not at his impetuous grandson. The child was just a byproduct of his generation. Grandpa Joe was frustrated with the weather. The clouds in the east were still blocking the sun, and their darkening nature gave him an eerie feeling that a storm was coming.

The rain, wind, and the darkness that accompanied it would only make their lives more difficult out there on the water.

"What was all that talk from the old mayor about sacrifice?" Asher asked, casting the line back out into the open water and attaching the reel to the side of the boat. "I mean, I didn't know what he was talking about."

Grandpa Joe sighed.

"Neither did I at the time," he said. "But now I do, now I do more than I'd like to admit."

Asher placed his hand on his grandfather's arm.

"You know, even though kissing is gross," the boy began. "I do like to hear about grandma. I like remembering her."

"Me too," Grandpa Joe replied, looking down at his grandson's smiling face. "You remind me of her in a lot of ways."

It was the truth, but the admission of it only made the weight on his heart heavier.

"Maybe we shouldn't finish the story," Grandpa Joe said suddenly. "Maybe it's for the best we leave it at that for now and focus on just fishing."

"No!" Asher's reply was immediate and doubtless. "You can't tell me a story like this and stop halfway through."

"I just thought-"

"No, fishing is boring. I want to hear the story."

Grandpa Joe thought about it in his head.

In his old age, doing two things at once had been growing more difficult, especially if one of those things was remembering. But the look on Asher's face was undeniable. The story must go on.

"Alright," Grandpa Joe said. "But you have to watch the lines closely and stop me if we get any bites."

"You got it!" Asher replied with enthusiasm.

"Where was I?"

"The monster!"

"Oh, yes."

Grandpa Joe let out a particularly long sigh.

"Well, it wasn't long until I was back at the police station..."

11

1972

"A monster with orange glowing eyes?" Sheriff Holmes said aloud in a skeptical tone.

"Yes!" replied Jonah emphatically.

The interrogation room they sat in was just an old office stripped to the bare bones, with only a few sparse pieces of furniture remaining; an old wood desk and a couple folding chairs. On one wall, a window with cheap one-way glass reflected Jonah's own image back at himself. Through it, he could see a faint outline of someone short and thin watching the interview from the hallway.

"You saw this creature," the sheriff read aloud from his yellow legal pad containing notes, the hand writing closer in style to hieroglyphics than the alphabet, and just as difficult to decipher. "At the pond and then miles away at the old well in the forest behind your house?"

"That's correct."

"Besides the eyes, what did it look like?"

Jonah struggled to find words to describe what had only been a momentary glance in the dark at a half-way submerged animal.

"It was big and long."

"Got that. Anything else more specific?"

"I think it was made of metal?"

Jonah didn't mean for it to sound like a question. He recalled the distinct sound it had made when the rock had glanced off its back. It had reminded him of the clattering of silverware into the kitchen sink.

"A big, long, metal creature with orange eyes."

Jonah didn't need to be a mind reader to see that Sheriff Holmes was taking his story about as serious as if he had told him he saw Santa coming down the chimney accompanied by the Easter bunny.

"But you weren't there at the party when it happened," the sheriff clarified.

"Yes, I told you," Jonah said, trying to hold back the frustration in his voice at having to repeat himself for the third time. "I was at home with my little brother and Olivia Wallace from school."

A tapping sound at the door made Jonah jump. Being back at the station, being in the interrogation room, the whole situation had him on edge.

"No more coffee for you," Sheriff Holmes said, standing up and exiting the room. Carelessly, the man left the door slightly ajar, giving Jonah a sliver of view into the hallway.

Jonah strained to see through the narrow opening from his chair. It was difficult to see much of anything. As silently as he could, he crept to the door and peered out.

Standing further down the hallway were the mayor and sheriff chatting. They were too far away for Jonah to hear, but their body language was telling enough. The sheriff stood up straight, almost at attention, as the mayor stood opposite with his hands wrapped tightly around the handle of his cane. A few rays of the morning sun caught in the emerald eyes of the metal panther carving, glistened almost magically.

Jonah fell backwards when a shadow darted in front of the crack.

Landing hard on the ground, he looked up to see the stern face of Deputy Brian Nibiikwe staring back at him. The deputy grunted loudly before shutting the door tight.

Jonah made his way back to his chair and sat down.

A few minutes passed before the door opened again and the sheriff walked back inside. To Jonah's surprise, he looked less annoyed than he had been when he had left.

"My deputy has just informed me that your girlfriend has corroborated your story," the sheriff stated, with no hint of emotion in his voice.

"She's not my girlfriend," Jonah corrected him without thinking, even if he wished it was the truth.

The sheriff rolled his eyes.

"It seems you are in the clear for now," he said as he crossed his fingers in front of his face.

"What about the creature?" Jonah asked, curious to know more.

"It appears to be another Grizzly attack," the sheriff replied.

"A Grizzly? No. I've been to Yellowstone National Park. I know what a Grizzly looks like. This was something else entirely."

"It's been confirmed by several experienced hunters in the area."

"Who?"

"Someone more qualified than some teenager with a penchant for rule-breaking."

"Then how do you explain what I saw? What the others saw?"

The sheriff lifted a page of his notepad.

"In your statement, you admitted to using marijuana. Is that correct?"

"Yes, but that doesn't explain—"

"Are you aware marijuana is classified as a schedule 1 narcotic?"

Jonah gulped.

"But—"

"Are you aware that first time offenses are punishable with up to a year of incarceration?"

Jonah didn't know how to respond.

"Now I remember when I was a kid. I remember the stupid things I did. After discussions with members of the town's elected officials…"

Jonah knew he meant the mayor. Everyone on the council deferred to his judgement.

"We are going to overlook that admission in your statement at this time, as it does not pertain directly to the case under investigation. But should you decide to interfere further or share your account with others, that may change. Do you understand me?"

"But what about what everyone else saw?"

"Ah yes, the other equally guilty parties."

"We can't all have imagined the same thing."

"Actually, you can. I'm sure you're familiar with the term reefer madness."

Jonah recollected the old black and white movie that his mother had forced him to watch when he was twelve, her laughable attempt to scare him away from using drugs.

"So we are classifying your statements as mass hallucination."

Jonah was stunned. He hadn't hallucinated anything. He had seen the creature's eyes before he had smoked the joint.

Sitting in silence, he realized no matter what he told the sheriff, it wouldn't matter. They had already written off his testimony as nonsense.

"What happens now?" Jonah asked.

"The town has organized a group to find the beast which we assume is still roaming in the vicinity. Curfew is in full effect until it is caught, and we are encouraging everyone to stay safe inside until this blows over."

"So I should just go home then?"

"Not yet."

The sheriff shifted uncomfortably.

"I do have one favor to ask of you."

Jonah's head perked up.

"Unfortunately, the parents of the victims are having a hard time coping with what has happened. It is my understanding that you were good friends with one of the deceased. We'd like to ask you to help us with officially identifying the body."

"You want me to identify Steve?"

"It's just a formality, an unfortunate requirement for the death certificate to be certified. I'd rather not put the family through any more suffering than I have to."

Jonah remembered the faces of Milton's parents when he had passed by them at the police station, their hopeless expressions of inexplicable pain and loss. The look of people realizing their world would never be quite as bright from that day forward.

He took a deep breath and wondered when he would feel the same. His friend's death hadn't quite hit him yet. It felt like a newspaper article about a bridge collapse in some town he had never heard of, tragic but distant. He couldn't imagine what Steve's parents were going through. They had left for the evening to go enjoy a night out, only to return home to the news that their only child, their son, had been killed.

Jonah remembered how seeing his father's flag-draped casket at the funeral had changed his mother. If he could go back and do anything to lessen her pain, he would.

"I'll do it," Jonah said.

"Great, come with me," the sheriff replied.

Together, they shuffled out of the room.

The walk-in freezer was cold. Jonah was dressed in his standard summer attire, shorts and a t-shirt, but inside it felt like midnight on Christmas Eve. The freezer belonged to the restaurant next door to the police station. Since the town didn't have a morgue, and with the sheriff not bringing in outside help, they had commandeered it as a makeshift holding area for the quickly growing number of dead bodies.

It was a tight fit, with tables shoved into the nooks and crannies. There was almost no space remaining for Jonah to maneuver, much less the rotund sheriff.

Three of the tables were currently occupied, white sheets covering very un-human like shapes.

The sheriff began lifting the sheets to check checking the toe tags.

"Here it is," the sheriff said, grabbing the top of the sheet on the table with two hands and pausing. "I'm going to lift it and then I'll need you to confirm the identity. Try to hold it together. If you feel like you have to vomit, there's a bucket on the floor at your feet. When you are sure, tell me the name. I'll cover it and we can leave."

Jonah nodded. Even the usually flavorless freezing air had a scent to it he couldn't get used to, the scent of death.

The sheriff pulled back the sheet and Jonah immediately felt the contents of his stomach gurgle.

There wasn't really a body to identify.

He recognized Steve's flannel shirt, the one he was wearing the previous night, except it was torn to shreds and stained with thick layers of red. Steve's chest looked deflated with gashes across the stomach.

"We couldn't recover all of his organs," the sheriff said, watching Jonah closely. "We assume the Grizzly got them after he was disemboweled."

Disemboweled, it was a retched term.

One of the arms was missing. Jonah assumed it had reached the same fate as the internal organs.

Both legs were there, but not attached to the body, one severed at the knee joint and the other at the hip. On the right one, Jonah could make out the scar on his friend's knee, a result of a childhood accident when they had been rough housing in Steve's treehouse and his friend had fallen to the ground, landing on a rake.

Jonah remembered it well, the spurts of blood like a fountain spraying from his friend's appendage. Yet somehow the ever-brave Steve had been laughing hysterically the whole time while Jonah screamed for help. Jonah reflected fondly on the memory. He almost felt like smiling; but the overwhelming disgust at seeing a dead body for the second time in a week overpowered it.

Sheriff Holmes cleared his throat loudly.

Jonah swallowed hard, even as the cold air burned his dry esophagus. Summoning enough courage, he brought his gaze to the head on the table.

It faced sideways, almost perpendicular to the neck, his auburn hair streaked with bands of gooey crimson. The chunks of flesh hanging from his cheeks looked almost like bad special effects from one of their trashy horror movies they went to see sometimes. The skin and fat looking waxy and manufactured.

Even with all the damage, Steve's facial expression was clearly visible. Jonah knew it. He had seen it a million times already. It was the face Steve made every time Jonah had been picked on in school, every time that Steve had run into the thick of the fight without a thought in the world for his own safety. It was the expression of someone rushing to the defense of those they cared about.

"So is it him?" Sheriff Holmes asked.

Jonah nodded.

"You have to say it out loud," Sheriff Holmes replied. "Or else it doesn't count."

"It's him," Jonah said quickly, wanting to get this part over with.

The reality of Steve's death had finally hit him, even if he had been told hours prior, seeing his friend's body just made it real. His legs felt weak, his knees wobbled. It took every ounce of his concentration not to collapse to the floor, a pathetic pile of human.

"You have to say his name."

"It's Steve Spiers," Jonah said, his voice almost breaking as the room seemed to shrink around him with every second that passed.

To his relief, the sheriff pulled the sheet back over the body.

"It's done," he said. "Thank you for your help."

Without another word, the Sheriff practically pushed Jonah out of the freezer and into the warmth of the restaurant's kitchen.

As he was escorted out of the family restaurant's back entrance, he caught a glimpse of his own reflection in the stainless steel cabinets that lined the walls. He was as white as a ghost.

The sheriff left him in the back alley behind the restaurant. The officer had offered him a ride home with one of the deputies, but the thought of being in the tight backseat of one of the police vehicles somehow horrified him more than anything else he could think of, especially since the last and only time he had been in one was with Steve.

Despite the mid-day sun high in the sky, boiling the asphalt under his sneakers, he preferred the long walk home.

At both ends of the alley, the streets were quiet and deserted. Everyone was already heeding the mayor's warning to stay indoors.

The alley stunk. The dumpster and grease trap from the restaurant combined to fill the space with a putrid, rotting stench that sent Jonah keeling over to expel the last of his breakfast from his stomach. Or was it the delayed reaction to seeing his best friend's dead and mutilated body?

Standing back up, with tears in his eyes, he wiped the bile from his lips with his sleeve.

A flyer on the nearby brick wall caught his eye. It was a notice from the mayor warning people about the algae bloom in the pond, urging them to stay away.

The blood in his body grew warm, dangerously close to boiling over.

He knew the rogue Grizzly story was a lie. When he had visited Yellowstone with his family, he had seen a deer carcass that had been killed by one, and it resembled nothing of what Steve's body had looked like.

The mayor and the sheriff were clearly working together to cover something up, but what?

Without thinking, he tore the flyer from the wall and ripped it to shreds in his hands. Then he tried to rip the pieces apart until there was nothing but a pile of stamp-sized scraps at his feet. The effort left him huffing and puffing as he stood alone in the alley.

Maybe not as alone as he thought he was.

Without warning, the back door of the restaurant opened, and a shadow appeared, towering over him.

Jonah looked up to see Rufus Hatchwell staring down at him with gritted teeth and almost every muscle in his body clenched.

So many times in his life, Jonah's fight-or-flight response had always steered him away from danger, avoiding confrontation in favor of living to fight another day.

In this moment, with his anger at the mayor still seething in his veins and the memory of Steve's lifeless body fresh in his mind, the will to fight filled him.

He brought his hands to his face, ready to take on the larger and stronger teenager. But he didn't care, he wanted to be just as brave as Steve had been in the face of something far fiercer.

Rufus's breathing was heavy and shallow as he stared down at Jonah.

That was when Jonah noticed Rufus's fists at his side. The skin was bruised and cut, smeared with blood. Loose pieces hung from his knuckles. It looked like Rufus had been punching a brick wall with his bare hands.

"What are you doing here?" Jonah snarled.

Rufus's expression didn't change.

"The sheriff asked me to identify the body," he said, his voice flat and emotionless.

Jonah remembered the other tables in the freezer, with their own sheets, hiding their own horrific remains of those he once knew as friends. He hadn't put much thought about it at the moment, his focus being on keeping it together long enough to identify Steve, but one of the other bodies was Milton's and that meant the other was...

"Unfortunately, the parents of the victims are having a hard time coping with what has happened." he heard the sheriff's words in his head.

Rufus's parents must be having as hard a time as Steve's, the mutilation of his twin sister Stephanie, an equally tragic event that no parent should ever have to endure.

"Me too," Jonah said at last.

They continued to stare at each other, but with each passing moment, the tension dissipated. The blood in Jonah's veins cooled and Rufus' stoic expression crumbled as they both shared a moment of grieving for their lost loved ones.

"The sheriff says it was a Grizzly bear," Rufus said, breaking the silence.

"Told me the same thing," said Jonah.

"It's bullshit," Rufus replied.

"I know," confirmed Jonah. "I saw it at the pond the night Milton was killed."

"What was it?"

"I don't know. But it wasn't a bear."

"I saw it too."

"Where?"

"At the party, I saw it standing in front of the fire."

"What did it look like?"

"I don't know. The fire behind it was too bright for me to see any details, just the long shadow and the eyes. They were—"

"Orange and glowing?" said Jonah, interrupting him.

Rufus nodded.

"I should have told the sheriff earlier," Jonah said. "I didn't think they'd believe me."

"They still don't," answered Rufus. "Half a dozen others told him the same thing I did. He thinks we were just stoned out of our minds. He thinks I'm lying when I told him I don't smoke."

The silence returned.

Rufus pulled a cigarette pack from his shirt pocket before dropping one into his palm and placing it to his lips.

"I thought you didn't smoke," Jonah remarked.

"I don't," Rufus replied. "This is my first one."

Jonah peered at the drops of blood dripping from Rufus's knuckles as he struck a match and lit the white stick.

"I'm sorry about your sister. How are you—"

"I'm fine," Rufus's reply was brief.

Jonah knew how the other boy felt. It was something he knew all too well. The energy it took to not scream at the top of your lungs or break every loose object in sight was truly exhausting.

"When my dad died, I was angry too," Jonah said, not sure if this would make Rufus feel better or not. "I was mad at him for going to war, for leaving my mom with a newborn, for not being there for us when we needed him. It just grew inside me until there was virtually nothing left, then one day I exploded, letting it all out."

"What did you do?"

"I broke every mirror in the house."

"Why the mirrors?"

"At his funeral, everyone kept telling me I looked just like him. So every time I looked in one, it reminded me of him and reminded me of why I was so angry."

"Did it help? Getting it all out?"

"For a little while, but it came back. I still do it sometimes. Take a piece of mirror out to the woods and smash it."

"I don't feel like breaking mirrors."

"I don't either, not this time," Jonah replied.

"So what do we do then?" Rufus asked.

The question lingered in the air between them, demanding a physical presence they both could feel. They both knew the answer. The only thing that would make either of them feel better was also the most dangerous idea of all.

Jonah grappled with it in his mind. Let the mayor and the sheriff handle. They'll know what to do. Except would they? Not if they kept believing it was some grizzly bear.

His heart was heavy, two recent deaths attached to his conscience, added to the abyss left behind by his father. He could carry it with him, letting it weigh him down, or he could use it to do something, to stop it from happening to anyone ever again.

"We kill it," Jonah said aloud.

"How?" asked Rufus.

"I don't know yet. But we can't do it alone."

Rufus nodded.

"What are you kids talking about?" said a voice from the street. "Kill what?"

A man had approached unnoticed, close enough to eavesdrop on their conversation.

Jonah recognized him immediately from his out-of-place Hawaiian shirt. It was the reporter from the police station.

"Who are you?" Rufus asked.

"The name is Bill Bradley," the man said, introducing himself. "No relation to the basketball player. I work for the newspaper in Madison."

"You don't look like a reporter," Rufus said bluntly.

"Well, I didn't originally come here in an official capacity," the reporter replied.

"Then what are you still doing here?" asked Jonah.

"Three teenagers dead," Bill began. "Mysterious circumstances, a Grizzly bear to blame. This smells like a good story to me."

"One of them was my sister," Rufus snarled, his fists clenched again.

"Hey man," the reporter said, putting up his hands. "I'm sorry for your loss. But I'm just doing my job. Speaking of which, do either of you care to go on record about what happened? Tell my readers your side of the story."

"No, we don't, you bottom feeder," said Rufus, his fists almost trembling.

"Just a few words," the reported pleaded. "Even anonymously."

"I said no."

"Was there anything strange about the bodies, anything that seemed a bit off..."

The reporter's voice trailed off as Rufus squared up with him, his breath heavy heaves again.

Jonah put a hand on Rufus's shoulder, trying to calm him.

"We can't do it alone," Jonah repeated softly.

Rufus thought about it for a moment, then must have agreed with Jonah. His breathing slowed.

"You want a story?" Rufus asked.

"Uh, ya," the reporter replied.

"Come with us then," said Rufus. "We'll give you a story."

12

1972

From the shade of his garage door, the only reprieve from the hot mid-afternoon sun, Jonah and the reporter sat on old moving boxes as they talked. The reporter was sweating profusely through his shirt as he listened, but it was impossible to determine what Bill's mood was since his eyes hid behind large aviator-style sunglasses.

Jonah was surprised Bill hadn't called him crazy already, as he shared everything he knew thus far. From the orange glowing eyes, to the metallic sounds that rocks and coins made as they bounced off the creature's long, slender hide; all of it sounded like it came straight from a pulp fiction magazine like Amazing Stories.

When he was done, he waited for the reporter to say something, but nothing came.

"You don't believe me, do you?" Jonah asked.

"Of course I believe you," Bill said in a most insincere tone.

Jonah just stared at him, unblinking.

"Alright," Bill said. "I think it's a bunch of kids with overactive imaginations. The mayor and sheriff's explanation of a Grizzly bear makes more sense."

"They are lying."

"Why would they lie?"

"I don't know yet, but they are definitely covering it up."

"It's not like they aren't doing anything about it. They are sending hunters out to look for it. I saw them staging at the police station."

"I don't think that'll work."

"Why is that?"

"I don't think they know what they're going after."

"Do you?"

The reporter gave him an odd look.

Bill had him there; Jonah was making it up as he went.

"Listen kid," Bill said as he walked out the open garage. "I'm at the motel by the station. If you guys end up doing something, come find me. I'm curious enough to follow you on this wild goose chase. At the least, it'll make for a great story about teenage shenanigans. Sound good?"

"Sure," Jonah said reluctantly.

"See you around," and the reporter disappeared, leaving Jonah alone with his thoughts and doubts.

Fortunately, he didn't have long to stew on the shortfalls of his plan as Rufus arrived shortly thereafter. Nathan and Neil followed behind him with expressions of apprehension.

Jonah greeted them as they took places near his dad's old workbench.

"Rufus says you have a plan to go after it," a voice said from behind Jonah.

Jonah spun around, surprised to see Craig standing there with his hands in his pockets.

"Working on it still," Jonah replied. "But we are going to go find it."

"And kill it," Rufus added.

"Ok if I come?" Craig asked.

"The more the better," said Jonah.

"I want to be the one that kills it for what it did to my best friend," Craig proclaimed.

The words stung Jonah a little bit, but something about how Craig's loud boasting gave Jonah a feeling it was hollow.

"You do know what we are going up against, right?" Rufus asked.

"I saw it," Craig said. "Out there in the forest."

"Do you remember anything that could help us?"

"Not really. It went by so fast."

Rufus growled in frustration.

"Well, first I think we should—" Jonah's voice stopped when he saw Diane's convertible pull up and park on the street. To his disbelief, three figures got out and walked up the driveway.

"Are we late?" Darci asked as she led the trio of girls under the cover of the open garage door.

"I didn't know—" Jonah began.

"I invited them," Rufus said before he could finish. "They were Stephanie's friends too. They deserve the right to avenge her as much as we do."

Jonah nodded as Darci sat down on a chair backwards and put her elbows on the back support. Diane leaned against a stack of cardboard boxes filled with his father's mementos. She looked angry, her mouth pursed tightly on her face. And last, Olivia walked over and stood next to Jonah.

He couldn't help but notice the dark circles under her eyes, a clear sign of hours spent crying. He wanted to reach out to her, stroke her back, hold her tight, comfort her, but with the rest of the garage staring at him so intently, he knew he couldn't.

"So what's the plan?" Darci asked.

"Plan, yes," Jonah took a deep breath before continuing. "By now, you've either seen for yourself or realized that what has been killing our friends is not a Grizzly bear, but something else entirely."

"What is it?" Neil asked.

"We don't know for certain yet," Jonah answered. "Just that—"

"How can you go after something you don't know what it is?" Neil interrupted him.

"I can only tell you what we do know," Jonah continued. "Four legs and a very long tail. Glowing orange eyes. It—"

"It has spikes on its back," Craig interjected.

"Spikes?" Rufus said with disbelief.

"I was right there," Craig said, defending himself. "It had a row of spikes down its back."

"I saw them too," Diane added.

"Fine, it possibly has spikes on its back," said Jonah, trying to regain the floor as the others whispered amongst themselves.

"It's somehow linked to the pond," he continued, raising his voice to compete with the other conversations forming. "I think I saw it in the well and I know that the well connects to..."

It was no use, no one was listening to him.

"Everyone shut up and listen!" Olivia suddenly yelled, and the garage fell silent immediately.

"Thank you," Jonah said. He opened his father's gun safe, the one that held their hunting rifles. "As you can see, we've got a few guns already."

"Won't we need a silver bullet or something to kill it?" asked Nathan.

"That's werewolves, you idiot," Neil replied, punching him in the shoulder.

"And vampires too," Nathan rebutted. "Why wouldn't it work on this thing?"

"Because werewolves and vampires don't have tails or spikes on their back," Neil said.

The two continued to bicker.

"Silver bullets are highly impractical," Darci commented, causing both Neil and Nathan to stop their argument and peer at her with surprised expressions. "They just don't have enough density to maintain their force and provide stopping power."

She suddenly stood up and walked over to the gun safe, pulling the rifles out, checking the chamber for a live round, peering down the sights, and then examining the rest of the firearm as expertly as a seasoned U.S. marine.

"If the creature does indeed have a hide that is thick or armored," she continued. "We'll need at least a Remington .223 round or larger to penetrate it. Given we don't know for certain, I'm hesitant to rely on these simple hunting rifles to be effective. I recommend something much more powerful."

She sat the rifle back into the gun safe and closed it. Turning around, she realized the entire group was staring at her with mouths wide open.

"What?" she asked. "Ballistics are a hobby of mine."

"Darci makes a good point," Rufus began. "Does anyone's parents have anything we could use more powerful than a hunting rifle?"

A communal shaking of heads in the negative followed.

Then Jonah had an idea.

"I know where we can get some more guns," he said.

"Great," said Rufus. "Why don't you and Craig—"

"What is this?!" said an alarmed voice from the open garage door.

Standing there, wearing her apron and with her hands on her hips, was Jonah's mother.

"I told you, you were grounded," she added, her voice angry and bitter.

"I can explain," Jonah pleaded, hustling to lead her away from the group and out of the garage.

As he passed, Rufus leaned in close.

"Get the guns. I'll get everyone else ready for later tonight," he said in a whisper.

Jonah nodded. He still wasn't certain how he would get them, but with his mother's glare piercing him, he knew he had bigger problems at the moment.

Inside, Jonah sat at the dining room table, awaiting a verbal lashing. She had ordered him to sit there and wait while she got Levi a snack as the 4-year-old sat watching television. She seemed to be taking her time preparing it, muttering to herself as she did so. Obviously practicing and preparing each word she would assault him with.

"First of all," his mother said, placing a plate on the floor in front of Levi before taking the seat opposite Jonah.

He braced himself.

"I wanted to say I'm sorry," she said.

Jonah flinched.

"I know I've been really tough on you this year," she continued. "And to be honest, I don't know why. I suppose it could be because I'm still at least a little angry at your father. He was so foolhardy, volunteering to go to war like that and leaving us, well you know what it's like around here now."

Jonah opened his mouth to say something, but no words formed. Whatever anger she had at him a few minutes prior had evaporated, and she was almost on the verge of tears.

"Even just now, I was so angry with you for having friends over that I forgot that you just lost your best friend last night."

The words stung Jonah; he understood how anger and sadness could swirl inside someone until it was almost impossible to distinguish between the two.

"And I'm not an idiot. I know it's been hard on you. The late nights at the diner, plus having a little one running around, makes everything just so stressful. Lord knows I could be doing a better job of controlling myself, I just wish your dad was still here, with us, helping me."

Jonah breathed deep, suppressing the growing urge to breakdown in front of her.

"But you've been helping me. More than a teenager really should. You should be out there, being with your friends, especially when times are tough. You should be a kid while you still can."

"I'm not a kid mom," Jonah said. It was the only thing he could think of to say.

"Yes, you are," she replied, her eyes swelling with tears. "You will always be a kid to me, my kid."

She put her hands on his from across the table.

"Just please, be responsible," she added. "You can't let anything happen to you. I don't know what I'd do without you."

Jonah nodded. Everything he had felt today, the sadness, the mourning for a friend, the anger; it had clogged together inside him like a dam. Nothing was getting through, even as the pressure mounted. In this moment, he wanted to tell her he understood, that he forgave her. But with the logjam holding fast, he could only manage a reassuring smile.

"So I know I asked you to babysit Levi," she moved on before he could finish processing. "And I know you're grounded. But I think after everything that's gone on, you should be able to go out with your friends tonight."

Go out with his friends? Did she overhear their plan to find the creature? She would never condone such a thing.

"Mom, I..." he tried to find a reasonable explanation.

"It was so kind of the school to open up the gymnasium for a prayer vigil in honor of Steve and what were the other's names?"

"Milton and Stephanie."

"So I've asked Mrs. O'Leary to watch Levi, so you can go. I have to work the overnight shift again."

Jonah was shocked.

"Just please pick him up from her house when you get home," she added.

"Yes, yes," Jonah stuttered. "Of course."

"Thanks sweetums," she said, stroking his cheek softly. "You really do remind me of him, of your dad."

Suddenly standing up, she swung her arms open.

"Now come over here and give your mother a hug before I have to go get ready."

Without hesitation, he walked around the table and hugged her tight.

She squeezed him back, placing her head on his shoulder.

Neither of them knew what tomorrow would bring, but in that moment, neither of them cared.

Jonah arrived at the motel around seven, parking his bike outside the front office. He had expected he would need to ask the clerk where the reporter's room was, but was surprised to find Bill Bradley sitting on the curb outside waiting for him. In the reporter's hand was a brown paper bag which Jonah could tell from the smell, contained some kind of cheap tequila.

"You ready?" Jonah asked.

"For the goose chase?" Bill replied, standing up. His voice slurred only slightly.

"I need your help with something first."

"What do you have in mind?"

"It's a little dangerous."

"Not a problem. I used to be a war correspondent."

"And pretty illegal."

Bill took a hit from a joint and blew the smoke into Jonah's face.

"Also not a problem."

"Great, then follow me next door."

The reporter, wearing his purple and white Hawaiian shirt, followed Jonah across the parking lot towards the police station.

The police station's front door was open. Other than the steady gurgling of the coffeemaker, it was completely silent inside.

Jonah was refusing to take any chances, and crept from the waiting area to where desks piled with paperwork sat empty.

A loud thud behind him made him jump.

Turning, he saw Bill steadying a trash can that was about to topple over.

"Shhh!" Jonah said with stern eyes.

Bill's eyes were red. He looked drunk and stoned already.

"Why are you creeping around?" Bill said, shrugging off Jonah's expression. "No one is here."

"How do you know?" Jonah whispered.

The reporter raised his eyebrows.

"Hello!?" Bill suddenly yelled.

Jonah panicked at the outburst.

"Hello?!" Bill repeated loud enough to wake the dead.

Jonah hushed Bill, but it was no use. He imagined a platoon of police officers would suddenly appear from nowhere and arrest them.

Except none did. The coffeemaker continued gurgling away, the only sound in the station.

"Told you," Bill said as he walked over to the machine and helped himself to a cup. He was quick to notice a bottle of Jack Daniels tucked away behind the machine, only partially hidden. He waited until Jonah's back was turned before he snuck a few pours from the bottle into the styrofoam.

"What are we doing here anyway?" Bill said as he sipped at the steaming liquid from the container.

"We need something strong enough to pierce whatever it is," said Jonah. "And I saw a ton of guns in the evidence locker."

Bill laughed out loud.

"You want to steal some guns from the police? You are crazy."

"I'll bring them back after we kill it. We just need something powerful enough to bring it down."

"You don't even know what it is."

"More reason to bring something big."

Bill seemed to mull it over in his head.

"So you think they just leave it open?"

"I overheard that one of the deputies is terrible about locking it up. I was hoping he had forgotten again."

"Leaving the front door open is one thing," Bill said, unsuccessfully holding back his laughter. "But leaving the evidence locker open when it's full of guns, no way. Not a chance."

"Just be quiet," Jonah hissed at him. "And keep a lookout for anyone coming."

"I can do that," Bill said with a smirk as he made his way back to the waiting area and sat down in a chair facing the parking lot. He sipped at the hot coffee gingerly.

Peeking under every desk as he walked towards the evidence locker, Jonah still half expected an officer to pop out of nowhere at any moment. He was surprised at how empty the station was, given all the recent deaths. Whomever was supposed to be here must be out on a call. They were continuing to run a skeleton crew at night, willfully oblivious to the danger. Even more reason for Jonah to get in and get out quickly.

Reaching the placarded room, he peered through the window and inside. For a small town in rural Wisconsin, it was surprisingly well-stocked with confiscated weaponry.

Putting his hand on the door handle, he tried to turn it. The handle didn't budge an inch. He applied more pressure, still nothing. Growing frustrated, he yanked and pulled on the door, but the thick metal door wasn't even rattling in the frame. It was useless.

Jonah felt immediately deflated. The entire plan had hinged on this. He would have to return to the group empty-handed, looking like a fool in front of Rufus, Diane, Olivia...

"Told you," Bill said from over his shoulder, causing Jonah to jump.

Jonah didn't want to respond. The reporter had been right.

"Lucky for you," Bill said, fishing into his jacket pocket. "I've got you covered."

Kneeling, he pulled out a small leather case and unrolled it on the floor. Several metal tools clattered to the ground.

"Oops," he said as he clumsily bent over to pick them up and place them back inside the case. It was a lock-picking kit, just like in the movies.

"How did you...?"

"Come on, kid, you think reporters always follow the rules? This little thing has gotten me the truth behind a story more times than I can count."

And he went to work, fiddling with the lock as he inserted and twisted the various metal utensils.

Jonah, not wanting to be useless, kept a watch for any signs that anyone was coming. Whomever was out could be back at any moment. Jonah was sweating as each second felt like hours.

"Bingo," Bill said as the lock clicked. "A piece of cake."

The door swung open and Bill was the first one inside with Jonah following.

"Holy smokes," he said. "Some of these are practically ancient."

He wasn't wrong.

As they walked past racks stacked with weaponry, it felt like they were on a museum tour. There were at least a dozen Lee-Enfields, Springfields, Colts, and Lugers; relics of the World Wars. But the deeper they went, the stranger it got. Several guns from the Civil War sat in the far back, buried under others, and even an old flint-lock musket that dated back to the days of the American Revolution.

"This is rad," Bill exclaimed, as he pulled an AK-47 from the rack and pretended to fire it. "I haven't seen one of these in years. You said the sheriff confiscated this stuff from hunters?"

"That's what he said," replied Jonah.

"You get elephants here often?" Bill said, holding up a rifle with a barrel almost as wide as his wrist.

"Just when the Ringling Bros. come to town," said Jonah. "Bring it with us. Throw the bullets in this backpack."

He grabbed his backpack the sheriff had taken as evidence from a hanging hook and opened it up. The fabric was splattered with dry blood, Milton's blood. Most of the contents had already spilled out onto the table, the Bugles and Cokes probably pilfered by someone on the sheriff's staff. Huge gashes on the outside rendered it virtually useless. Jonah panicked. His father's watch was nowhere to be seen.

"One of the deputies must have taken it," Jonah said aloud, frustrated.

"Taken what?" asked Bill.

"My dad's watch. They were keeping it as evidence, but it's not here."

"We have to worry about that later. We can't use that. It's sliced to hell."

"I brought another."

Luckily Jonah had come prepared, grabbing Levi's pack as a backup on the way out the door.

"Fill this one then," Jonah said, turning around and facing out the door so that Bill could load it up while he kept watch for any officers returning from a call.

Being much smaller than his own, the straps cut against Jonah's shoulders as it grew heavier and heavier with each handful of cartridges that Bill poured inside.

"Some .762s for the AK," Bill said aloud.

"The AK?" Jonah questioned. "Are you sure that's—"

The AK-47 being thrust into his arms stopping him from finishing his sentence.

"What about—" Jonah began again, only to be interrupted by the strap of the heavy elephant gun being thrown over his shoulder.

Bill was clearly not paying him any attention.

"These will do very nicely," Bill murmured as several loud and heavy objects were added to the already bulging pack.

"What was that?" Jonah asked, struggling to turn his head to see.

"Don't worry about it. Just try not to bump into anything," Bill said with a smile.

That did little to quell Jonah's nerves.

Before long, the backpack was filled to bursting, and they left the evidence room, carefully closing the door behind them.

Jonah's back and legs hurt. Carrying the two guns and pack of ammo was exhausting.

"Think you can carry the guns at least?" Jonah asked.

"This is your caper, I'm just helping you along a bit," Bill replied.

Slowly, they headed towards the exit.

As Jonah passed the bathroom door, he heard a noise that made his heart sink: the distinct sound of flushing coming from the men's room.

Behind him, the door swung open, blocking him against the wall and separating him from Bill.

"What the hell are you doing here?" Jonah heard the voice of Deputy Brian Nibiikwe from the other side of the door, filled with surprised anger.

"Oh, just looking for the sheriff," Bill said calmly

Jonah turned his head, knowing they had been caught red-handed.

Except the deputy was facing away from him, confronting Bill. He didn't even know Jonah was there. Over the deputy's shoulder, Jonah could see Bill's eyes urging him to keep going.

Slowly and steadily, Jonah took as silent a step forward towards the front door as he could. Step after step, he prayed he could get away unnoticed.

"The sheriff isn't here," the deputy announced. "You shouldn't be either."

"Well, the front door was open," replied Bill. "So I helped myself to a cup of coffee."

"The coffee isn't for the public."

"Then I suppose the whiskey wasn't either?"

"What? How did you? Are you drunk?"

"Maybe, are you?"

"I should arrest you."

"Wouldn't be the first time. But I'm pretty certain that the state prosecutor might be very interested in my story. The drunk deputy, passed out in the bathroom while on duty, several kids killed, virtually no investigation..."

"You wouldn't dare."

"How do you know?"

Only a few more steps and Jonah would be out the door. Bill was doing a phenomenal job of keeping the deputy occupied.

Reaching for the handle, he pulled the door open slightly and got one shoe into the fresh outside air when...

"Freeze," the deputy's voice boomed from behind him. Jonah's hands jumped into the air, the guns clattered to the ground.

"Now turn around slowly," the officer commanded.

Jonah slowly complied, facing the deputy with his eyes fixed on the ground in shame. His goose was cooked.

"What the hell are you doing, Jonah?" Deputy Nibiikwe asked.

"I, I, I," none of the lies that ran through Jonah's mind made any sense. Borrowing the guns as props for a play they were putting on at school, performing an authentic battle reenactment in his backyard, each one was just as ridiculous as the truth.

"Slowly put your hands behind your head and—" the deputy began.

"We are going after it," Jonah blurted out.

He looked up to check the deputy's reaction. From the dark stains around the man's armpits, the thick beads of sweat falling from his forehead, and the disheveled nature of his hair; it was apparent the deputy was coming down after another night of heavy drinking.

"We already have hunters going after the Grizzly," the deputy said, not lowering his gun.

"We both know it's not a Grizzly."

"What? Of course it is."

"You tried to warn me the other night. Warn me and Steve."

"Yes, to stay out of the forest, away from the pond. It's dangerous out there."

"But there was something else too, something you didn't tell us. Something you couldn't tell us."

"Of course not, I was just—"

"I've seen it, so has half the kids in town."

"Seen what?"

"You tell me."

"You know I can't let you leave with all of that," the deputy said. Jonah could tell the deputy was struggling to keep his composure.

Jonah took a deep breath. What would his dad say? What would his dad do in this situation?

"I am leaving with it," Jonah said, doing his best to stop himself from trembling as he spoke. "Me and my friends, we are going to find it and kill it. You can shoot me if you want, but we're not stopping until that thing is dead."

Bill's eyes were wide with astonishment.

"If I can't stop you from trying," the deputy said, tensing the muscles in his arms. "Then I guess I need to help you."

To Jonah's surprise, the deputy lowered his gun and placed it back in its holster.

"What did you have in mind?"

13

1972

Jonah rode in the front seat of the police car as they drove down the forest access road towards Tranquility Pond. He held on tight as they went, ruts in the dirt road tossing him and the rest of the passengers violently at unexpected intervals. Bill sat in the back, doing his best to keep the guns and Levi's backpack full of ammunition from flying into the air. Deputy Brian drove, seemingly oblivious to the turbulence. Between the two older men, the vehicle rank of booze and the fresh air from the open windows was a welcome lifeline for Jonah.

They drove in silence except for the grunts of discomfort and clinking of shells from the backseat.

Jonah couldn't hold back any longer.

"Do you know where my dad's watch is?" he asked the deputy.

"What?" the deputy replied in confusion.

"It's missing from my backpack in evidence. It's a gold pocket watch. But it's broken, not worth anything. I want it back."

"No one logged a watch into evidence with your backpack."

Jonah didn't believe him. How could the watch just vanish like that?

"I want it back."

"I didn't take it."

Jonah's fists clenched. He could feel the anger bubbling inside him again. Being unable to tell if the deputy was lying or telling the truth infuriated him.

Bill must have noticed.

"So what is it exactly?" the reporter asked from the backseat, trying to diffuse the situation. "The creature we're going after."

"There's no word in English for it," Deputy Brian replied. "But my people call it the Mishipeshu."

"Can you spell that?" asked Bill as he tried to scribble onto a small notepad he produced from his shirt pocket.

The deputy ignored him.

"It protects the waters of the pond, which in our culture was the gateway to the spirit realm."

"What does it look like?" asked Jonah.

"My grandfather always said it was a great and powerful mountain lion," the deputy replied. "But my grandmother thought it was a snake with legs."

"Well, which is it?" Bill interjected.

"Oral traditions don't work that way,' answered the deputy, annoyance growing in his voice.

"Well, that's hardly helpful," said Bill.

"Still think it's a just wild goose chase?" Jonah asked the reporter.

"Maybe, but turning into one hell of an interesting goose," Bill replied.

Even in the faint cabin light, Jonah could see a glint of excitement in the reporter's eyes. Leading him to the realization that guys like Bill didn't just seek out danger, they thrived in it.

"In either story," asked Jonah, returning his attention to the deputy. "Do they mention any weaknesses it may have, anything we can use against it?"

The deputy shook his head.

"It is said that the Ogimaa, the chief, had a weapon that could kill it," he explained further.

"And your brother never told you?"

"He did not."

"So your great grandparents or ancestors or whatever had a weapon that could hurt it," Bill said, interjecting again. "It obviously was a primitive tool of some type."

"That would make sense," the deputy replied.

"They didn't have guns," Bill continued. "Specifically, they didn't have really, really big guns like these."

"That's correct."

"So I don't care what it is then. Nothing I know of could survive a blast from either of these bad boys."

The deputy took another deep breath. Jonah could tell he was holding back his own opinion on the subject, holding back concern. Jonah shared it. But what else could they do? Bill wasn't wrong. There was nothing on the planet strong enough to withstand the small arsenal in the backseat. There was no reason to believe the elephant gun or the AK-47 wouldn't be enough.

"What does it want?" Jonah took his turn to ask the next question. "I've lived here my entire life, and nothing remotely like this has happened before."

"They say it only emerges every seventeen years," said the deputy. "Usually when the summer days are at their longest."

"Has it attacked your tribe before?" Jonah asked.

"Yes," the deputy replied. "It is why my people live so far away from the town. We avoid the creature at all costs. I myself thought it was just a silly legend until that family was found dead by the water when I was a boy."

"You mean the father that killed his family and then himself?" Jonah could hear Bill's pen scratching frantically at the notepad in the back.

"That's not what happened…" The deputy's voice trailed off.

"Another goddamn lie," Jonah snarled.

"The mayor, he's the one who keeps everyone in line with the story," the deputy replied. "The sheriff goes along with anything he says."

"Is that why I saw him with all of those big game hunters at the Elk's Lodge?"

"Yes. They have set a trap for the creature away from the town, using live deer as bait. They hope to lure it far enough away so they can kill it."

Jonah remembered the herd of deer he had passed on the way to the pond. They were so bold and fearless. Hardly the behavior of animals traveling through a predator's territory.

"You don't think that will work, do you?" Jonah asked. "That's why you stayed behind?"

The deputy nodded.

"They don't really listen to me or my people. None of the other animals fear the Mishipeshu, nor should they. Man is the only threat to the spirit world."

The memory of Craig jumping into the water, upsetting the water's pristine surface, glanced through his head.

"Do you think by going into the pond with my friends, we somehow awakened it?"

"I don't think so."

"Why not?"

"My family has been here many generations. We have countless stories about the Mishipeshu. It always awakens every new generation."

"Like a reminder.."

The deputy nodded.

"Deputy Nibiikwe," Jonah began before hesitating. A question lingered in the back of his mind, but he wasn't sure yet how to ask it.

"You can call me Brian," the deputy replied. "After letting you leave the station with all of those guns, I doubt they'll let me keep my badge."

"Brian," Jonah began again. "Why are you doing this? Why are you helping us?"

The deputy took a long breath before speaking.

"My grandmother used to tell me a story. It was about a time when our ancestors confronted the legend. It's not a happy story. Facing the creature in broad daylight, our fiercest warriors turned and ran. In the process, we allowed an innocent child to be taken by it. To us, defending the innocent is paramount. Our cowardice brought great shame. I'm helping you because I have also brought great shame to my family, and maybe this is my one chance at redemption..."

He paused before his voice could break. Taking a deep breath, he continued.

"For me and my ancestors."

Jonah couldn't believe what he was hearing.

"Do you mind telling it to us?" Jonah asked. "The story from your tribe."

The deputy looked at Jonah for a moment, as if his eyes were pleading to not make him relive the tale in detail. Jonah knew it was too painful, that the deputy would refuse.

"It happened before there was a town here, when my tribe had a village near the pond. My ancestors..."

Jonah listened intently as the deputy spoke, hoping some detail from the legend would provide a clue to the monster's weaknesses that they could exploit, but the deputy would have to hurry. It wouldn't be long before they reached the muddy banks of Tranquility Pond.

As the deputy's police car arrived, Rufus and the others looked like deer in the headlights. Ready to scatter different directions to avoid arrest. It wasn't until Jonah emerged from the front seat did their concerns ease.

"It's alright," Jonah said aloud, his hands raised. "It's just the deputy. He's agreed to help us."

Rufus particularly looked distrustful at first, but as the deputy helped unload the guns and ammunition from the back of the cruiser, his skepticism waned.

"Holy crap, is that an elephant gun?" Neil exclaimed with wide eyes. "It's bigger than my—"

"Shut it," Rufus said forcefully, and Neil recoiled to a quiet spot in the group's rear.

"What have you guys figured out thus far?" Jonah asked.

He expected Rufus to explain the plan immediately, but was surprised to see Darci step forward.

"We found a shallow depression on the other side of this hill that we think will work," she began. "It's surrounded on three sides by higher ground that would make excellent vantage points and, on the other, by a direct route to the water's edge. We would also be upwind, giving us another key advantage."

Jonah and the others listened attentively.

"It didn't seem to be bothered by the fire at the party, so obviously it's not afraid of it. So we'll start a campfire in the basin to give us better visibility. We've also raided Craig's mom's liquor cabinet and improvised some Molotov cocktails."

"Wait, how do you know how to make those?" asked the deputy.

"Read about it in a magazine," Darci said quickly before continuing. "They likely won't do much damage to it, but they should serve as ample distraction. Now Sun Tzu says, 'In the midst of chaos, there is also opportunity.' That's what we need to create, enough chaos so that we can hit it with something big. That elephant gun should do it, but if not, I have a backup plan."

She pointed to Craig's shiny red Ford F-100 parked several yards away. The blood immediately drained from Craig's face.

"According to the manufacturer's book in the glove box," Darci began.

"You went through my glove box?" Craig asked. She ignored him and continued.

"That truck weights 4,500 lbs, give or take. With the forward momentum of the downhill slope plus the engine's acceleration, it should make a powerful battering ram that should be able to destroy anything it hits."

"But it's brand new," Craig pleaded. "It's my graduation gift."

"You haven't graduated yet," Darci replied.

"I will next year," he said.

"What happened to all that talk back in the garage about wanting to be the one to kill it?"

Jonah held back the urge to chuckle.

"Ya, of course," Craig said. "Anything to avenge Steve."

His nervous expression cast serious doubt on that.

"How are you planning on luring it in?" asked the deputy.

"Olivia and Diane rounded up a ton of frozen meat from their parents' freezers as bait," Darci replied.

"It won't work," the deputy said, shaking his head. "The Mishipeshu—"

"The Mishi-what?" Rufus asked, interrupting him.

"It's what his people call it," Jonah clarified. "A Mishipeshu."

Rufus held back a bewildered expression, but didn't speak up again.

"Why won't it work?" asked Darci.

"It only hunts humans," the deputy replied.

"That is problematic," said Darci.

Jonah could see her mind racing as she contemplated how to get around the obstacle. At last, she seemed to have exacerbated all options and looked to the group with solemn eyes.

"Any volunteers to be bait?" She asked.

No one was in any hurry to step forward.

Jonah wondered what his dad would do in this situation.

"I'll lead the column," Jonah imagined his father's voice volunteering as lead scout of his platoon in Vietnam. Always willing to be first in line when danger came knocking, always one to put his life in front of someone else's. Always the one to blend bravery and stupidity.

"I'll do it," Jonah said, deciding to give it a shot.

The entire group turned to stare at him, making him suddenly very nervous.

"You sure?" Rufus asked.

"Someone has to," Jonah replied.

Rufus put his hand on Jonah's shoulder and nodded in thanks.

The moment was interrupted by the sudden outburst of wailing from Olivia.

Before anyone could react, she took off towards the forest access road, her loud sobs audible in the quiet night.

Both Darci and Diane started after her.

"No," Jonah said. "I'll go talk to her."

They both stopped in their tracks.

As the rest of the group dispersed to make final preparations, Jonah jogged to catch up with Olivia.

"Wait up!" Jonah said, as he got close enough for her to hear him without having to yell.

Olivia just kept walking, the faint glow of the town's lights in the distance ahead of them.

"Please, just talk to me," he said, tugging on her elbow.

She swiped her arm out of his grasp.

"Hey, stop," he pleaded, this time running in front of her to block her path.

She ran straight into his chest, not seeing him through the tears that flowed like a waterfall from her eyes.

Jonah stumbled for a moment, but was able to steady himself in time by wrapping his arms around her shoulders in a bear hug. He expected her to squirm away, like she had done with her elbow, but she didn't.

Instead, Olivia nuzzled closer to him, burying her face in his thin flannel shirt.

"What's wrong?" he asked.

Wrong question. Olivia's sobs increased in intensity and volume.

"Olivia, please," he pleaded. "Talk to me."

"Why did you do that?" she replied, pushing herself away and pounding at his chest with a weak fist.

"Do what?"

"Volunteer like that."

"It was the right thing to do."

"No, it wasn't. It was the stupid thing to do."

"I don't think that's fair, I—"

"You're going to die."

Jonah's stomach turned over. He tried to ignore it. He knew he needed to be brave, even if every particle in his body told him to turn, take Olivia with him, and run.

"Darci has a good plan. I'll be just fine. Trust me."

"That's what my dad said too, before he volunteered to fight in that stupid war."

Jonah understood why she was crying. He probably had a better understanding of what she was going through more than any other teenager in the entire town. But what could he possibly say to comfort her?

"My dad said something similar when he left," Jonah replied.

"Then why are you doing this?"

"Because it's exactly what he would have done if he were me."

Her sobbing subsided as she looked up at him with red, tear-soaked eyes. The moon's reflection glimmered in her gaze, its bright light overhead feeling as if it shined just for them.

Jonah was at a loss for what to do next. He felt hopelessly confused, indecisiveness paralyzing him.

Lucky for him, he didn't need to do anything at all.

Standing on her tip-toes, she kissed him under the star filled night sky.

For that long minute, as their lips touched and mouths connected them together, all the problems of the world melted away.

The sadness of losing their friends.

The worry over what would happen next.

Even the painful scars of their fathers' deaths seemed to have subsided.

As their mouths separated and she nestled herself in his chest again, only one thought dwelled in his mind. It was a promise to himself and to her.

I'm going to marry this girl.

He didn't know how long they stood there like that.

Barely audible, hidden behind the sounds of crickets and owls, he could only just make out her whispers.

"I still think you're being stupid."

Returning to join the others, the couple lingered for a moment, their hands touching, afraid to let go, afraid it would be the last time. Olivia was the one who had to break the connection. Jonah certainly couldn't muster enough willpower to do it. Leaving him behind, she ran to join Darci and Diane; who were busy pouring alcohol into glass soda bottles for the Molotov Cocktails.

As she kneeled to help them, all three girls exchanged various expressions; a secret conversation only women could understand. Olivia's eyes must have told them all they needed to know about what happened on the road. Diane couldn't help herself and giggled slightly. It reminded Jonah that they were all still just a bunch of kids.

It was hard, but he knew he had to take his eyes off of Olivia and get to the campfire. He began the slippery trek up the hill.

Along the way, he passed Neil and Nathan gathering fallen tree limbs for firewood. Without Rufus around to keep the order, they were playful with one another as they worked on their assignment. They kept trying to compare the size of the log each had found to another body part, one upping one another each time they found a larger piece of timber. It was a crude game, but not one Jonah would have put past himself a few years prior while romping around by the old well with Steve.

At the top of the hill sat Craig's truck with Craig inside. Jonah could see the football player's reflection in the side mirror. He was smoking a cigarette in the cab, one hand stroking the Ford logo embedded in the steering wheel. Craig's eyes stared further down the hill with a vacant, distant expression.

Their other vehicle, the police cruiser, had been moved to the rise on the opposite end. It was empty, with its lights illuminating the bottom of the basin where Deputy Brian, Bill the reporter, and Rufus worked in a small clearing, building up the bonfire.

Being careful not to slip, Jonah made his way carefully down to join them.

As he approached, he noticed tense voices arguing with one another.

"I should be the one with the guns," the deputy said, clinging to both of the weapons in his arms.

"We need a shooter on both hills. You can't have both guns," Rufus replied.

"Yes, but I'm the only one here who's had official firearms training," rebutted the deputy.

"I'm sure the creature will keep that in mind before it chooses its next victim," said Rufus, looking annoyed. "Help me out here Jonah, what do you think?"

Jonah assessed the group for a moment.

"Rufus, your dad took you hunting for bull moose a couple summers ago, right?" he asked.

"Yep, nearly bagged one too," the other teenager replied.

"What does that have to do with—" the deputy began to say.

"And Rufus, you have a forty or fifty-pound weight advantage on the deputy?"

"That I do," the large boy said in a rather pleased tone.

"Then you can take the elephant gun," Jonah said.

"I don't think that's a good idea," the deputy said.

"Brian," Jonah began, speaking to the deputy in a voice of friendship. "You've risked so much being out here with us already. Please, Stephanie was his sister, his twin sister. Let him do this."

The deputy seemed like he was about to contest again, but begrudgingly he handed over the elephant gun to Rufus.

"I'll take the AK," Bill the reporter jumped forward, as if the deputy would just hand it over to him.

"Not a chance in the world," said Brian.

"Why not? I was a war corespondent in Vietnam. You know how many of these I've seen? Hell, I was at Hamburger Hill when—"

"I've watched you do nothing but chain smoke that joint for the last half hour. There's no chance I'm giving you a weapon."

Bill's eyes attempted an appeal to Jonah.

"The deputy is right," Jonah said to him.

Bill scoffed out loud in defeat.

"I've always wanted to fire one of those things." Bill said to himself in frustration as he trudged up the hill to the police car.

"I'll put him on the radio," the deputy said. "Any sign of the creature and he'll call it into the others."

"We are ready up here," they heard Darci yell from the top of the hill. "What about you guys?"

"Us too," Jonah yelled back.

"You guys better get in position," he added, facing Bill and Rufus.

Rufus was the first to move, easily lugging the heavy rifle on his shoulder as if it weighed nothing. As he passed Jonah, he put his hand on his shoulder.

"I'm sorry for not saying it earlier," Rufus said. "But I'm sorry about Steve. I'm sure he was a good guy. He had to be if my sister liked him."

Jonah smiled and nodded back.

Rufus rustled up the hill and out of sight.

The deputy and Jonah were left alone. Neither looked at each other, both opting to stare into the dancing flames as they licked at the yet to be charred wood.

"You're a brave young man," Deputy Brian said, breaking the silence. "I'm sure your dad would be proud."

"Thank you," Jonah said, steeling himself, holding onto the focus of what would come next for them.

He was surprised when Brian took a step closer to him and held out something in his hand. Jonah reached down and picked it up.

"It's my service revolver," the deputy explained. "A Smith & Wesson. I'm afraid it won't do much damage, but it might buy you some time."

Jonah nodded a thank you. He couldn't find the words to fit the moment, so he just remained quiet.

Brian soon disappeared from the fire, leaving Jonah alone.

Taking a seat on a nearby stump, he looked out over the pond just fifty feet away. He could see why Brian's people would think the lake was the gateway to the underworld. It was always so serene, always so quiet, leaving the water's surface reflective and impenetrable looking. Anything could be lurking beneath its surface. What other mysteries did it hide?

Well, there was one mystery he intended to take care of that night, one mystery he intended to snuff out. For Milton, for Stephanie, for Steve, and for whomever countless others had unwittingly been victim to this monster. Its time was going to come to an end, or else Jonah would die trying.

14

1972

It had been almost an hour and there was no sign of the creature. Jonah was growing nervous. He was running out of firewood, the initial tower of timber burning quicker than they had thought. The surrounding hills were still and quiet, no sign of movement. With the fire so close, it was impossible for his eyes to adjust to the darkness outsides its perimeter of light. The others could have chickened out and left him alone for all he'd know.

He pushed any thoughts of his friend's cowardice from his mind.

Most frustrating of all was that nothing had stirred from the waters of the pond. No glowing orange eyes had appeared, no suspicious floating logs had emerged, not even the faintest of ripples across its surface had disturbed it. He was beginning to doubt their plan would work.

Except he knew it had to.

Growing bored, his mind drifted off to memories of his father. Their own trips to the woods to camp and hunt. They had hunted all sorts of wild game: deer, elk, wolves, even bears. They all seemed so tame in comparison to the Mishipeshu.

He caught himself from laughing out loud as he remembered one trip in particular. His father handing him a plastic bottle of a strange liquid, he sniffing it to ask what it was only to fumble it when his father had told him it was deer urine. The contents had spilled everywhere, all over clothes. His father had thought it hilarious, his mother not so much. They ended up throwing out what he was wearing and it took an entire week of tomato soup baths before the scent lessened enough for him to be let out in public again.

Hmmm. That gave him an idea.

Jonah sniffed at his shirt. It still smelled like his mother's laundry detergent. That sanitary scent with only a hint of lavender perfume. The only thing he was going to attract smelling like this was the Ajax Laundry Detergent Knight.

That's what was wrong. There was no scent to attract their prey.

Walking to the edge of the firelight, he unzipped his pants. With the knowledge that everyone around him was likely watching him closely, he found that peeing suddenly became very difficult. Closing his eyes, he imagined himself alone, standing at the edge of a cliff, aiming at the forested valley below as clouds passed by. Eventually, he found success. Moving in an arching path, he marked as much of his territory as he could. Thankfully, he had been holding it in for a while so there was plenty to cover the perimeter.

Now all he needed was a little breeze…

"What the hell is he doing?" Rufus asked himself from the top of the hill. He was crouched next to a bush, watching Jonah closely. The elephant gun in his hands at the ready, and the brightly colored child's backpack next to him stuffed with the gun's enormous shells.

Neil and Nathan were behind him, cowering quietly in a bush while watching his back.

The girls were another thirty feet away and had failed to hold back their giggling as they all got a pretty good look at Jonah, hopping around as he peed on every bush and plant in sight.

Was he putting on a show or something? Rufus thought to himself.

Not wanting to let it distract him, he kept his eyes fixed on the water, ready to fire at the slightest sign of movements on its surface. The beast would come from the pond. Darci had assured him of that.

It was warm out; Rufus was sweating. The moisture clinging to his palms made holding onto the rifle stock difficult. He wiped his damp hands on his wrestling team t-shirt, but it made little difference. It was just as soaked through with sweat as the rest of him. Damn Wisconsin humidity.

Relief came in the form of the wind reversing direction. A cool breeze began to emanate from the pond, almost whistling as it traveled through the clearing and up the slope, hitting Rufus square in the face with a refreshing chill.

The minutes stretched on, and in the quiet loneliness, he grew anxious. When the time came, would he be able to execute his part in the plan without error? In wrestling, he had often practiced for four hours or more a day to perfect his technique. Though he had fired a gun before, he didn't do it every day.

He decided a little practice wouldn't hurt, and it would help pass the time.

Making a whispered boom sound as he pretended to pull the trigger, he reached over to the backpack to pluck another one of the shells and pretended to reload the elephant gun. Another boom, another shell. Another boom, another shell.

It was feeling almost seamless. He could locate the bag without having to take his eyes from the gun sights.

Boom, another shell. Boom, another shell. Boom, another…

He reached for the bag, but his hand found nothing but air.

That was strange.

Had someone snuck up and grabbed it? Was it one of Neil's stupid and ill-timed pranks?

Looking sideways to check the bush where the two knucklehead friends of his had taken cover, he held back the urge to curse when he saw it was empty. They must have snuck away when he wasn't looking. There was nothing left of them but a few muddy footprints leading towards the road.

Where the hell did the bag go then?

He froze when he heard a strange sound behind him.

Maybe one of them kept their nerve and came back. Probably Nathan, that one was always more afraid of Rufus than he was the wrath of God.

Turning, he prepared to give the boy a verbal berating.

Except it wasn't Nathan. Instead, Rufus found himself face to face with the creature that he had been waiting so patiently for. Face to face might have been the wrong word. The creature's head was stuffed inside the backpack, the shells and contents of it spilling to the ground. Rufus could hear it sniffing, loud heavy snorts, muffled against the fabric that snapped and strained against its face.

Not wanting to draw attention to himself, he slowly swung the gun around to point it in the direction of the monster. Though only several yards away, under the dense canopy of the forest trees, it was nothing but an ominous dark shape against an even darker backdrop.

Carefully, his finger found the hammer and swung it back.

Click!

In the forest's quiet, it might as well had been a warning shot.

Before he knew it, Rufus felt something hard hit him in the chest. It was the hardest he had ever been hit before; it felt like a truck had run him over. As the sensation of the ground disappeared from under his feet, and the world spun around him, he got the impression that he was floating.

Jonah saw it first, the human-like silhouette flying through the air before quickly losing altitude and hurtling down the side of the hill. A long black stick-shape trailed behind it, bouncing slightly as it landed. The elephant gun.

Which meant the flying body was Rufus.

A moment of silence passed, Jonah's mind unable to process what had just occurred.

He jumped when Levi's backpack fell to the ground at his feet near the fire. His bewildered eyes darted to it immediately. It was torn open, most of the bullets gone and only a few sparse items zipped into the outer pockets remaining.

A sickening feeling formed in the pit of his stomach. He was supposed to be the bait; he was the only one of them supposed to be in any real danger. Things weren't going according to plan.

The sounds of screams filled the air.

"The girls," Jonah said in alarm under his breath.

Without a second thought to slow him down, he pulled the deputy's service revolver from his belt. Taking aim at where Rufus had been flung from, his eyes searched frantically for anything non-human he could take a shot at. But with the branches blocking most of the moonlight, all he could see was darkness.

"Damnit, give me something to shoot at," he said to himself.

His wish was granted.

Two floating orange eyes stuck out from the black veil that strung across the treeline.

"I'm the bait, asshole," he said as he pulled the trigger.

In quick succession, three shots range out from the revolver. Two disappeared into the night, but a lucky one resounded with an audible clink as found its mark.

"That's right, I'm over here," Jonah muttered as the orange eyes began moving down the hillside in his direction. Slowly at first, but quickly speeding up, he realized the dark silhouette that had formed underneath it was almost at full sprint.

He backed towards the water's edge.

The creature was maybe thirty yards away, then twenty, now fifteen. Without Rufus, there would be little chance of stopping it before it got to him. Jonah braced for the impact.

The sound of the girls' screams were muted momentarily by an even louder noise. A hail of bullets erupted from the other hill, the sound of an automatic rifle firing in bursts. From the muzzle flashes, Jonah could see the deputy's stoic face behind the stock. If his eyes were still bloodshot, Jonah couldn't tell.

Sparks flew off the side of the creature as the bullets pelted its thick hide, like the sound of a hailstorm on a tin roof. Jonah instinctively hit the dirt, not wishing to be shredded by any of the shrapnel that sprayed in every direction.

The booming noises assaulted his ears, clogging the rest of his senses as he panicked, not sure of what to do next. It was the closest Jonah had ever gotten to what it must have felt like to be a fresh boot on the ground of a real battlefield in Vietnam. The closest he would ever be to knowing what his father had endured.

The deputy's fire had stopped the creature in its tracks just within the halo of light cast by the bonfire. It was the first time the creature had held still long enough in the moonlight for Jonah to get a good look at it.

It stood on all fours, roughly six feet tall, from its feet to the spiked ridge that ran the length of its back. Craig had been right after all about the spikes. Its tail, which was long and serpentine, slithered and writhed, snapping like a whip as the monster braced against the gunfire and snarled in frustration. It had no fur, just a thick scaly hide that reflected the dancing flames of the fire in bronzed hues. The eyes glowed bright orange against the creature's face. Black fur jutted from in between the copper plates on its head and cheeks, with whiskers that stuck out from the snout. Rows of sharp teeth glistened in the light. A steady stream of saliva dripped down the creature's fangs that must have been at least eight inches long.

Jonah could see why the deputy's ancestors thought it was puma or cougar. Its movements reminded Jonah of a nature documentary he had seen once. In it, a herd of wildebeest's lack of fear had thwarted a lion's initial attack. Just like Jonah had seen in the documentary, the creature was now studying its belligerent prey, planning a new tactic that relied less on fear alone to succeed.

As the AK-47's magazine ran out, Jonah could see the deputy's face turn frantic as he tried to reload the gun with its barrel still smoking. He had just finished shoving the new clip into the AK when...

Thunk!

A rock hit Brian square in the forehead, knocking him to the ground instantly.

The creature had thrown it using its mouth, swinging its head around violently to launch it the 40 yards up the hill with deadly aim before returning its attention back to Jonah.

The service revolver trembled in his hands as he tried to take aim and fire again. Fire what he knew to be rounds that would do nothing to the creature's thick copper scales.

But before he could squeeze the trigger, an umbrella of fire engulfed the monster. The sounds of breaking glass followed each other in succession, as bottle after bottle rained down from the hillside onto it.

It snarled as each Molotov Cocktail burst, the scales on its back glowing as they became super-heated.

Jonah looked up to see the three girls yelling and cheering each other on as they launched their salvo. They looked and sounded more like they were on a bowling team together than locked in a struggle for survival with a supernatural beast.

Eight, nine, ten cocktails. Whatever they were doing was working. The beast was so enamored in scraping away the hot fire from its hide that it had completely forgotten about Jonah.

The explosions lit up the hillsides brighter than the bonfire had. It was so bright that Jonah could see someone moving slowly amongst the brush and rocks halfway up the hillside.

Rufus was still alive, and he was looking for something.

Jonah squinted. *Could it be? Yes, there it was.*

The elephant gun, another ten yards and he would have it. But Rufus must be hurt, bad. Lightning quick on a good day, he was moving slower than Milton playing dodgeball in gym class.

Eleven cocktails, twelve...

The salvo stopped as the girls ran out of ammunition.

Worse though, the flames on the creature's back were burning through their fuel quickly. The flames growing smaller with each passing second. Rufus didn't have enough time.

"Craig!" Darci yelled from the hill. "Craig! Plan B! Plan B!"

Craig's truck exhaust roared to life. He had virtually a straight shot at a distracted target. If he hit the pedal now, he'd knock the thing clear into next Tuesday.

Seconds passed, but the truck didn't move.

"What the hell are you waiting for?!" Darci screamed.

And to their collective anguish, they all watched as the truck's headlights slowly retreated from the hill and disappeared into the forest.

No words could adequately describe the expression of disgust on Diane's face as she watched Craig drive away, abandoning them.

None had much time to dwell on it. The creature's roar erupted louder than the exhaust, snapping them all back to attention. The fire on its back had gone out, the glowing hot metal of its scales steaming in the night air. Its eyes were fixed on the three girls at the top of the hill, the source of its latest torment.

Two steps, three steps. It shimmied slightly as it dug its claws into the soft earth. It was so cat-like in its movement that Jonah knew what would happen next. Years of chasing Mrs. O'Leary's tabby around the yard had taught him well.

It was about to pounce.

Jonah checked Rufus's progress. He was still several yards away from the where the gun lay. He needed more time. More time to load it, to aim, to fire.

Jonah shot off the last three revolver rounds at the monster's face. They dinged off the scales on its neck with it barely noticing. The girls had disappeared into the hillside, frantically mixing more Molotov Cocktails. By the time they had made one, it would be too late.

"Over here!" Jonah yelled, but the creature gave him no notice.

A fresh hail of bullets from the AK-47 returned, pelting the creature. Jonah looked for their source, thankful that Brian was alive, except it wasn't Brian's face lit up by the muzzle flashes. It was the reporter, Bill.

His face was smeared with fresh mud and his hair was tied back in a bandanna made from his Hawaiian shirt. He looked like an aging version of the commandos from the patriotic newsreels that ran at the cinema, still glorifying a war that everyone knew had already been lost.

Instead of holding on the hill, enjoying the safety of a ranged, covered position, Bill ran forward as he fired. The psychopath was charging the beast. Jonah wasn't sure what he was trying to accomplish. The bullets weren't any more effective than Jonah's revolver. Maybe Bill thought if he got closer, he could do more damage, or maybe he just imagined himself as one of the soldiers in the wild stories he had written about during the war.

He stopped fifteen feet from the creature, falling to one knee, screaming at the top of his lungs as he burned through the clip in a matter of seconds.

The screaming continued even as the bullets stopped, accompanied by the clicking of the empty magazine.

The creature quickly recovered from its braced position and faced Bill, whose scream quickly ran out of air as he looked into the monster's eyes with sudden shock and fear.

With a sweep of the creature's long tail, Bill's body flew through the air and landed on the muddy beach twenty feet away. It remained there motionless, possibly dead. It was impossible to tell from this distance.

Only temporarily distracted, the creature returned its gaze to the girls. Coiled in its stance, dug its feet into the dirt, and prepared to pounce. It was ready to end Jonah's promise to marry the girl of his dreams, and Jonah felt powerless to stop it.

A single gunshot rang out from the hillside, a single explosion that sent a shockwave through the shallow basin, waves across the pond, and scattering sleeping birds in treetops for miles. Everyone in earshot, including Jonah, fell to the ground, clutching their ears as shooting pain accompanied by a loud ringing filled every one of their senses.

Jonah's vision blurred, and he struggled to get back to his feet. His head ached like it was being split down the middle.

Though just a fuzzy black spot in his vision, he could still make out the silhouette of the beast against the firelight. A most unholy sound coming from its gaping mouth. A cross between the snarling of a cat and the roaring of a bear.

Every second that passed, Jonah's vision healed, and every second he could make out a new horrifying detail.

The bullet had punched a hole clear through the side of the creature's face, knocking out one of its eyes. A black oil-like liquid spewed forth from the wound as it swung its head wildly, spraying the foul liquid in every direction. Some splattered onto Jonah, and he immediately recognized its smell. It was that of death and decay.

A plate from the creature's neck, torn off by the force of Rufus's bullet, lay on the ground, the bonfire's flames dancing in the copper's bright reflection. Rufus had hit it dead on, the force of the elephant gun enough to penetrate even the creature's thick hide.

However, it hadn't been a kill shot.

Jonah tried to stand up, but found himself falling back to the ground as a feeling of vertigo hit him hard, his equilibrium completely out of sorts.

The monster was also moving, snarling, and baring its teeth at him as it approached.

Jonah closed his eyes and waited for the end to come, for it to take him to be with his father.

Except it didn't. Passing right by him, sluggishly the creature limped towards the water's edge.

"It's trying to go back into the pond!" Darci yelled. "We have to kill it before we lose it."

"I'm out of bullets," Rufus roared back. "Where are the bullets?!"

Jonah didn't have to look far. Levi's little backpack stood out like a sore thumb on the ground only a foot away from his face, a few bullets still inside. He considered trying to throw the whole thing to Rufus, but that was twenty yards away. How was he going to do that in his state? The bag was nothing more than a few strips of cloth, barely keeping themselves together.

A strange bulge in one of the side pockets caught his eye. It certainly didn't look like a bullet. Bill must have packed a little extra something just in case the guns weren't enough.

Jonah pulled it from the bag.

With every ounce of concentration he could muster to avoid falling back down, he stood up, holding the little green pineapple grenade in his hand. He tried to take aim at the creature, but the world swayed and spun as he tried to focus. He was just as likely to miss and throw it straight at the girls or Rufus in this state.

Jonah took a deep breath and closed his eyes. This was his moment. He couldn't fail; for Steve, for Stephanie, for Milton.

When he opened his eyes again, he wasn't standing near the pond. He was in his front yard. The afternoon sun was lingering in the sky, his skin basking in its comfort and warmth. His father was there too, standing near the white picket fence with a smile on his face.

It was a memory, a memory of the first time his dad had taught him to throw a baseball.

The grass underfoot was freshly cut, the smell filled his nostrils. They had just come home from a Wisconsin Timber Rattler game. The best minor league team for miles. Jonah could still taste the ice cream on his lips, a treat from the 9th inning, a celebratory prize for the team's victory.

"Give your old man the best you got," his father yelled as he punched a fist into an old leather baseball glove.

Jonah looked down at the white leather ball in his hands. The texture was rugged yet refined. The raised seams were pleasurable to grip, his fingers traced them instinctively. From the faded white and embedded dirt, Jonah knew it must have been used a million times in its life, but despite it all, it was still just as good at doing what it needed to do as the day it was made.

"Come one Jonah!" His father yelled in encouragement again. "Give me the heater!"

Something kindled inside of him. An impossible urge overtook him. The want, no, the need to throw the ball.

Jonah pulled his arm back, just like the pitcher for the Rattlers had. He swung his arm forward with all his might, just like the pitcher had. The weight of the baseball disappeared from his fingertips, spinning in the air in slow motion in front of him. The cheers of his father echoed around him, only replaced by the loud clap of the ball as it wedged itself deep into his father's glove, the plume of dust erupting from the impact.

Then Jonah fell to the ground, wrapped his arms over his head, and yelled as loud as he could.

"Everybody down!"

At that last moment, returned the world of the pond and the night; he saw the one good eye of the Mishipeshu look back towards him in alarm before his entire world ceased to exist.

15

1972

As Jonah opened his eyes, an angelic figure floated above him, greeting him with a comforting smile. It filled him with relief.

Back at the pond, he had known he was living his last moments on this earth. He had accepted it. After all, his father had never been afraid of death. Why should he have been? Plus, going out while throwing a WWII surplus grenade at a legendary monster that had killed three of your friends seemed like as good a way to go as any. His only worry had been whether heaven or hell awaited him.

Thankfully, the angel hovering over him proved that he had, despite years of tormenting his poor mother, somehow escaped eternal damnation. The white mist of clouds flew past him as he imagined he was being transported at a phenomenal speed through the skies towards a banquet of friends and loved ones. Even better, the angel escorting him to the pearly gates looked remarkably like Olivia.

"Wake up Jonah!" a voice boomed in his ear.

But I am awake, he replied, except not out loud. It was a voice only he could hear in his mind.

The slap to his cheek ended the euphoria. The peaceful world of clouds evaporated, replaced by billowing smoke escaping to the night sky overhead as the bonfire slowly died out.

"He's awake!" An excited voice cried out.

The first face he could make out was Olivia's, who, despite the dirt stained tears smeared across her cheeks, looked more beautiful than she ever had before.

"You did it," the deputy said, his face appearing over her shoulder. A trickle of blood on his scalp dripping from where he held a piece of white gauze tight to it with his palm.

"I did?" Jonah questioned. He wasn't clear what 'it' was.

He tried to sit up.

"I was able to get the sheriff on the radio," said the deputy. "He and the mayor are on their way."

"Shit," Jonah said. "Are we going to be in trouble?"

"I don't know," the deputy replied. "Let's just take this one step at a time. You got hit pretty hard by the blast."

The baseball hurtling through the air towards his father's glove passed through his mind.

"Where's the creature?" Jonah asked, suddenly growing concerned.

"You got it good," Brian replied. "From where I could see, you caught it behind the neck plate, wedged the grenade right in there. We found copper scales all over the place. The rest of the body got caught in the current and sucked into the pond. I reckon you blew its head clean off!"

"Great," Jonah said, sounding as if he had just been told he heard scored a B on a test. None of it felt real yet.

He glanced around at the faces he could see. One immediately stood out as missing.

"Where's Bill?" Jonah asked, not seeing the reporter.

"Oh, Bill," Deputy Brian said, rolling his eyes.

The deputy helped Jonah stand up and, with his arm over his shoulder, led him to the beach where Bill's body lay a little way down the shore. Diane was crouched over him, holding up his head.

Jonah could see specks of bright copper glittering in the mud and sand at his feet. The waves hitting the shore lifted the glimmering flecks momentarily before pulling them back into the water, as if reclaiming them.

As they approached the wounded reporter, Jonah could hear the man frantically grunting.

"Jonah, Jonah," Bill muttered. "I'm glad I got to see you before I died."

A white bandage was wrapped around his bare chest, though it didn't look to be bleeding too bad.

"I told you," Deputy Brian said with annoyance in his voice. "You're not going to die."

"Don't sugarcoat it for me," Bill said, still sounding hysterical. "I can take the truth. I know I've lost too much blood. I can already see the light forming in the distance. I'm stepping towards the light."

He held out his hand towards the sky, reaching for some invisible object.

"That's just the moon jackass," the deputy said.

"Jonah, tell my mother..." Bill stammered on, but Jonah was no longer paying attention.

He was staring at the limbs of an enormous black willow tree as they hung out over the pond. He remembered the gnarled and oddly shaped branches from just a few days prior, when Steve had brought him to the exact same spot.

Freeing himself from the support of the deputy, he limped over to the base of the tree on his own and knelt to the ground.

"What is it?" The deputy asked.

"This is where we found him," Jonah muttered quietly.

"Found who?" interjected Diane. She was also ignoring Bill's crazy mutterings.

"Milton," Jonah replied. "We found his head right here at the base of this tree."

"I'm sorry," the deputy said, any hints of joy gone from his voice.

Jonah stayed on his knees for a long moment, staring at the trunk, which was splattered with the foul black blood of the creature.

A sparkle of moonlight caught something in the mix of sand and mud at the tree's base.

Jonah plunged his hands into the earth, without care for what digging in the cold, hard clay might do to his fingernails. He scraped and clawed with abandon until his hands at last grasped the metal buried below.

"What is it?" Olivia asked as she took a step closer, cautious of Jonah's strange trance.

Wiping the smooth object clear of the mud, he held it up to the moonlight for all to see.

"It's my father's watch," Jonah declared. "I thought I had lost it."

It glistened in the moonlight, the gold somehow glowing brilliant and white.

Holding it up to his ear, he listened.

Still not ticking, still broken, just as it had been when the military had returned it to his family.

Nothing had changed.

A sudden wailing from the clearing diverted everyone's attention.

It was Rufus, who was sitting on a stump with Darci, as she dabbed at the wound on his chest with a piece of his torn shirt.

Jonah tried to rush forward to see his friend, but only managed a few steps before lightheadedness overtook him and he stumbled. Thankfully, Olivia was close and caught him.

"We got to get you home," she said in his ear.

"Not yet," he replied, the shooting pain throughout his body suddenly numbed by her soft touch.

I'm going to marry this girl.

"How you doing Rufus?" Jonah asked as they got closer.

"Dislocated shoulder, maybe broken ribs," Darci spoke for him.

"I'm fine," Rufus replied sternly, trying to stand up.

"Oh lord," said Darci, forcing him back to his seat. "A mythical beast just beat the crap out of you. You shot a gun that's one step below bazooka. Stop with this machismo bullshit, who you really trying to impress?"

Rufus tried to reply, but the pain in his side was too unbearable and all he managed was a silent wince.

"You guys should get going," Deputy Brian said. "I'll take care of Bill until the cavalry gets here. I think your pal Rufus needs to see the doctor in town. He'll live, but that's a nasty busted shoulder. His wrestling days might be over. I'll try to hold off the mayor and the sheriff till tomorrow at least. Give you all a chance to get your stories straight."

"Agreed," Darci replied. "Diane can give us a lift in her convertible."

"I think have blankets to cover the seats with," Diane added in a worried tone. "Wouldn't want to get blood on them."

"Diane!" Darci scolded her.

It took both Darci and Diane to pull the grunting Rufus to his feet to begin the trek up the hill to where the cars were parked.

Olivia tried to pull Jonah forward to join them, but he forced her to stop.

"Wait," Jonah said, a thought occurring to him. "I'll be right back."

"But—" Olivia didn't get a chance to air her protest as Jonah forced himself to pull away from her and stand on his own.

She and the rest of them watched silently as Jonah limped slowly and steadily towards the pond, leaving a lone footprint with a parallel dragline in the mud in his wake.

Reaching the edge of the water, Jonah paused and looked out over Tranquillity Pond. The shockwaves from the grenade had long since dissipated, and the water had returned to its perfectly glassy surface texture. He hoped that the bomb had done its job and that the body of the Mishipeshu was out there, sinking deep into the mud and decomposing, fresh food for the fish.

Looking down into his own reflection, he expected to see the face from the mirror that he recognized and fought with every day since getting the ill-news; the face of his father staring back at him. Had he lived up to his father's legacy? Had he made his father proud?

Except his father wasn't staring back at him. The person who looked back at him with the mud-caked face, scared temple, and bruised eyes was someone else entirely, someone new that Jonah didn't recognize.

He wasn't his father anymore, nor was he going to try to be. He was himself now, the man that he would be for the rest of his days. With the watch clutched tight in his palm, he knew what he had to do.

"Give me the heater!" he thought he heard a voice say from the pond.

Without hesitation and with one colossal toss, he hurled the watch out over the water. It hung for several seconds in the air as if floating before plunging back to earth, hitting the surface with a splash, and being lost to the depths of the pond forever.

Turning, he re-joined Olivia, welcoming her assistance in walking, and the five of them trudged up the hill together towards Diane's car.

"When I get my hands on Craig, I swear," Rufus snarled as he struggled with the muddy terrain.

"I'll be right there with you," added Jonah.

"Get in line," said Diane, catching everyone by surprise.

After a long moment, they all laughed.

Though almost every joint, muscle, and nerve in his body hurt, Jonah could barely feel the cut on the side of his head Rufus had given him a week prior. It felt like a lifetime ago.

Rufus fell asleep in the backseat of the convertible as they drove. The steady stream of bright porch lights passing by at a feverish pace hurt Jonah's head.

"Your house is closest, Jonah, so I'll drop you off first," Diane announced.

"Thanks," Jonah said. He wasn't feeling great, he just wanted to lie down.

"Wait, are you feeling nauseous?" Darci asked. "What about double vision? A headache? Light or noise sensitivity?"

"Um," Jonah stammered. "All of the above?"

"You probably have a concussion," she replied.

"I don't think so," said Jonah, his voice sounded unconvincing. "I just need to rest. After I grab Levi from Mrs. O'Leary and get him to bed."

"You shouldn't be alone tonight," Darci explained. "Someone should stay with you. You probably shouldn't be responsible for a four-year-old in your current state, either."

"What are you talking about?" Jonah said as the car pulled up to his house and came to a stop. "I'm perfectly fine."

In that moment, it felt like a reasonable way to display how fine he was. He would just hop out of the car, graceful, land on his feet, and no one would worry another second about his condition.

When he face-planted into the grass of his own front yard, inches from the pavement it had the opposite effect.

"Definitely a concussion," Darci said with a look of concern.

Rufus groaned in pain in the backseat.

"We have to get this one to the doctor," said Darci.

"I'll stay with Jonah," Olivia said, jumping out of the car to help him to his feet.

Jonah could see Darci's eyes narrow at the same time that Diane's lit up with excitement.

"I don't know if that is a good—" Darci began.

"Great idea, see you tomorrow!" Diana said before putting the car back into gear and speeding off down the street.

"That was weird," Jonah commented, as Diane's convertible's taillights disappeared around the corner.

"Which house is Mrs. O'Leary's?" Olivia asked, her voice soft and sweet in Jonah's ear.

"Um, that one," Jonah said. He began staggering towards the neighbor's front door.

"Uh-uh," Olivia said, stopping him. "You look like you got ran over by a delivery truck. I'll get your brother. Go ahead and wait for us by your front door."

"You got it," Jonah said, feeling slightly delirious as he carefully navigated the front steps.

It wasn't long before Olivia appeared on the sidewalk that led up to their door, carrying a pajama-clad child wrapped around her torso. It reminded him of just how sweet she had been with Levi in the bathtub the night after the forest party. He felt butterflies in his stomach, or maybe it was just the nausea, he couldn't quite tell. All he knew was that he liked the way she made him feel.

"Shhh," she hushed, almost sensing Jonah was about to say something.

He promptly closed his mouth and opened the front door, ushering them inside.

Jonah collapsed onto the couch immediately, his head still swimming, while Olivia ascended the stairs to put Levi to bed.

His eyes drooped, his head snapping back as he felt himself nodding off. Not wanting to fall asleep and leave Olivia alone after such a horrifying night, he forced himself to stand up and keep moving.

Pacing the hallway that led to the kitchen, he passed his father's portrait at the base of the stairs.

"You guys do have a lot of things in common," Olivia's said from the top of the stairs, startling him.

"I think he had better hair," Jonah said, trying to crack a joke. He felt oddly aloof.

Olivia giggled.

"He might have," she added with a smile as she descended. "You have sticks and mud in yours."

Jonah could watch her walk down those stairs over and over again for the rest of his life and be completely content. She didn't walk; she floated.

Every step so planned, so dainty. She didn't feel real; it felt like he was still dreaming, and a very nice dream indeed.

She didn't stop until she was a few inches from his face, close enough that he could feel the heat coming off her body.

"How are you feeling?" she asked.

"I'm, I'm," words suddenly made no sense to him. He sounded like Levi trying to pronounce a really long word he had heard on television, sounding it out slowly until it all came together.

"I'm fine," he managed to say.

"Good," she said with a slight nod.

It was now or never.

Leaning in, he planted a kiss on her lips.

He immediately became distraught when she pulled away.

"I'm sorry," he stammered out. "I didn't mean to. I thought—"

"No, it's not that," she stopped him.

"Then what is it?" he asked, so confused by what was going on that he wasn't sure what to do next.

"Don't take this the wrong way," she said, her eyes betraying nothing but kindness in her gaze. "But you really need a shower."

Of course, the creature's blood was still splattered on his skin and soaked into his clothes.

"I understand," he said, suddenly feeling self-conscious. "I'm just going to go upstairs, brush my teeth, hop in the shower, try to rinse off whatever happened tonight before it becomes permanent."

"That's probably a good idea," she said, her pearly teeth almost glowing in the dim hall light.

He made the move to walk past her, but her hand stopped him in his tracks.

"Would you mind if I joined you?" she asked.

"No, not at all," Jonah replied. He had hoped heard that right, he wasn't sure if a concussion could cause hallucinations, it probably could. But every sense in his entire body was going off like he was center-stage of the biggest firework display on 4th of July.

Carefully, she led him by the hand up the stairs. With the bathroom door closed and the light clicked on, the hot steam of the shower began to squeeze its way through the gap in the frame and...

"I'm going to skip ahead real quick," Grandpa Joe said.
"Really grandpa?" Asher groaned. "Just tell me what happens."
"Not a chance in your life."
"But that's not fair."
"You'll live."

Jonah and Olivia collapsed onto his bed, both feeling the exhaustion of a long night overtaking them.
"My mom is going to kill me if you're here when she gets home," he muttered.
"Can I borrow your bike?" Olivia asked.
"As long as I get to come see you tomorrow to pick it up."
"I'm sure that can be arranged."
It was a moment he hoped would last forever; her arm over his chest, his hand gently stroking her bare shoulder. Their voices softening slowly with each passing minute as sleep approached.
I'm going to marry this girl.
His mind couldn't get the thought out of his head.
"When does your mother get home?" Olivia asked.
"Her shift is done at seven," Jonah replied as he yawned.
"I'll be out of here by sunrise, I promise," she said through a yawn in kind.
"Just a few hours of sleep will do us good."
"I know."

And they both drifted off into a sweet slumber, wrapped in each other's arms.

J onah didn't dream as he slept, he was far too exhausted for that. When the chirping of the birds drew him into the waking world, he instinctively reached over to feel for Olivia's soft skin next to him. His fingers found nothing but a warm patch where she had once been.

She must have just left, her promise to be gone by sunrise kept.

Rolling over, he pressed his face into the pillow and his nose filled with the delightful scent of Olivia's lavender perfume.

With one sleepy eye, he looked out the open window, where the first rays of light had begun to find their way onto the trees of the forest. His mother would be home soon.

Forcing himself to endure the pain in his muscles and head, he sat up in bed and looked at the alarm clock. Almost 6:45 in the morning.

That was late.

Not for him, of course. Jonah slept in past eight most mornings if he could get away with it. It was late for Levi, who was usually up before the birds and begging for sugary cereal in front of the television.

Putting on a fresh shirt, fresh being a relative term, and gym shorts, he made his way across the hall and to Levi's room.

The door was wide open.

Jonah peered in and saw the bed was empty, the messy sheets thrown off as they were every morning.

The child must have already gotten up and gone downstairs by himself.

Descending the stairwell, Jonah could hear the television on, the sounds of gunfire blasting as a western played on it.

"Can you turn that down?" Jonah asked grumpily to Levi, walking blindly as he tried to wipe away the last throws of sleep from his eyelids.

Except the spot in front of the TV where he expected to find Levi was empty.

Jonah's eyes struggling to function. He sauntered over to the set and flicked it off. Silence engulfed the house again.

"Levi?" Jonah yelled.

No answer.

He tried calling out again, but no one responded.

Wandering into the kitchen, he was surprised to find the backdoor wide open. Levi must have gone outside to play.

"Levi," Jonah continued yelling as he walked onto the back porch. "You know you're not supposed to be out here without—"

He stopped when his barefoot stepped in something wet on the deck. Jonah peered down as he lifted his leg. A warm, crimson liquid stuck to the pad of his foot before dripping to the floor.

It was blood.

Jonah gasped.

A thick pool of blood had formed on the deck, about an inch deep. He followed its trails with his eyes as streaks of it traveled down the stairs that lead to the back lawn, splattered across the blades of grass, and disappeared into the thick forest.

Jonah couldn't think, he couldn't breathe, as he stared down in horror at the scene; every part of his body immobilized.

He didn't move when he heard the front door lock click and the hinges creak as it opened.

"Jonah!" his mother yelled.

He could hear her the tapping of her heels against the kitchen linoleum.

"I was able to get off work a bit early," she began as she opened the fridge and pulled out a carton of eggs, setting them on the counter. "How about I make a good old-fashioned egg and pancake breakfast, just like..."

Her voice lost sound as she stood next to Jonah.

They both stared in silence at the ground where Levi's blood-stained teddy bear sat in the pool of blood, its head ripped open and the stuffing spilling out.

"Where's your brother?!" his mother screamed at him.

"I don't know," Jonah stammered, coming to his senses. "It took him."

"What took him?!"

He didn't know what to tell her; he didn't know how to describe it. Every word in the English language somehow seemed wrong.

"Go find him!" She yelled, unable to take the silence a moment longer. "I'm calling the police!"

Shoeless and wearing only his underwear, Jonah took off, bounding down the back porch steps and into the grass, following the streaks of blood at as fast a pace as his breath would allow.

He lost the trail in the treeline, but it didn't matter; he knew where it was going.

Sprinting with no regard for his own safety, he ran the path he could trek blindfolded in the dark, the one he and Steve had walked a thousand times as children together.

His lungs burned. He didn't care. His feet bled and ached as sharp stones cut at his soles. He didn't care.

He only cared about one thing: getting Levi back.

As the thicker part of the forest waned and the trees became less dense, he caught the first glimpse of the bright sunlight illuminating the clearing where the old well sat.

There, the trail of blood resumed, the tall grasses painted red in a long line that culminated at the stone and mortar circle in the center.

He was running so fast that he could not stop in time; slamming hard into the side of the wall, almost toppling over and falling inside. Catching himself, he stuck his head over it, hoping to find the figure of Levi alive and safe, staring back at him.

"Levi!" he screamed.

The soft gurgle of the running water was the only sound that replied to him.

He continued screaming at the top of his lungs. It could have been hours or only minutes, he did not know.

Nothing replied to him.

When his voice was gone and his lungs would no longer let him deprive them of air, he collapsed against the wall of the well, heaving heavy breaths.

The tears fell down his cheeks freely in a current as strong as the underground river that fed the well itself.

Memories swam in his mind, flashing through in quick succession like some morbid episode of 'This Is Your Life'. Each one another scene in a long list where Jonah had treated his younger brother with apathy, disdain, and malice.

He buried his head in his hands, wishing more than anything else in the entire world that it had taken him instead.

When at last the tears subsided, he wiped at his cheeks and opened his eyes.

Between his legs, a small pool of water had formed in the depression left by one of the creature's footprints. In it, a round gold object shined bright in the morning sun.

Jonah reached down and picked it up, holding it in front of his face with disbelief.

It was his father's watch, the one he had thrown into the pond.

And in the quiet of the forest clearing, one sound stood out from the rest.

The tick-tick-tick of the watch as the small hand made its way around the dial.

The clock had started again.

16

2023

"We never found Levi's body," said Grandpa Joe as he watched Asher's face. The boy's jaw hung open and his eyes were wide. "The whole town, including the mayor, helped us look for him. We scoured the pond, we had divers and everything, but it was no use. The creature had taken him into whatever dark underwater lair it called home. Through it all, none of us realized the truth. Not me, not clever Darci, not Rufus, not the deputy, not even the mayor in all his wisdom. It wasn't until years later that I realized the truth."

Grandpa Joe drew a heavy breath before letting it out slowly with a pained sigh.

"All it had wanted was Levi. It killed Milton because it smelled Levi's towel. It killed Steve and Stephanie as they lay under Levi's favorite blanket. Our plan to lure it into the clearing hadn't worked, because Levi's backpack was next to Rufus instead of me. We had been fools. The thought never even entered our minds that it wasn't actually after us."

As if on cue, the serenity of the pond's surface suddenly filled with bright light as the clouds parted and the full orb of the sun became visible overhead.

"That can't be the end, grandpa," said Asher. "That wasn't a happy ending."

"Not all stories have happy endings," Grandpa Joe replied, sharpening his eyes on the water. He could feel it coming, even if he couldn't see it yet. It wouldn't be long now.

"But in your stories, it's always the naughty boy who gets eaten or the bad guy that falls off the cliff. Levi didn't do anything wrong."

"You're right, he didn't. Other than maybe being a bit too addicted to television, he was the perfect child."

"Then why did he die at the end?"

Grandpa Joe paused to think of an answer.

"I guess that's just how the world works sometimes. The young and the innocent get caught up in things outside their control, in things they didn't start or even really understand. Shit happens. When you get old, you learn to accept it."

Asher seemed confused more than ever.

"Should we go back?" Asher asked, his shoulders growing hot under the summer sun. He suddenly wished he had worn a t-shirt underneath the overalls.

"Can't leave now," Grandpa Joe replied. "It's about to be the best time of day for catching a fish." He rummaging around in his bag and pulling out a bottle of sunscreen, throwing it to Asher.

Asher's original fascination with the pond was gone. He peered over the side of the boat with suspicious eyes.

"That didn't really happen, did it?" Asher asked, rubbing the sun screen onto his shoulders.

"I told you it was all true," replied Grandpa Joe.

"None of your stories are true, grandpa."

"That one was."

"Sure."

Asher did his best to feign disbelief, but Grandpa Joe could see the worry growing in the boy's face.

"Did you ever see it again?"

"A couple times."

"Why not just leave it alone? You always told me if you just leave nature alone, it will leave you alone."

"I wish this worked like that. See, I don't think this thing is natural. I don't think it comes from our world."

"Cause that's what the deputy told you?"

"His people were here long before the town was. They would know better than us."

"You skipped that part of the story, the part when he told you the legend."

"I did?"

"Yes, you did. Can you tell me that part now?"

Grandpa Joe glanced at the pond. The surface remained still. Time was growing short, but the boy had a right to know.

"Please grandpa," begged Asher. "Pretty please."

"Fine, alright," said Grandpa Joe.

Asher settled back and smiled. The boy did love his stories. One more couldn't hurt. It was the least he could do.

17

1785

The midnight wind carried the lemony-scent of the magnolia trees and honeysuckle through the flap in Ziigwan's tent, filling it with pleasant memories of her childhood. Running along the river, her friends chasing one another, each in turn pretending to be a mighty stag or hunter as they tossed sticks and branches as pretend weapons. It would usually have made her smile.

Not tonight.

The bindings around her wrist and feet were metal, crudely forged, sharp, and already creating blisters on her skin that had started to bleed. At least she was no longer naked, Tobias allowing her some protections from the hungry eyes of the men who had ogled her with grotesque stares as she was led back to camp to stand trial.

No one believed her.

Many of the men had been quick to jump to their own conclusions, hurling accusations that she had lured Silas to the pond in order to mutilate him to appease her savage gods. It hadn't helped her case that she was naked and still very much soaked in the man's blood.

Tobias had been quiet, seemingly unable to push back against the will of his own men. Only when they had proposed stringing her up from the nearest tree by the neck had he stepped in to demand a trial for her back at camp.

"Under the laws of god and man, we must allow justice and due course," he had said. It had stymied the men's demands for swift vengeance, at least for now.

Forced to the confines of the tent with nothing but stale bread and a bucket of water, it had been two days wait while the rules of the trial were set and agreed upon by the white settlers. Other preparations had also been made. She could hear the sounds of felling trees and saws. The men were building something and she could only imagine what machinations their minds had designed for her death.

Her thoughts wandered back to the waters of the pond, to her visit to the spirit world under its surface. In her time of need, the spirits had come to her protection. With Silas only moments from ending her life, they had intervened and taken his life instead. For that, she was thankful, her only wish being that their powers extended beyond the banks and into camp, where she needed their help once again.

But part of her knew that help would never come. Her people had stories about this area, stories about the protector that guarded the gateway. It rarely left the water except only to hunt.

Footsteps outside caught her attention. Perhaps it was Tobias coming to tell her he had convinced the others to believe her. Not likely. More likely it was one of the other men, sneaking inside to have their way with her in the night since she could no longer fight back. She knew their stares; she knew what each of them secretly wanted. Though chained, they would find her hardly a helpless target.

She was surprised when a faint whimpering sound emanated from the other side of the canvas.

Through the narrow slit, Samantha, Tobias's wife appeared, her young child wrapped tightly to her chest. The whimper had come from the baby, who was stirring at the movement of its mother. It was starting to cry.

Samantha hushed it, stroking the child's hair softly. When the baby had fallen back into a peaceful slumber, the woman at last spoke.

"How are you doing?" she asked.

Ziigwan had barely slept. Her stomach rumbled, and her lips were cracking from dehydration.

"I'm alright," she lied, not wanting to betray any satisfaction to the white woman that she was suffering.

"It's just awful how they are treating you. I mean, just a few days ago they were praising your hunting skills. Now they leave you in here like this."

Ziigwan gave her an icy stare. She didn't like the feeling inside her that this was some form of white man trickery, a false ray of kindness to make the coming cruelty all the more painful.

"Tobias told me everything," Samantha continued, growing impatient at the lack of verbal response. "About Silas following you, about the pond. As far as I know, he got what was coming to him. Just the other day, I caught him staring at me while I was feeding the baby. He didn't even have the courtesy to look away when I saw him. He just watched and smiled until I left. The man was positively revolting."

Ziigwan knew what she meant. No one would mourn for Silas. He was a free-loader, boozer, and obnoxious. Except here she was waiting to stand trial for his murder, for no reason other than the fact he was a white man and she was not. If the tables had been turned, she doubted he would have had to face the same fate.

"Why are you here?" Ziigwan asked bluntly. Though the sentiments were comforting in a superficial way, she knew the white woman wouldn't be offering them if she did not have an ulterior motive.

"Tomorrow morning is the trial," Samantha explained. "Tobias is worried about the men, the effect it will have on them…"

He's worried about them?! Ziigwan twitched as anger pulsed through her body. A fresh bead of blood ran down her hand from her iron bindings as the jagged metal tore at her skin.

"So am I. They are all so superstitious, they get spooked so easily. If even a few of them were to run off, it could doom the entire company, leave us dangerously short handed and force us to return home. And well, that could ruin us, him and I."

Ziigwan listened with her lips pursed tight, holding back her anger at every well-spoken word that flowed from the woman's mouth like silk.

"That's why I'm here," Samantha continued, barely aware of Ziigwan's growing fury. "I wanted to ask you to plead guilty."

Ziigwan couldn't believe her ears. Plead guilty?

"It would certainly save us all a lot of trouble. Tobias can make sure when the punishment happens that its quick and painless. We can even arrange for you to repent before the end, and a Christian funeral. It's the least we could do. The Bible says anyone who takes Jesus into their heart is capable of salvation, even if you have been a heathen your whole life."

If the woman wasn't carrying a child across her bosom, Ziiwgan might have heaved herself on top of her and beaten her with her bound fists right then and there. She didn't believe in this silly Christian god. Why would she repent now as his people carried out a grave mis-justice upon her in his name?

"We just don't want you telling your story and getting the men all worked up for nothing, that's all," the white woman continued, oblivious to the growing hatred the prisoner harbored for her.

Ziigwan had thought the woman elegant and beautiful at first, sweet and caring. She saw that was all just a facade, a performance to hide the rotten and selfish person inside. The child on her chest would grow up with the same selfishness, the same rotten core as her parents.

How she was a fool to trust in Tobias's justice. He was no better than Silas.

"Think on it, please," Samantha said, turning to the flap. "It's really what's best for everyone. It's just like the Bible says. Jesus Christ laid down his life for us. And we ought to lay down our lives for our brothers and sisters."

Your brothers and sisters.

As the woman and child disappeared back into the darkness of the night, Ziigwan finally let loose her bottled up emotions. Jerking and kicking violently, she used it to try to drown out the pain and break her bonds so she could escape. She knew there would be no fair trial, that her story would fall on deaf ears, that the white man's justice was anything but.

The iron was stronger than her.

The bindings did not break, but only bit into her deeper.

As her body grew motionless, exhaustion overtaking her, her eyes slowly drew to a close.

The night was quiet. Not even the crickets were chirping. The lone sound was a pair of owls in the distance, hooting at one another, chatting in excited anticipation for what awaited Ziigwan.

Their songs were the last sounds she heard before letting sleep overtake her.

She was awoken at dawn by the sounds of a great amount of movement around the camp. Men hollering and yelling at one another, large pieces of timber being moved to and fro. There was a palpable level of energy floating in the cool morning air.

She didn't have to wait long for two of Tobias's men to fetch her and pull her into the morning sunlight, which had just crept over the trees. With the sudden abundance of light and her bound hands unable to shield her eyes from it, she had much difficulty seeing where they were going as she was dragged through the clearing.

The men's voices grew quiet as she drew near. She could only make out a few of their whispered words.

"Savage."

"Sinner."

"Harlot."

"Murderer."

They only reinforced what she already knew about what was to come.

Ziigwan soon found herself shoved into a chair. By now, her eyes had adjusted to the bright morning light and she could see more clearly.

They were in the clearing where Tobias's men had constructed a makeshift well upon their arrival in order to pull fresh water from the earth. A half dozen long benches cut from birch trees had been carved the previous evening and hauled into three rows with a center aisle between them. An additional table and chairs had been constructed and placed to her right. Just like her, they faced the benches where an audience of men from the camp sat with weary and tired faces.

The only other structure in the clearing was also the largest. Near the table, on the opposite side of where she sat, was a single log standing almost six feet into the air, with branches neatly cut and piled at its base. Shoved into the gaps between the branches were dry grass and twigs.

Tinder.

She recognized a pyre when she saw one.

The ways and formalities of the white men never ceased to bewilder her. In her tribe, a cut throat did the job faster and cleaner than what they had built for her. Why bother going through the energy and effort? Were the men that swayed by such symbols that it mattered?

She might never fully understand them, not with her limited time remaining.

One of the men rung a small bell and the audience members stood up and turned around. They all watched with eerier reverence as Tobias and his wife, bearing their young child, walked down the aisle side by side. Upon arriving at the first bench, Tobias kissed his wife's hand and helped her to an open seat before making his way to the center table and taking his own.

Only after he had seated did the rest of the audience sit down.

Ziigwan could see how the whole scene afforded deference and respect to Tobias, who presided over the group as he pulled out several papers and laid them on the table in front of him.

"We are here today in order to determine and enforce the Lord's justice," Tobias spoke, his voice sturdy and powerful. "Standing accused is Ziigwan Nibiikwe..."

His pronunciation of her last name was so poor that she almost wondered if he was referring to a different defendant.

"Of the murder of Silas Underwood in cold blood and without provocation," he continued. "Using this knife."

From his pocket, he produced her Kingfisher knife and placed it on the table next to his papers. The blade still had Silas's dried blood on it from where she had slashed his cheek.

"How do you plead?" Tobias asked her.

His face turned to gaze upon hers for the first time since the beach.

The lies hurt, not because they were untrue, but because they were spoken by someone she had until recently trusted and respected.

His eyes betrayed that the lies pained him as well. She would have felt sorry for him if not for his own part in carrying out this grave injustice.

"Not guilty," she said loud and clear for everyone to hear, taking special care to stare directly at Tobias's wife sitting in the front. She was smiling before the declaration and after it, not betraying any sign of remorse or disappointment. She hated the woman more than ever and whatever horrible brat of a child she carried with her like some shield.

"Very well, we shall start with the testimony of the witnesses," Tobias commanded, and the trial continued.

One by one, the men who had been at the beach to witness the horrors of whatever had killed Silas stood up and gave a short account of the events from their perspective. They often added additional details that were completely unfounded and only painted the picture of her as a savage in more fantastical lies.

"She had a piece of his skin hanging from her lips..."

"Her knife had been stabbed clear through his still beating heart…"

"She covered herself in his blood so she could ransom his soul…"

"She had cut off his…"

Each one more disgusting than the previous and in some cases, contradicting one another. Yet as each man told their lie, the crowd of men gasped and nodded in shocked dismay at their testimony.

Ziigwan tried not to listen as more men stood and more men lied, instead trying to appreciate the forest she loved one last time. The smells carried on the winds, the sounds of birds chirping at one another, the diverse shades of green.

Despite the dozens of trees already cut down, the forest refused to let any of its beauty suffer. It would endure, born long before Ziigwan or the white man, it would live on long after their bones were dust. She sought comfort in the thought.

At last, there were no more men to draw their accounts. At last, it would be her turn to tell the true story.

Maybe she could sow enough dissent with her tale that it would break up the company. Why should she hold back any of it? She didn't owe them anything anymore.

"If that is the last of the witness testimony," Tobias began. "Then we will move onto sentencing."

Ziigwan lurched forward.

"I have not spoken yet," she proclaimed.

Tobias peered over at her.

"Your testimony is unnecessary," he said with cold, unfeeling eyes.

"Why not?"

"There is more than enough for me to pass judgment."

"But—"

"It is under the purview of our creator and almighty lord," Tobias kept on speaking as if she wasn't even there, turning his attention to the audience. "That…"

"This is not justice!"

"That the defendant, Ziigwan Nibiikwe, is guilty and is to be sentenced to death by the cleansing fire of our Lord. May God have mercy on her soul."

Her continued protests were drowned out by the cheers of the crowd as they stood up to celebrate.

The two men who had stood guard next to her during the trial picked her up by the shoulders and dragged her struggling body towards the pyre that had constructed. Once there, they removed the chains around her hands and feet, replacing them with thick cord bindings that strapped her tightly to the trunk.

As she thrashed and riled against the post, she began to realize how little it mattered. She could not escape and a man holding a lit torch was quickly approaching.

The audience from her trial had formed a small half-circle around her, Tobias, his wife, and their child front and center to watch her final moments. The agate brooch pinned to the child's blanket, the same brooch that Ziigwan had coveted all so recently, the same brooch she now wished for nothing more than to smash to pieces against a hard stone.

The strength of her anger faded, the gap it left behind filled with sadness. Her tribe had been right, she could not trust the white man. She belonged with her own people, living a quiet life of peace. Tears poured forth from her eyes.

She shut them tight, not wanting to give the settlers any more of her. She had already given them enough.

Ziigwan let the sounds of the chirping birds fill her mind. Better to imagine flying free in the air with them than endure the reality of the fire.

Strange, she thought to herself. Amongst the chirping of the birds were two more familiar sounds. The owls, that ones whose conversation had lulled her to sleep the night before, were back at it. Except it was daytime. What were owls doing awake?

Curiosity got the better of her. She opened her eyes.

The settlers were still crowded around her, watching her closely. Tobias and his family were still at the front, her chief magistrates of injustice. But the torchbearer, who was serving as executioner, had stopped in his tracks. It quickly became apparent why, sticking from the center of his chest, was an arrow. Based on the color and pattern of the eagle feather attached to it, she recognized it as belonging to her people.

After a moment, he dropped the torch and collapsed to the ground, causing an uproar of chaos as the flame lit some of the dry brush at the crowd's feet alight. Bodies ran in every direction.

White man criss-crossed as they ran for their flint stock rifles that had been carelessly left behind near the court benches. Others grabbed axes and hatchets from the ground and prepared for attack. A might yell emanated from the forest as a dozen of her tribesmen burst forth at full speed from the concealment of the trees and charged the white men.

Tobias's wife screamed, her baby cried. They cowered together as Tobias led a counter charge against the attackers.

The grass of the clearing quickly splattered red with the blood from both sides. The smell of the honeysuckle and marigolds replaced by the lingering burning of gunpowder as flint stock muskets fired.

Ziigwan noticed these details only as a background to her biggest concern. The dried grass that had lit so easily where the torch had fallen to the ground had begun to spread and was steadily approaching the mound of fresh tinder beneath her feet.

Thankfully, in the battle, no one payed her much notice any longer. With all her remaining strength, she wiggled and writhed against the bindings. They were strong, but the cords that made up her restraints had been fashioned from young branches. They still held some of their youthful flexibility and, bit by bit, she could feel them yield and stretch.

It was now or never. With all her might, she pulled her right hand, trying to pass it through the loosened restraints. The broken bones in it from where Silas's axe had smashed it cracked and sent shooting pains through her body. Except those same broken bones also made the hand soft and malleable, able to fit through smaller spaces.

It pulled free of the bindings, which allowed for her other hand, still intact, to slip through as well. With her one good hand, she worked at the tight knot that held her legs in place.

The world around her was muted and distant as she focused on freeing herself.

Listen to your body. Don't let it bend before you are ready. Nothing else matters.

Blood returned to her numb toes as the cord came undone around her ankles, and just in time, too.

With a mighty roar, the grass and twigs under her suddenly became alight. Ziigwan jumped off the small mound, landing on the table where Tobias had passed his false judgment. Hitting it hard with her shoulder, the table split in half under her weight, spilling her and its contents to the ground.

Opening her eyes, she was relieved to find her Kingfisher knife laying on the grass beside her. It may not be much, but it had served her well in defending herself against Silas. Perhaps it could serve her well once more.

Snatching it with her good hand, she scrambled to her feet and prepared to join the fray.

Except the clearing no longer showed any signs of a battle. It had grown still and quiet.

The warriors and trackers of her tribe held clubs and tomahawks at the ready but frozen in place. Same as the white settlers with their rifles, little columns of smoke burning from the flint stock wicks. They all looked so different from one another. How could there ever be common ground between them?

There was one thing that they all had in common, one identical trait that every person in the clearing shared. They all looked completely and utterly terrified.

The funeral pyre, Ziigwan's intended fate, was billowing a light gray, almost white smoke that hung low to the ground, giving the surrounding area the appearance of a misty fog rolling through the valley.

The outline of the well the settlers had dug was barely visible in it. However, the silhouette standing next to it stood out, dark and foreboding. It was taller than any two men, towering over the warriors still frozen in their battle stances. The two glowing orange eyes pierced the smoke like lanterns in the night.

At its feet was Tobias's wife and child, cowering on the ground.

Ziigwan was the next closest, her knife in hand, and prepared to strike. Tobias and the rest of the mixed groups of white men and native warriors spread out in a fan from there.

For a long moment, no one dared moved.

It wasn't until the baby's cry pierced the veil of silence that the creature let out a mighty roar that made Ziigwan's blood run cold.

The white settlers were the first ones to run, all but Tobias dropped their weapons and sprinted into the trees at the opposite end of the clearing. The creature took a step forward, one brilliantly lit paw stepping out of the smoke and into the direct light; its copper scale armor reflecting the bright sunshine.

One of the warriors from Ziigwan's tribe fired an arrow at it, but the stone tip crumbled as it glanced off the creature. Another threw a spear with similar effect. The creature barely registered the attacks, choosing to sniff the air instead.

Her people, known for their great courage in battle, began a slow retreat, step by step. They chattered in her native tongue back and forth, debating whether to leave or stay and fight.

One warrior yelled her name, beckoning Ziigwan to leave with them. They had come to rescue her, to bring her home; not to do battle with the protector of the spirit realm. Their weapons would be of little use against it. They needed to go.

She did not move.

The child's cries grew louder, the mother unwilling to look up and face the beast that lapped at the scent of the air with its tongue.

Tobias inched closer to them, a musket in hand. His hands visibly trembling.

Ziigwan's were too. She concentrated on holding the Kingfisher knife tight.

The creature lowered its head and took another tentative step forward, its face only a few yards from Ziigwan. If she lunged, she might be able to stab it in the eye before it could react. Blinded, they would have a chance to escape; all of them.

She tried to will herself to act. She tensed her muscles, planned her move, and told her body to jump without concern for her own fate.

Except she didn't. She remained perfectly still. Something had taken over her heart, something she hadn't felt since she was a little girl, fear. No matter how much her mind thought and planned, her heart would not let her act.

And why should she? They had been prepared to take her life just moments ago, burn her alive. She owed them nothing.

Tobias did not have the same problem. He did not struggle to act.

Raising the rifle up, he took aim and fired at the creature. The metallic sound of the bullet bouncing effortlessly off the copper on the creature's neck elicited nothing more than a spiteful growl in response.

From the south, a breeze picked up and, with it, the billowing smoke from the pyre completely engulfed the clearing.

Ziigwan struggled to breathe, dropping to the ground in an effort to find whatever clear air she could fill her lungs with. The smoke burned her eyes, making the world dissolve into shades of gray.

The child cried louder between coughs.

Until it didn't.

Ziigwan crawled forward towards where the sound had last originated from, only to find Tobias's wife kneeled on the ground, sobbing between hacking coughs. Tobias hung over her, holding her as he searched for any break in the fog that would allow him even a few meters of visibility.

As she got close, she realized with painful dread that something was missing. Not something, someone. The blanket in Samantha's arms was empty. The innocent child no longer nestled securely inside it.

She crawled past them, hoping it was not too late. Pleading with herself to do something, anything to find the baby. The outline of the well was faint ahead of her.

Loose rocks and ember grasses scratched at her arms. She ignored them and trudged forward until she could reach out and touch the rocks they had built the well from. They were sharp and jagged under her fingers; she didn't care.

Pulling herself up and over, she hung her head over the well, peering down into the darkness below. The air was wet and cool, a reprieve from the hot, dry smoke she had just endured.

Two orange globes stared back at her from deep below, floating in the darkness.

They hung there for a moment, studying her, paralyzing her with fear, piercing her soul.

Then they were gone. With a splash, the darkness turned perfectly still, an empty void once again. The only sound that remained was the echoed cries of a baby that grew fainter and fainter with each passing second.

Pulling herself from the well, she found the smoke had dissipated somewhat, as much of the initial tinder had been burned through. Only the central log, black and cracking, remained.

The shadow of Tobias appeared over her shoulder. She turned, ready to wield the knife against her judge and jury.

"Stop," he said instead, holding out both hands in front of him. They were empty, his rifle discarded and laying on the ground. "I'm not going to hurt you."

She didn't believe him. He reminded her of Silas, his feigned proclamations of peaceful intent that only precluded the violence to come.

"Where did it go?" he asked, his voice trembling as tears streamed down his cheeks and into his thick beard.

Ziigwan glanced to her right, a few rays of light glistening in the distance as they reflected off the surface of the pond.

"What is it?"

Ziigwan shook her head. She did not quite know herself how to describe the creature to the man in any way that he could understand.

Tobias nodded and turned away.

It was the last time she ever saw Tobias. She returned to her tribe, ashamed at her own failure to act, ashamed that she had given in to fear.

18

2023

"Isn't Tobias the name of that guy on that plaque in the town square?" Asher asked.

"Yes, it is. He gathered the settlers and founded the town of Tranquility Pond," Grandpa Joe said. "He ended up having seven more children. All of them joined him on his crusade to kill the monster."

"Well, did he?" asked Asher.

"Based on what I've already told you, what do you think?"

"I don't know what to believe. Your stories aren't usually this long or complicated. I don't know what's real and what you just made up."

"All of it's real."

The boat descended into silence as Asher tried to decide whether or not he believed his grandfather.

"I think you lost your bait," Grandpa Joe said, breaking the silence.

Asher reeled in his line and checked the hook. It was indeed bare.

His mind still caught up in the story, he fished clumsily in the tackle box, searching for the container of fresh worms.

"Ow!" he yelped. A sudden jab of pain caused him to pull his hand back. A tiny drop of blood trickled from the tip of his finger.

"Careful," Grandpa Joe said. "Lots of sharp things in there."

Asher peered inside and saw the source of his wound, an old rusty hook that wasn't safely stored in its compartment like the rest. He held it up to the light to examine it, including the drop of red on its tip.

"Sorry about that," Grandpa Joe said. "I've been looking for that old thing. Sometimes it's the old things you lose that come back to bite you. You better wash it off in the water."

Asher was apprehensive about doing so. From the well of the boat, he felt safe, and the quiet water that surrounded him suddenly felt ominous and foreboding.

He thought about the story, about how the monster appeared every seventeen years. Math was never his strong suit in school. He tried to count backwards in his head but lost track in the 90s.

The story isn't real. Why would Grandpa take him out here if it was?

His thoughts argued back and forth in his head, reason and irrational fear, the two forever locked in battle against one another. Meanwhile, his grandfather stared on, not betraying any emotion or thoughts, waiting and watching to see what Asher would do.

What was he doing? He was nine-years-old; he wasn't afraid of monsters. His grandfather was just messing with him, wouldn't be the first time.

It was no different then when his grandfather snuck off into the woods one night while they were camping and made howling sounds like a werewolf just to freak him out.

He wouldn't fall for the same ruse again.

Leaning carefully over the side of the boat, he dipped his hand into the water to wash away the blood. He wasn't some kid anymore. Monster stories wouldn't work on him.

"So what have been doing all this time?" Asher asked, deciding to play along and show how brave he was. "Just letting it come into town and gobble people up?"

"Rufus and I tried to kill it a few times," Grandpa Joe replied. "But we gave up. We are too old to fight anymore. If we hadn't killed it by now, we were never going to."

Asher's finger must have been cut deep. A steady flow of blood still gushed from the wound, creating a small stream of red in the muddy water that sunk into the depths and out of sight.

"So now we just try to do our best to keep it at bay," Grandpa Joe continued. "Keep it from hurting too many people."

"How do you do that?"

"We give it what it wants."

Asher's face hit the water first, stunning him.

He kicked and flailed as he tried to figure out which direction was up and which direction was down. The water was so cold, cold as ice, despite it being the dead of summer. The cotton of his overalls swelled as they absorbed the water, becoming heavy and clumsy.

Thankfully, his mother had insisted on him taking swim lessons every summer since he was young. Gaining his senses back, he found his equilibrium and pushed himself back to the bright light of the surface.

What was Grandpa Joe thinking? He had gone far this time.

His mother was going to have a heart attack when she finds out Grandpa had pushed him into the pond as a prank.

Hitting the surface, was relieved to gulp at the fresh air, filling his lungs. He coughed out some of the water he had swallowed in the initial shock and immediately went to work looking for the boat so he could climb back in and dry off.

Except the boat wasn't there. It was twenty yards away already, his grandfather paddling it quickly towards the shore.

"Not funny, grandpa," he yelled as he struggled to keep his head above water with the wet overalls proving difficult swimming attire.

His grandfather wasn't laughing. The old man was in the boat, rummaging around in one of the bags. Maybe he was looking for a life preserver?

A fish brushed up against Asher's leg, causing him to twitch his body away in surprise. That was weird. Shouldn't the fish be afraid of him?

Another one swam past him, his time against his arm. Then another one, and another one.

The surrounding water suddenly frothed with fish. They were practically jumping out of the water all around him.

What was this? Another one of grandpa's silly tricks?

He peered at the boat and was surprised to find the silhouette of his grandfather standing in it at full height. In his grandfather's hands was something something long and black, a fishing rod maybe, no, thicker. The way he holding it was wrong too. It looked like he was holding a gun.

Then it clicked. His grandfather was holding one of the guns from the pack in his hands. He was peering through the sights, aiming it carefully, directly at Asher.

Asher panicked. Why was he doing this? It wasn't safe to point guns at people!

Then he felt something brush up against him, pushing him sideways in the water. It was large, too large to be a fish.

He frantically began to swim towards the boat, not wanting to wait around to find out what it had been.

Asher had only gotten a few strokes in when he screamed out in pain. Something had bitten into his calf, he could feel its teeth sinking deeper and deeper into his skin.

He thrashed, he kicked at it, but nothing worked. In a few moments, his screams had become swallowed up by the waters of the pond as he his head sunk beneath the surface.

---

*I*t was done.

Jonah's shoulders and chest rose up and down as he breathed heavy breath after breath into the quiet summer air.

He had hoped for a clean shot, one more chance to get the beast before his time was up. The M82 in his arms was getting heavy. He had worked all year to get it from a buddy of his in the Marines. It wasn't legal for civilians to carry, but in the U.S. obtaining such a weapon only took two things: time and money.

His only worry was if he would get a second shot. His frail old body might not be able to take the kickback, the damn thing was usually shot from the prone position. It had an effective range of 2,000 yards. Accuracy would not be an issue from this distance.

"Come on, Asher," Jonah said aloud, holding back his trembling finger from inadvertently pulling the trigger. "Fight it, make it come back to the surface."

Except it didn't.

The seconds ticked by, Jonah's arms growing more tired with each until eventually he couldn't take it anymore. He sat the gun down back in the boat and collapsed onto the bench.

His chest hurt, his heart beating quicker than it had in years. It had grown weak, just like him.

Rufus and he had tried. Lord knows they had tried, but the monster was damn near indestructible. They had laid mines in the lake, shot it with a light machine gun, Rufus had even hit it with poison arrow from a crossbow. Nothing had worked.

But they knew it was mortal. It never fully healed from what they did to it in 1972, but they still didn't know how to kill it.

In 1989 they had failed, only succeeding in pissing off the creature enough to go on a rampage through town that ended with fourteen men and women dead, along with one child missing. The missing child had been the son of the owner of the plant, who soon closed everything down and moved on to another town. Too many painful memories for them in a town like Tranquility Pond.

The town spent the next seventeen years slowly dying, but not Jonah. He had prepared for the next hunt, the next chance to avenge Levi. Meanwhile, Rufus had made his own plans, including ensuring that the youngest child in town would be situated near the lake on this day in 2006.

Jonah had failed again, barely putting a dent in the monster before it had snatched that poor girl and disappeared into the depths.

Sad as it was, Rufus had convinced him one missing girl was better than another dozen or more killed. With that, his only remaining friend from 1972 had retired from the monster hunting game, leaving Jonah all alone.

He had considered recruiting new helpers, younger men who could pick up the mantle after he was gone. But the men of the younger generation were soft and lacked conviction. As soon as one would agree to help, they would suddenly announce their departure as the date approached.

Jonah was heartbroken when the time came and the youngest child left in town was his own flesh and blood, his sweet and loving grandson. He could take his grandson away, hide him in the city, let the creature hunt for someone else's child.

But he wasn't going to do that, he wasn't raised to do that.

With the mayor long dead and Rufus no longer willing to fight, it fell on Jonah's shoulders to make the sacrifice that had to be done. So he had reluctantly brought his grandson along, recruited the boy to fight in a war he understood little of.

At least Asher's final few hours were happy ones, spent in the splendor of nature and not in front of some video game screen.

The fish had stopped their frantic escape from the depths and the pond's surface grew quiet once again.

Jonah looked over the side of the boat, at his reflection on its surface.

He didn't recognize the man staring back at him. The bald scalp with sparse wisps of white hair looked familiar enough, the wrinkled skin that barely clung to his muscles and bones was to be expected, but it was his eyes that looked most out of place. The fire of 1972 all but gone from them.

Jonah should get back to town soon. He would need to console his daughter.

She knew what was going to happen to Asher. Grandpa Joe hadn't sugar coated any of it. But just like when Olivia had died after battling with cancer for near a decade, no amount of preparation could prepare someone for the moment the news actually breaks.

He sat down and picked up the oars.

Asher's lungs ached as he held back the urge to breathe. The brown, muddy water all around him would hardly provide any relief. He pounded with his fists at whatever held tight to his leg. It had done little good. He was being dragged down to his death.

Suddenly, the world of water around him changed. Gone were the browns and greens that limited visibility to nothing more than a foot in front of your face. The water had become crystal clear. He could see the bottom of the pond, another thirty yards below him. He could see fish swimming in giant schools that darted and danced in unison.

Through the muted sounds of bubbles, he could hear what sounded like a song being sung in a foreign language from very far away. It seemed to get louder the deeper he went.

He had maybe another thirty seconds before he passed out and it would all be over. What could he do? His fists did nothing against the jaws clasped to his leg. He had no weapons.

Except maybe he did.

Remembering the blade that the dark-skinned man had given him, he pulled it from his overall pocket and didn't hesitate.

Thrust after thrust, he stabbed at whatever held tight to his leg. The knife seemed to glance off something harder, stronger, with each try. Until it didn't.

He could feel the squishing as the blade sank deep into something soft.

Whatever had grabbed his leg immediately let go and kicked furiously, pushing himself towards the surface.

The brown water returned. He couldn't tell where the surface was. He just hoped he was going in the right direction and kept kicking as hard as he could.

His eyesight grew dim, he was losing consciousness. The burning in his lungs was unbearable. It felt like the world was being swallowed up by the pain and darkness.

Bursting from the surface of the pond, he gasped for breath.

Never had the sun felt as good on his skin. Never had the musty, humid summer air filled him with as much joy. In that moment, it was all he could think about.

Regaining his senses, his mind no longer obsessed with the need for oxygen, he was reminded that the danger had not fully passed yet.

Whatever had grabbed him was still under the water. Asher needed to get to the boat.

Turning his head frantically, he spotted it. It was maybe twenty or thirty yards away, almost to the shore.

The man inside, his grandfather, had stopped rowing and was staring back at him with a dumbfounded expression.

Asher didn't care, he just started swimming towards it.

His leg where the creature had sunk its teeth into him ached horribly. He could feel a steady stream of blood pouring from it, weakening his muscles. Asher shut it out of his mind. He just kicked, and kicked, and kicked.

He didn't know how far he had gone, or how much farther he had to go. His vision was too blurry to gauge distance with any accuracy.

Something grabbed his shoulder. He had been so focused on swimming that he hadn't noticed the creature had caught up to him.

With the knife still in hand, he turned to swing at it but was foiled when he felt his body lifted into the air.

He was done for.

Asher landed in the bottom of the boat.

"Are you alright?!" Grandpa Joe yelled above him.

"Grandpa!" Asher replied, wrapping his arms around the familiar face.
"Did you get it? Did you kill it?"
"I don't know. I stabbed it, that's it."

Grandpa Joe looked at the blade in Asher's hand. Black blood still clung to the blade and dripped down the hilt. It smelled like a rotting corpse.

"I don't want to go back in the water," Asher cried. "I don't want to go back."

His grandfather looked at him, tears streaming down his own cheeks.

"It's alright," Grandpa Joe said. "Let's get you out of here."

"Won't it come for me?" asked Asher, growing hysterical.

"We'll just keep driving. We won't stop until we are hundreds of miles from any lake or river. It won't get you, I promise."

Asher sprung forward to hug his grandfather, clinging to him as if for dear life.

Letting go, his grandfather immediately rowed the boat towards the shore. It was only another ten yards, and then another twenty up the embankment to the truck. And who knew how hurt the creature was? They had a good chance to make it.

With a mighty roar, an explosion erupted from the water, the boat tipping over and spilling both of them into the shallows. Asher landed hard in the soft mud, temporarily dazed.

Scrambling to his feet, his eyes darted everywhere, searching for his grandfather. Instead, he found the creature that had attacked him in the full light of the sun. It was exactly as his grandfather had described it. Bright, shining scales of copper from its head to the end of its tail. A long, panther-like body, copper spikes lined down its spine. The only difference was the glowing orange eyes. There were none.

Where the two eyes would have been, one had grown over with a patch of copper skin and the other was a black wound that spewed forth the same foul smelling blood that dripped from his knife. Asher must have somehow stabbed out its other eye. It was blind.

Its tail whipped behind it, snapping like thunder, as it swiped with its claws at the air in front of it, frantically searching for Asher.

Maybe if he remained perfectly still, it wouldn't be able to find him. He held his breath and hoped.

The creature's movements stopped, standing on its four legs. It lifted its nose to the air and sniffed.

One sniff, two sniffs, with each one its nose changed direction, eventually narrowing in, pointing directly at Asher.

It may not be able to see, but that didn't mean it couldn't smell him.

It took a step forward, then another. Its long paws barely made a ripple on the water, none of its movements made a sound.

Asher considered running, but the sound would surely give away his position. He couldn't stay still either. He didn't know what to do next.

Both he and the beast heard a loud clicking sound from nearby, turning their heads in unison in the direction it had come from.

The quiet of Tranquility Pond erupted as what sounded like a cannon went off.

Asher thought he had gone deaf, the world suddenly overtaken by the ringing in his ears.

He could see his grandfather laying in the mud, writhing in pain. The military style gun lay at his side, half submerged, the barrel smoking.

The monster had been the receiver of the shot, where it hit directly in the creature's shoulder. The copper scales dented and caved into a wound where black blood drizzled slowly out of it.

Grandpa Joe had hit it dead on and still it lived, and it was pissed too.

Reeling onto its hind legs, it hissed and growled. Surprisingly, its underbelly was not armored like the rest of it was. It was covered in dark fur, so dark it almost looked like an extension of the creature's own shadow.

Grandpa moaned as he turned over and reached towards the gun. Swinging it around, he pointed the muzzle towards the still reeling creature and pulled the trigger.

Nothing happened.

He pulled at the bolt and tried to fire again. There was only another loud clicking sound.

The creature had heard it too, its attention suddenly no longer on the wound in its shoulder but towards grandfather.

"Run," Grandfather Joe yelled. "While it's distracted."

He continued to fiddle with the gun, trying anything and everything to get it ready to fire again.

Asher froze as he tried to think of what to do next.

It was hard to see anything. Jonah's right eye was bleeding, making the world a blur of red-tinted shapes. He hadn't been strong enough to hold a gun like that. The recoil had punched the scope into his right eye, crushing the bone of his orbital sockets. He might even have to lose the eye.

That was the least of his concerns.

One particular dark red shape was growing larger in his vision. From the snarls and growling, he knew it was the Mishipeshu. For over fifty years, he had been hunting it and it was time for that hunt to come to an end, one way or another.

Only one of them was going to be leaving the pond alive that day.

There was a slim chance it could be him, if only he could get this goddamn gun to work.

He had made the mistake of not taking it out to practice before today. He knew it would have tons of recoil, much like the elephant gun Rufus had fired in 72'. Jonah just hadn't realized how much.

Other than his eye, his right shoulder was probably dislocated. Making troubleshooting the gun jam all the more difficult. As he fumbled with it, his only hope was to distract it long enough for Asher to get away, to find help.

Damn the consequences, his grandson didn't deserve this. He was just a kid.

Using only his left arm, he swung the gun around in front of him. If it wouldn't fire, at least he could use it as a club.

The Mishipeshu stood right above him, sniffing the air, listening intently.

"Come on, you son of a bitch," Jonah yelled at the top of his lungs. "Come get me. I'm ready for you."

The monster stood up on its hind legs, one of its paws high in the air, ready to swipe it down right onto Jonah's chest. It would most surely crush him, cave in his sternum and ribs. Hopefully, it would be quick.

Jonah braced himself.

The Kingfisher knife that the dark-skinned man had given Asher cut deep into the Mishipeshu's underside. The monster fell to the ground and landed on its side.

"So deadly it can pierce shadow," the man had told him.

From the wound in the fur, torrents of black blood spilled into the pond, buckets of it. Asher pulled his hand away, leaving the blade lodged inside.

His grandfather had told him to run, but he hadn't listened. Even despite his grandfather's betrayal, he still loved the man, and there was no way he would leave him to die.

Backing away from it, he kneeled at his grandfather's side. The old man's white hair was stained red and brown, his face bloodied and bruised. He looked like a boxer after losing a fight.

"Is it dead?" Grandpa Joe asked.

Asher pondered how to answer. The creature certainly looked dead, but he wasn't getting close enough to say for certain.

Pulling his grandfather up the shore and onto the muddy bank, Asher was surprised to hear yelling emerge from the forest behind him.

"Holy crap, you did it!" yelled Mayor Hatchwell. Even in his old age, he was practically skipping towards them with a smile on his face. "Shit, is Jonah alright?"

"I don't know," Asher said, tears in his eyes.

Grandpa Joe's breathing was shallow, his skin pale.

"I'll take him to the hospital," the mayor said as he got close.

"No," said Grandpa Joe without hesitation. "I'm fine right here."

"But you're bleeding, we have to—"

"No Rufus. I want to stay here a bit longer. Asher, help me sit up, will you?"

Both the mayor and Asher helped prop Grandpa Joe up against one of the boulders on the beach.

"You finally got the son of a bitch," said Mayor Hatchwell, tears glistening around his eyes. He held Grandpa Joe's hand tight.

"Not me," grandpa replied. "Asher did it."

"The kid?!"

Grandpa Joe nodded.

"Well, isn't that something? How'd you do it?"

"The knife," Asher replied.

Rufus gave him a look of disbelief.

"You mean I took out a second mortgage on my house to buy enough firearms to try to blow this thing to kingdom come, and you killed it with a knife?"

"It's a beautiful, crazy thing," said Grandpa Joe, his face wincing.

"I guess so, I guess so," the mayor said.

Grandpa Joe smiled.

"For Levi," he said, tears in his eyes.

"For Stephanie," replied the mayor.

A long second passed.

Grandpa Joe let out a long breath, like he had been holding one in for a long time.

Then something in his eyes changed. The light didn't quite reflect the same way in them that Asher remembered. His chest stopped moving.

"Rest well, my friend," the mayor said, bowing his head.

Asher stood up. Having just watched his grandfather die, he wasn't sure what to feel much less what to do next.

Walking over to the creature, he reached into the black ooze that had formed and pulled the knife from its body.

The pond, which was usually so still, looked different to him. Ripples and waves were everywhere on its surface. They pulled with a gentle current that Asher could feel in his toes.

Slowly, he watched the body pull away from the shore, the current carrying it away into the depths. Back to the dark where he had heard the strange voices singing that foreign song.

If the pond really was the gateway to the spirit realm, then it was returning home to where it belonged. He didn't feel happiness, he didn't feel relief, nor loss or sadness for that matter. He didn't feel really anything at all.

All he felt was numb.

THE END.

From the Author

Is the Mishipeshu real?

The legends and lore of the Mishipeshu (Mishibijiw in Ojibwe) are certainly real to the Ojibwe people. Known as the 'water panther' or 'great lynx', there are quite a few versions of the creature as passed down from the tribal elders, with some regional variations mixed in.

By no means is my depiction of it the end all, be all, true version of the legend. Instead, through my story, I tried to combine the amalgam of the various versions together, being as true to all as I could muster given the constraints of writing a coherent fiction novel.

Of special note, the Mishipeshu is not traditionally seen as an evil entity within the Ojibwe culture. From my research, it is most often depicted as a protector or benign entity. Please do not get the notion that it is some boogeyman-like legend, for it is not.

I went to lengths to double and triple check my translations, word choices, and depictions to be accurate of the Ojibwe people's culture. However, I am human, and any mistakes I may have made in the process come from a place of absolutely no malicious intent.

I highly suggest anyone interested in learning more about the Ojibwe and their rich heritage to contact the tribe itself, the Minnesota Historical Society, and the Milwaukee Public Museum for more information. I personally found their legends and stories fascinating and incredible, well worth a read.

Why the Mishipeshu?

I set out to the write this story based on my desire to tell an old-fashioned monster tale. I had a setting already picked out and a rough idea of what my creature would look like. I actually searched through over a dozen oral histories from tribes in the region looking for my "monster" and it was the Mishipeshu that I found most striking. As the story progressed and I tried to imagine myself in the time period; the Vietnam War became the topic I really found the characters to naturally revolve themselves around. Everything that happened to Jonah/Grandpa Joe really came about because of the impact the war had on his home. This eventually drew a parallel to the monster itself, which became a symbol for the inevitability of war to occur throughout human history and cultures globally around the world.

Why every 17 years?

I heard a statistic once that the average time between major armed conflicts across the globe was roughly 17 years, which ironically coincides with the amount of time it takes to replenish an entire generation of young men. I never fact checked this, but it didn't need to be 100% accurate for the point to hit home.

Why did it only hunt the youngest child in the town?

In my opinion, this is true of all wars. Child soldiers in Africa. Dead parents (civilian and soldier). War takes the most from those who understand the least about it.

Is the Kingfisher Knife real?

There were several depictions of a Kingfisher knife in the original stories. However, I was unable to find any example of an actual knife being fashioned from the parts of a Kingfisher bird. My belief is that it is largely symbolic and no such knife exists. But what do I know? In my opinion, being proven wrong is one of the rare thrills left in life to experience. If you can make one, I'd love to see it.

Milton Keynes UK
Ingram Content Group UK Ltd.
UKHW021903130824
446844UK00013B/955